DEATH SECRETS

ALSO BY JANUARY BAIN

DEATH SECRETS

AN ANNE HALE PI THRILLER
BOOK 1

JANUARY BAIN

ROUGH
EDGES
PRESS

Death Secrets
Paperback Edition
Copyright © 2024 January Bain

Rough Edges Press
An Imprint of Wolfpack Publishing
1707 E. Diana Street
Tampa, FL 33610

roughedgespress.com

Paperback ISBN 978-1-68549-613-5
eBook ISBN 978-1-68549-612-8
LCCN 2024938781

For Don

DEATH SECRETS

ONE

Anna Hale cranked up the volume on her headphones, desperate to study for her high school English exam scheduled for the morning, but the hypnotic beat couldn't mask the loathed voice of her stepfather growing louder by the second.

"You whore! Sneaking around and giving me those pious looks. You don't think I don't know better. I should throw you out right now, you and your bitch of a daughter!"

The soft sounds of her mother trying to pacify him were indistinct, impossible for her to hear.

Pass out already, old man.

She tried forcing her mind on the textbook, but the lines of printing blurred, making it hard to concentrate. If the subject at hand was a math or science quiz, she'd ace both without much effort. And that one computer module they'd had this semester had fascinated her. She yearned for a career in data processing, discovering all the secrets. That was if she got a choice. Her stepfather was threatening to make her leave school early to help bring more money into the household. She rolled her eyes in disgust. The guy just couldn't hold down a job. Never his fault, like his shitty attitude wasn't a factor. Or that his breath so often stank of booze, and his body of stale sweat.

The conversation from earlier between her and her mom bothered her like a harbinger of things to come, making it harder to focus. *"I've made arrangements. If anything happens to me—go next door. Alex and Cindy Pace will look after you. And you get along so well with Josh and the twins."*

Her mom had talked over Anna's every denial of anything ever happening to her. Anna was going to keep her mom safe. Learn karate or something badass at the gym to give her the upper hand. But her mom had made her promise and she had gone along with it. Anna didn't want her mom worrying more than she already did, not that she wouldn't stay and help her if worst came to worst. She'd never desert her mom. They had to stick together, no matter what.

Another loud series of barks drew her attention away from her favorite daydream of getting a high-paying job, of taking her mother far, far away. She'd also warned her to stay out of it, that her stepfather couldn't help himself having to work at a job he hated, but Anna's stomach churned with the effort. She wiped her damp palms on her patched jeans, straining to hear, the test long forgotten.

She pressed hard with her fist through her ragged T-shirt, making the talisman she wore around her neck dig deep into her chest. It was just a crude image of a wolf stamped into a cheap metal disk and tied to a bit of cord she'd found lying by the sidewalk, but it meant something to her, something that reminded her of her namesake, her real father. Bartley Wolfe.

A loud crashing sound of something falling erupted downstairs. She dumped the headset and jumped off the bed, then raced down the narrow staircase in her sock feet, her pulse hammering in her ears, her head about to explode. She rounded the sharp corner that composed the L-shaped kitchen and living room, the clean but faded linoleum with most of the square-shaped pattern worn down to gray splotches, slippery beneath her feet. Her disgusting bear of a stepfather stood over her mom, his meaty fists raised like a boxer, his pugnacious face darkened by raw hatred.

The man who liked to fight at the local gym or bar was not in the ring now, but at home, one that his mother had tried very hard to make as nice as possible on a shoe-string budget. She could take a few items from the half-bare cupboard and turn them into something good in no time, having a long-acquired knack for stretching things. The food was prepared with love, the essential ingredient she always said would keep them full.

Her mother had fallen to the floor, or more likely been pushed, knocking over a chrome chair with a torn cushion that she had duct-taped to keep the stuffing inside. The dingy fabric was bulging out again like gray matter, the cover torn.

"Mom, are you okay?" She rushed to her side.

She looked so tiny, so worn out, though she'd had her when she was only sixteen. She tried to speak and failed, her mother's eyes pleading with her. A stream of blood dripped down the side of her face making Anna's stomach roil with worry.

"Take my hand. We'll go next door. Get help." She

crouched, put her arms around her, and tried to get her to sit up. Before she could manage it, her stepfather was on her, slamming her hard and knocking her off her feet.

"You got something coming as well, you little bitch."

A ringing in her ears drowned out any further words, but the blows to her body and face echoed deep inside. She tried to roll over onto her mother, arms flailing to protect her, and she partially succeeded just before the world went dark.

The stench of something burning woke her. It took a few seconds for the haze in her mind to clear, to realize how dim the light in the kitchen was. She began coughing uncontrollably, her lungs trying in vain to force the heavy smoke out. Her heart raced with the effort, eyes streaming tears. Her mother was so still, curled up on her side, her body half over hers.

"Mom, wake up, we gotta get out of here!" She crawled onto her knees and shook her shoulder, but she didn't move, didn't respond at all.

The sounds of sirens in the distance. Help was on the way. But she had to do something. Now. She touched her throat, felt a faint pulse under her fingertips.

"It's going to be okay. I'm going to get you out of here." She tried to pick her up, but her arms flailed like a rag doll. She was heavier than she thought.

She'd have to pull her mother along the floor. At least the smoke was less dense near the ground. Sweat dripped in her eyes, stinging. She ignored the pain and began tugging her mom toward the back door. It was only a few feet. If she could just get her outside, into the fresh air, she would come around.

But she never did.

TWO

PRESENT DAY—ANCHOR, ALASKA

Anna hammered her stepfather with another right hook, ignoring the pain that ripped through her shoulder, sweat dripping in her eyes. She didn't see the beat-up old punching bag swaying and jerking before her, but the face of a killer. Nineteen years, six months, and twenty-four days she'd been waiting for the appeal process to end, for justice to be served. She hit the bag again so hard on the backswing that her knuckles cracked wide open, payment for her being too impatient to bother with gloves. *Damn it.* Now there was blood dripping on the garage floor. After grabbing a rag from the dustbin, she wound it around her hand.

The door to the adjoining house opened and Tia stepped out onto the cement. Anna waited for her to speak, her breathing ragged and harsh.

"I packed a bag. I'm going with you," Tia said, her stance defiant, her blue eyes flashing with meaning, her normally loose blonde hair up in a tight bun. Her go-to hairdo when she meant business.

Not this again. Unease coiled in her stomach.

A bang on the garage door alerted her to other company. Bad timing. But when had her life ever been anything but bad timing? She ignored the inopportune knock, needing to have her say first.

"You can unpack right now. I told you. I need to do this alone." She braced herself for any objection. This was her burden to bear. Alone. She wouldn't let that monster take anything more from anyone she loved.

"Why do you have to be so stubborn? I can help you, just like you're helped me these past months." Tia raised her voice. "Stop pushing me away!"

They had grown so much closer since she'd come to live with her. She'd gone from being her adopted sister to being her closest friend. But Anna's stance on thinking it best to keep Tia away from the troubles from her childhood had caused a few arguments of late, a deep rift. Her sister wanted to be there for her, repay the favor of having come to live with Anna. But Anna intended to do this alone, face the beast one last time. Then try to put it behind her. She'd used the anger his actions had caused to fuel her life, to drive her forward, making her unlovable at best, but focused on helping others which gave her some sense of being part of the community. Her early experiences had made her an introvert, no denying that. But it had made her a great study of human character.

"No need. Your students need you more than me. Don't worry about it." She had taken Tia in after the breakup with her boyfriend. Glad to do it. Some small payback for all the times the Pace family had helped her in the hard years since her mom was murdered.

"You don't need to be the strong one all the time,

Anna. It's fine to accept help once in a while. And I'm sorry I yelled." Tia shook her head and stomped back inside the house.

Her heart rate slowed down as the worry over the confrontation dissipated. A sense of forlornness replaced it.

"I'm sorry," she whispered, talking to the empty garage. Was there a right thing to say? She felt the pressure on her back, the plane scheduled to leave in the morning. Now was not the time when she was under stress to change her plans, it was the time to steady the course. Surely, Tia would forgive her once this situation was done with and things got back on track.

The knock came again. Anna groaned and went to find out what was most likely their neighbor Jay Loewen, wanted at this time of night. The guy was always borrowing something. At least he usually returned the items. But the last thing she needed at the moment was a conversation with the busybody about the heated discussion he must have overheard between her and Tia. She'd kept her early life private from friends and acquaintances, never divulging the secrets of her past. Ashamed maybe. But most of all she wanted the chance to start over, her new life untainted by events that happened back in Kentucky.

She glanced again at the door where Tia had fled. Well, it hadn't worked at all like she'd hoped; word had gotten out and spread like wildfire in the small town of Anchor anyway, causing problems for her and the Pace family. It had made her shy away from others, worried she'd brought the monster with her whether she wanted to or not.

THREE

WALLS UNIT, HUNTSVILLE PRISON, TEXAS—FOUR HOURS TO LIVE

Anna scanned the area around the prison, observing two passersby in deep conversation. *Risk assessment: low.* Sergeant Carter had been the one to teach her to observe body language, to pay close attention to gut instinct. She had done it for so many years it had become second nature, taking a moment to observe possible trouble before it began. Protected her ass on more than one occasion.

She rolled her mom's wedding ring—the only keepsake she had of hers—around her finger before taking it off and stashing it in the glove box for safekeeping. She wished she hadn't argued with Tia before she left. But she needed to do this alone, see justice done. Not that it was going to bring her mom back. Nothing could do that. Not even the elusive closure everyone spoke of. If anyone had lived that night, it should have been her mom.

"Damn it!" she cursed and practically shoved herself

out of the vehicle, her anger pushing her right up to the doors and inside the maximum-security institution. The hackles on her neck tingled as the steel entrance sprung shut like a death trap behind her, the clank of metal-on-metal jarring and final. She shoved away the image of a caged animal prepared to gnaw off its own limb to escape. A wolf does not feel self-pity. *Do or die.*

Locked in with murderers, an overpowering stench attacked her nostrils, a mishmash of ripe urine and flop-house sweat underscored by cheap disinfectant.

"Halt." A burly prison guard stepped up and faced her, one hand upraised, the other hooked on a thick belt that held a taser and other instruments of the trade. He pointed at the electronic scanner. "Walk through there."

Anna did as required. Then she exited the device before the guard frisked her. The man gave her a sharp look before checking the ID she handed over.

"You're here for an arranged visit with prisoner number 139247, Albert George Norman?" the man asked, his eyes dark and unblinking.

"Yes, sir."

"Haven't seen you here before." The guard gave her another thorough look up and down in that intimidating manner essential to the profession. Fair enough.

"Haven't had a reason to before now." Truer words were never spoken.

The uniformed man shrugged, his eyes narrowing. "Happens more than you think. Say, you remind me of an actress with that dark hair and exotic eyes. Very iconic. She played in *Zorro*." The man snapped his fingers. "Right. Catherine Zeta Jones. All feisty and charming the pants off that guy in that movie."

Inwardly, she groaned. If only she had a nickel for

every time she heard that line. But her exotic looks compared to Jones's was a match she could handle, the famous actress more spirited than not on screen.

"Wish I had her bank account, but I reckon I'd settle for a week being chauffeured about in Cannes or Sundance with all the perks," she said. Attending a film festival, though not something on her bucket list, would definitely be an improvement over what awaited her today.

"Wouldn't we all. You can go in now. He's waiting." The guard gestured with a meaty thumb, his lips quirking upward even as he worked to suppress a smile.

Anna braced herself, offered up a brief prayer and pushed open the door, entering the long narrow space with the dingy, white-washed walls. Two large guards were situated, one at each end of the room, their expressions closed off though their eyes proved they were alert for trouble.

She glanced to her right and came face to face with her nemesis through a solid plexiglass partition. She watched the prisoner's eyes widen at the sight of her. *Not so scrawny now, asshat.* The outward appearance of the man chained to the table had changed, but Anna could still see the evil hidden inside. The hair, white and thinned, combed in greasy strands across his mottled white and brown scalp. But the eyes, they still flashed sharp as knives, almost as cutting as his words had been.

She picked up the house phone. The prisoner took his time answering with hands that shook, his mouth pinched by a network of wrinkles etched deep in his flesh.

"So, girly, you finally got off your lazy ass to visit your old stepdad. Here at The Walls, we gotta saying: never trust anyone not of your blood."

"You've lived too long, old man, and you're going to die too easy." Time to get this over with and done with. She needed to be back in Anchor, back to taking down the bad guys, helping the needy and innocent. It was the only thing that brought true meaning to her life. Something to make up for failing her mom, for her failings as a woman, and as a person.

"That may well be, but you have to live with what you failed to do *long* after I've departed this earthly plain," the old man cackled before the coughing fit hit him hard. The sound harsh and mucus laden. It rattled his sunken chest as he struggled, his eyes reddened and wet with the effort. The handcuffs and ankle chains seemed superfluous. The man was past being able to do much of anything, physically.

She waited him out.

"I'm going to die soon anyway. The county could have saved themselves a few bucks on that injection shit if they'd waited another month. Heard it costs a heap more now that drug companies are going all ethical and won't sell them the good shit anymore," he said.

His eyes darkened as he pressed his pinched lips together tightly. "Takes longer too. You'll like that, won't you? See your old man suffer more. Maybe you'd like to see me fry? Good old-fashioned electrocution more up yer alley? The smell of burning flesh. Or maybe a hangman's noose?"

"Like you made my mother suffer? Nothing will make that right. *Nothing.*"

"You think living in the shithole over at Polunsky for two decades ain't torture enough? Waiting, knowing I'm going to die when they get around to it? Shit girl, you don't know nothin'."

For all her good intentions, visions she couldn't avoid

of that awful night stuck her hard, fueling a raw-edged, cold anger that surged deep inside her belly. It had torn her life apart. Changed her forever no matter how much Alex and Cindy and their twin daughters, Zoe and Tia, and older brother Josh tried to keep her on the right path.

But the darkness had not altered one iota in the spirit who sat across from her, although now housed in an old man's feeble body. *Unrepentant* according to his psychological assessment and everyone else who came into contact with him. No redeeming qualities, playing the trickster at will, charming when it suited his needs, deadly when it didn't. This was the man who had taught her that not all people were human. Some were cold relentless psychopaths housed inside a human mask.

Anna ran a hand over the small area of rippled flesh on the back of her neck hidden by her white shirt collar, her hair pulled up into a ponytail. The fire had consumed everything, determined to devour her until a first responder had dragged her out, the man suffering his own burns in the process. *No good deed goes unpunished.*

It had taken a defibrillator unit to bring her back from the other side stronger and wiser about people with the idealism knocked right out of her.

"Have you done anything with your life, girl?"

"If you count giving two tours of duty to my country, spent in Afghanistan and Iraq as doing something. And one Silver Star for valor in combat during the battle to retake the city of Kunduz in 2015. Plus, a degree in criminology." Pride stirred at what she'd accomplished despite his humble beginnings. None of that could be stripped away, not even by the monster sitting opposite her.

The prisoner grunted. "What do you do for a living then? Something easy, I'm thinking."

"I'm my own person, started a business. Private investigator agency up in Anchor, Alaska." She'd recognized the need to walk her own way after her deployment ended. She'd considered and rejected law enforcement, instead turning to private business. The stint in the Army had given her valuable skills she intended to get the most out of, skills she was grateful for.

The old man did not seem impressed or was screening his reactions. His eyes flicked to her collar. "Left my mark on you."

No, the wolf did, the metal disk burning its image deep into my flesh that fatal night.

"You ever wonder why I did it?"

"No need to know," Anna said. Though motive was valuable when she was looking to compile a profile for an unsub, this was one case she knew too much about. It didn't warrant discussion.

"Well, if it's any solace to you, I wouldn't do it again. Even though that bitch had cheated on me. I'd run as far from the two of you as my skinny legs could carry me."

"I tried to stop you." Remorse and guilt burned red hot in her soul for a moment before she could shut it down. She had been fourteen, not capable of interfering with a full-grown bull of a man, but that didn't keep the guilt at bay. Sleepless nights counting the *what-ifs.* What if she'd been stronger? Smarter? A better daughter?

"And did it work?" he taunted, his eyes rheumy and angry. "Killed the bitch anyway, maybe because of it. Might not have if you hadn't done what you did. If I wasn't seeking retribution for the way you treated me— your own stepdaddy. Ever think of that?"

"Every day."

The man grunted, satisfied. Hacked into a handker-chief held between his handcuffed paws. Anna observed bright specks of red blood before he stuffed it back awkwardly into a pocket of his prison-issued orange jumpsuit, hampered by the metal restraints that jangled with every movement. He appeared to be gathering strength while observing him through eyes that pinpointed with shots of hellfire. Premonition of a final evil tore through her. Too late, the venom was now even fouling the air.

"You know you don't have your daddy's blood, girl? You come by your bastard looks honestly. Your saintly bitch of a mother cheated on your daddy when she was la-tee-dah-ing in some tourist resort in Mexico the summer before you were born. That's why he left her. Why he doesn't love you. She ever tell you that? I thought not. I suspect you got lots of relatives somewhere else in the world. Not so high and mighty now, eh." The old man who she'd once called her stepfather cackled again, his handcuffs rattling, knowing he'd scored a direct hit.

Just when she'd thought she was immune to anything this bastard had to say. Her hand tightened on the phone, straining the tendons in his wrist. "You're lying!"

"Check it out. I'm telling you the truth as no one else fucking will. Not too late to check out your family ties. Find out how many half-siblings dangling from that tree. Hell, I even got one of my own whelps out there some-place if his mama ain't lying."

She struggled to keep her game face on. She and her birth father, a man she barely remembered except in photographs, had shown a pale man with blond hair she hadn't looked much like. Bartley James Wolfe. Her mother was fair as well, though they shared the same brown eye color. Could there be some truth to it? But even as she asked herself the question she knew, deep down. The man was telling the truth about this one thing. Trying to lash out before he died—do more harm. A part of her had always suspected her mother had been hiding something from her. Just not this.

"You gonna at least see I'm buried proper and not a statistic in that Captain Joe Byrd Cemetery? You owe me that much. Maybe atone a little for your sins against me, girl."

She didn't answer, unwilling to ease the mind of a murderer. She hung up the phone and left the room with a nod to the guards, a part of her wishing she hadn't come. But a person must do what she's called upon to do, to see justice done.

———

5:10 P.M.

Anna followed the others into one of two viewing rooms that butted up against the execution chamber. She was numb and found that to be a useful state. When asked which of the two areas available for viewing she wanted to be in, she'd chosen the victim's side, not the prisoner's, finding it annoying to be asked the obvious. As the small group found their seats, the lights were switched off, leaving them in darkness. She heard quick intakes of breath around her, nervous rustling. Not unexpected—it had been explained to them what was about to occur— but still, the reality was harsh and sudden.

The chambered room the witnesses faced was well lit, a focus for adjusting eyes. Steel bars and glass were all that separated them. The cement brick walls in the small, brightly lit room were painted dull green. The prisoner was already there, strapped down to the white gurney, IV lines attached to both his widespread arms. He was accompanied by the warden and a guard.

Anna sat mesmerized. Her heart fisted in her chest. Thump-thump-thump. Each heightened beat another second ticked off.

Then everything began happening in even slower motion, one movie frame at a time. The warden stood behind the prisoner while the guard held a position by his feet, their movements deliberate, choreographed. Chaplins weren't allowed in anymore after a Supreme Court ruling decided all religions should be accounted for or none. Texas chose none.

It was then she noticed the microphone suspended above the prisoner's head.

"Any last words?" the warden asked.

"Distrust all to whom the impulse to punish is strong. Wise words to live by from Friedrich Nietzsche," the man said with enough piousness in his tone to make her release what scant sympathy she housed for an old man about to take his last earthly breath.

The warden covertly signaled for the executioner in the next room to release the lethal dose. The drug began entering the prisoner's bloodstream by remote injection. No mess, no fuss.

Drip. Drip. Drip.

Exacting and horrifying.

She willed herself to continue feeling nothing, same as she had been doing for years. Most days it worked.

"I feel cold. So, I'm not going to hell after all. Fuck you," the prisoner growled just before losing consciousness.

A human life slowly ended before her unwavering eyes. Anna watched but observed nothing leave the man's body. Nothing to show the exact moment of death. No effervescence of soul or spirit drifted up, just a used-up old man lying still on a gurney. A pathetic ending really.

———

6:06 P.M.

Prisoner 139247 was pronounced dead. No one cried. No one mourned. Except for those that had to attend, the press and prison officials, she was the only so-called family there. And she was also a victim. But she would do one more thing. Something her mother would have wanted as much as it pained her to do it. See him properly buried. Maybe then she would find that elusive closure.

Nine o'clock that night, she found himself the only witness to the burial. A few weeks back she'd arranged for the plot, making sure it was far away from decent folk. She felt she was burying a part of herself in the grave, the naive teenager that once believed all people were good inside, as the priest said his piece over the mortal remains of prisoner 139247.

Impatient now for it to be over with and to catch her plane back to Anchor, she glanced over at the narrow roadway where she'd parked the rental vehicle. The action caused her to notice a cruiser with two police officers driving slowly past the graveside. The driver pulled up and parked, though neither cop exited the vehicle. The man of the cloth continued speaking a few words over the coffin, his voice calm and resolute. Her attention was pulled elsewhere. *What are they doing here?*

"Would you care to throw some dirt on the coffin?" the priest asked, his faded eyes kind and inquiring.

"No, thank you, sir." She shook the man's careworn hand and strode away.

"You did the right thing. I know it must have been hard for you."

The words made her turn back around. The memory of the harm done by the monster when he had been let out on bail came back. How her former stepdad had bullied and threatened the family that had taken her in. The fallout on neighbors that were going to testify against the murderer of her mother.

It had caused their move to Alaska, to get away from the sudden notoriety. Thank goodness her mother had the foresight to have Alex and Cindy Pace made her legal guardian in the event of her death. Anna had always understood that Alex Pace wanting to start a risky business with a couple of old friends from his college days, mining for gold from paydirt, was only a plausible cover for the move to the northernmost state of the union. But the three amigos, as the three venture capitalists liked to call themselves, had steadily increased their profits before Alex had died of a heart attack last year. At least there was that. If she had also been responsible for their fortunes taking a nosedive, it would have been another crushing defeat to bear.

"It's done now. Much later than it should have been, but I intend to move on. I won't let him win."

"Good." The man's scant white hair ruffled in the slight breeze. "Take care."

"You as well, sir."

She walked toward the rented truck, one eye on the police car. As she drew near, both doors opened and the officers stepped out. Something had happened. Something bad. Their faces, though stoic, gave the game away.

"Anna Hale?" the taller of the two asked.

"Yes."

"I'm Detective Ian Simpson of the West Central Police Detachment. You have an adopted sister, Tia Olivia Pace, living with you up in Anchor, Alaska?"

The professional tone of the officer held sympathy, making her even more on edge. "Yes, sir. Is she okay? Why are you here?" she demanded. She wanted to shake the information out of the policeman.

The older officer's lips were pressed together as though what he had to say was too upsetting and he needed a moment.

"Please, dear God, just tell me. Is Tia all right?"

"I'm sorry to have to inform you that Tia is missing under suspicious circumstances." The policeman's expression was creased with concern. His younger partner said nothing. He wouldn't even meet her eyes, his Adam's apple moving up and down.

"What are you talking about?" She said the words, but they didn't connect with her brain, with who she was thirty seconds ago. Something or someone else was taking over. Talking for her. A crow squawked nearby, the sound unsettling. Surreal. A harbinger of death, a murder of crows. She'd turned her phone to silent mode for the day, needing to keep her wits about her. Now she fished it out of her pocket and realized she'd missed a sleuth of messages while it had been on silent mode.

"What happened?" She should have been there. She should have let the asshat go to his grave alone. Her mother wasn't here to judge her, so why had she felt such compulsion to see it through? To do the right thing and see justice done. The very air was vibrating now, the sound of thunder back in her ears. But too late. Lightning had already struck.

"There's no easy way to tell you this. The person or persons involved left a letter of intent and a black rose on the front seat of a vehicle registered to her. The evidence all points to an abduction."

The air went so still she was certain time had stopped.

Then black spots filled her vision and one of the officers grabbed for her.

"You okay, miss?" He held her up to keep her from slipping to the ground, her knees collapsing beneath her.

Am I okay? No. She knew then it was never going to be okay again.

FOUR

ANCHOR, ALASKA

The man checked the road in the rear-view mirror. One car approached on the lonely stretch of highway, the one he'd been hoping and praying for the past half hour, knowing her schedule.

"For by grace, you have been saved through faith. And this is not your own doing; it is the gift of God, Ephesians 2:8." He repeated out loud the oft-heard words of a thousand sermons he'd been forced to attend as a young boy, vindicating his actions. A gift indeed. A kindergarten teacher. What a poor use of her talents. She was far too fine to have to work out of the home. A porcelain doll who deserved the best treatment. The treatment he could provide. She'd come to love him in time when she was treated like a real princess.

He stepped from the vehicle, adjusting his collar against the onslaught of the north wind. Anchor, Alaska, was an icebox this time of the year. He made sure his wig was secure against the stiff breeze's disruptive presence.

Soon he would not be lonely. Comfort. It was so close he could taste its sweet flavor, causing his mouth to water.

Sticking out his thumb, he held his breath. Would she stop? Offer assistance? There was never a guarantee he had calculated right. Now it was up to *Him*. He looked skyward, his eyes watering from the freezing arctic air. *The Lord is my shepherd; I shall not want. He maketh me to lie down in green pastures: he leadeth me beside the still waters. He restoreth my soul: he leadeth me in the paths of righteousness for his name's sake. Yea, though I walk through the valley of the shadow of death, I will fear no evil: for thou art with me; thy rod and thy staff they comfort me...*

A few seconds passed, each heartbeat an agony as he recited the words. This was the perfect time. It had to be now if it was meant to be.

Yes.

The car containing the precious cargo he coveted was slowing now down, before pulling off the road and parking behind him. He allowed himself a brief moment of satisfaction. She had been chosen. She was the one.

FIVE

ANCHOR, ALASKA

Anna clutched both armrests, straining to hold on to herself as the small Boeing 737 circled the airport. *Would the goddamned plane never land?* At least with the town having just over twenty-five thousand residents, it wouldn't take her long to get home. Normally, this would be a happy moment, but with what awaited her? Not a chance in hell.

Why hadn't she been here? She stared out at the snow-covered ground fast approaching, incapable of seeing anything but Tia's beautiful face reflected in the glass. If anything happened to her, she'd live with the crippling guilt forever.

The terminal was a nightmare as she forced her way through the labyrinth. She found herself confronted by two cops as she exited the main gate. Browne and Karloff.

"About time," Karloff grumbled, a man she'd mistrusted since he'd bragged about his mistreatment of a drunk, forcing the prisoner to sleep in his own vomit. His perfunctory manner grated at the best of times. This was not that time.

"Just tell me, have you found her?" The hours on the plane, waiting for an update on what was going on had been a nightmare.

Browne shook his head, making unease slither and tighten into knots in her belly.

"Let's go. We have some questions for you down at the station," Karloff insisted.

Anna narrowed her eyes at the vastly over-weight officer, clamping down on all emotion. Maybe she should thank him for that small favor? The luxury of allowing her feelings to run away with her was not what this situation called for.

"Good to see you too, Karloff." No way she could keep the sarcasm out of her voice. "What, no condolences, officers? Isn't that how these interactions usually begin? Just before you go out of your way to follow your own agenda?"

Sergeant Jack Browne grimaced, his cheeks reddening. "Sorry about this, Anna, and about your adopted sister. We'd like you to come down to the station. We need to talk about some things concerning the case. Tia was living with you for a few months now, right?"

"You playing good cop now, Jack?" Anna asked. "Since I'm not under arrest, I'll take my own vehicle thank you very much."

"You got something to hide, or maybe you think you're too good to ride with us? Let's go Jack. I told you this cowgirl wouldn't cooperate," Karloff said. The bully lumbered away without looking back.

"Ignore Karloff. We'll see you at the station soon as you can get there," Jack said.

"I'd like to head home first." She cleared her throat, unable to keep the faint hope at bay.

"Fine. But don't be too long. You know Karloff. He'll just head over to your place."

"I'd recommend a muzzle and a sturdy leash."

Jack's expression turned to stone. "Karloff's only doing his job."

Anna didn't answer, letting her silence speak for her. She strode away from the man and out the airport's side exit. The cold slammed her in the face, making the scars on her neck burn, but she ignored the discomfort and climbed into her icebox of a truck. Guilt for being away at the worst possible time was eating her alive.

The half-ton truck wouldn't turn over when she tried the starter, making her curse a string of choice words. After a few more futile attempts to start the engine, she hammered the steering wheel with the palms of her hands before breaking down into tears. A few minutes later she swiped them away and blew her nose. This was not the time for weakness, but the time to act. Tia needed her.

SIX

"Why are you here, Buck? What do you hope to gain from these sessions?" Doctor Molly leaned forward in the armchair, poised and perfect, her expression pensive and duly interested. Her accomplishments were hanging in full view behind her, university degrees, photo ops of the pumping of the flesh, candid shots of her and her niece. All perfectly nauseating now that he had the goods on her. He just needed to wait, spring it at precisely the right moment.

The Buck savored the underlying frustration clear in her tone. He knew damn well why he was here. To waste sixty minutes of his precious time once a week, otherwise his younger wife was pulling up stakes. Plus, it made him look good, a man who was willing to go the extra mile for a marriage hiccup was a man to be trusted. More to the point, another divorce wouldn't help his chances in the spring election.

"Teresa insisted, and I went along with the game plan." He shrugged and adjusted the crease on his pantleg. If this didn't work, he had other ideas to guarantee his return to office as the town's mayor. His old man had never once said he was proud of him, not until he'd won that first election. He'd not give that validation up for any woman, no matter what he had to do to silence her. *Whatever it takes.* He owned that motto right along with his father.

"You've been coming here for weeks now and have yet to share your real feelings about your wife's ultimatum. Did you feel it unfair in anyway, that she insisted on your coming to see someone for the marriage to continue? Is that a point of contention for you?"

Hmm, new tactic. He had to give her bonus marks. It had been somewhat amusing to watch her ply her trade. Good thing she was an outstanding-looking woman with those flashing green eyes and thick auburn hair she was always fussing with. Maybe if Teresa left him in the end, which was looking more and more likely, he would have asked the sexy doc out. She'd have looked good on his arm and was currently unmarried. Too bad that could never happen now. Ah, but he did savor the coming victory. Playing with her was going to be such fun. He'd always wondered how a woman like the doc had made her way so far up north when she obviously was better suited to southern climates.

"Unfair? No. I look forward to these conversations once a week. Nice break from the pressures of mayorship."

She tucked an auburn lock of hair behind her ear, smoothing down a few errant strands. "Maybe you would benefit more from seeing someone else? In three months of therapy, we seem to have hit an impasse these past few weeks."

I'm not going through this shite again, not for anybody. "What do you need from me? I've explained my position. I want to do whatever I can to make Teresa happy." He added a charming, earnest smile that popped his dimples for good measure. Females were always so predictable, especially those that thought themselves immune. Maybe especially them.

"'Happy' is not something you can make someone else feel. They need to find that emotion for themselves. As I've explained before, you need to consider more specifics. What can you do to make her feel more valued? Her words heard?"

"I've listened to her liturgy of complaints many times over. Taken notes." He crossed his legs at the ankles, admiring the shine on his new shoes he'd worn for the release of the city's budget earlier in the day. Yeah, he'd listened to her endless squawks about how undervalued she felt. After all she did for him. How she was eye candy for events and her opinions didn't matter. *Play to your strengths, baby.* Since when was looking good a crime? Of course, she had now outlawed that particular term of endearment for her, saying that being called "baby" was demeaning. Why the hell had she agreed to marry him in the first place? Yeah, right, she wanted a sugar daddy. Now she wanted to change the rules, pretend she could play a far bigger part in his success. Not fucking likely. He knew his town. What it took to be successful. Hadn't he been mentored at the hands of an expert. His own father, a cold man who never had a kind word for his family but knew how to get things done. How to keep people in line. A legend in his own time, something that The Buck was striving for. Power meant he could get away with anything if he did it right. Hell, he already had done the unthinkable with none the wiser.

"How did you respond? Did you change any of your habits? Change is hard for anybody. The first step toward real change is listening to the other person, hearing how your actions make them feel. Teresa feels she'd undervalued. She wants to become an active participant in your relationship. She married young, her whole life ahead of her, one could say idealistic even. Now, she's maturing. Recognizing that she needs more of a say in how your lives will unfold together going forward. For instance, how does she feel about you running for re-election?"

"She's not interested in the campaign. Thinks the position of mayor on top of all the businesses I run or own a piece of takes up too much of my time. She wants me home more, but she knew what she was getting into. My political investment in this town brings goodwill, from the funeral business to the strip mall, they all do better for it."

He sat back in his chair. He just needed Teresa to hang in there till spring, then she could go her own way for all he cared. But if she thought he would pay out half of the funds that his father worked so hard to acquire, never home even on Christmas Day, then she had another thing coming. Over his dead body would he allow that to happen. Better yet, hers.

The doctor frowned. "So you see things as trading one thing for another? You're not invested in this community because you're called to serve, but for what it can do to help your business interests? Am I hearing you correctly?"

"Sounds like you're questioning my motives, doc. No, it's not just that, it's also because I have a vision for this town. I want to see my community thrive. Be there for the people who need me. They deserve my best efforts.

No reason why it can't be a win-win, right?" Was she buying it?

Apparently so because she began twirling a shiny lock of hair around long slender fingers. Fingers that would look perfect wrapped around a certain body part.

"I do, however, have to question *your* motives and credentials, *doc*," he said.

She stared at him as if he had suddenly turned into a two-headed monster. "What on earth do you mean?"

"Perhaps you're not aware that I'm the main investor behind the Yellowbrick Road Casino?"

Her eyes narrowed almost imperceptibly. He decided in that moment she'd be good at poker, just not as good as he was.

"No, I did not know about your business interests in the casino, but I don't see why that has any bearing on your therapy?"

"Ah, but I think it does, very much so. I did a little investigating of my own. Seems you're in deep trouble from gambling money you don't have. A psychologist who can't even treat herself successfully. Does that about sum it up?"

She stared him down. "You have no right to dig into my confidential records. I intend to repay every cent owed. Who told you about this? I want a name," she hissed.

"Doesn't change the facts, baby. You're in hot water up to your eyebrows according to your financial records. And you know what, that's not even the worst of it. You're hiding a far darker secret than being a lousy gambler. Are you not?"

Her eyes became two hard bits of emerald glass, watching him like a predator watched its prey. A shiver ran down his spine. It was almost like there was someone else hidden deep inside that delicious package. Huh, it must be a trick of the light.

But oh my, it was fun to turn the tables. He sat back in his chair. He had her now. No need to marry this one.

"If you wanted to bed me, Buck, you could have just said."

SEVEN

Anna sat alone in the dingy interrogation room and rubbed at the cramp that had a death grip on her neck. They'd been at it for hours, the detectives and her, going over and over her story that would never change. How could it when it was the truth? And what part did they not get? She was not in town when Tia went missing. If they thought letting her stew alone would help their case, then the devil was alive and well and living in Anchor City. The walls of the box-like room vanished as she tried over and over to envision how this could have happened. Tia had been on her way home when she was taken. No signs of a struggle, according to the report. She'd just vanished into thin air. But someone must have seen something? The quandary was eating her alive. Why waste time on her? With her abilities, she should be out there helping them solve the case. Instead, they'd locked her up like some kind of animal. *I need to get out of here and go look for her.*

To keep her mind occupied and sharp, she began to count things, the tiles first, finding the floor had a ten count each way, making the final tally one hundred. The number that signified the end of one chapter in life and the beginning of another. She could not accept that, unless the next chapter included Tia, alive and well. That's what she focused on, the whole family together again.

She'd just finished counting the large number of holes in the ceiling tiles when Karloff came lumbering in without his partner, his bulk oppressive in the small space. Perhaps he enjoyed using it to intimidate people? Anna didn't react, ignoring the man. She did wish though she had access to all the cards the cops were holding back from her, waiting for her to slip up. Such a waste of resources. She wanted the case solved far worse than they did. She wanted Tia home with a desperation that left a bitter taste in her mouth. *Please, give me the time to become a better person. To learn to be more patient and understanding. To be a better sister and friend.*

The cop lowered himself into a chair that creaked in protest under the impressive weight. How did the man manage to haul around all that bulk without having a heart attack?

"So, your stepdaddy finally cashed in his chips. You get a kick out of that? Knowing he's now pushing up daisies?"

The man was a walking, talking cliché. "No flowers will ever grow over that miserable carcass." Anna noted the man's watery eyes and bulbous nose. Cirrhosis of the liver looked about ready to set in.

"Be that as it may, seems to me nurture counts for more than nature. Your life led up to this moment, you know, her being taken out on that lonely stretch of highway. We're checking on how long her car was abandoned. To see if you had time to do the deed before leaving for

33

Texas." Karloff narrowed his eyes to mere slits, the flesh pockets around them more pronounced as he drilled his sausage fingers on the metal tabletop.

"Are you saying my shitty childhood caused Tia's abduction?" Anna shook her head. "That makes no sense at all." She sat up straighter. "Look, she was fine when I left her this morning. Surely by now you know she taught all day and was on her way home when this happened?"

Karloff shrugged, a smirk tugging at the edge of his mouth as he shifted his bulk. "Here's the thing. She didn't go in to work today. Took the day off sick and they called in a substitute teacher to cover for her. You didn't know about that? Strange."

Why didn't she say something to her? She'd been sleeping before she'd left to catch her early flight. Her throat tightened at the memory of yesterday's disagreement and she jabbed her fingernails deep into the flesh of the opposite hand.

"But her car must have been seen by someone if it had been there all day? And why did she go out then? If she was ill?"

"Exactly. Lots of things are in play. Did you kill her *before* you left for Texas?" Karloff said the words so softly that it took a second for them to register. "It would explain the damaged knuckles on your right hand."

"I did not kill Tia!" The denial exploded out of her. Damn it. She hated losing her temper, especially in front of Karloff. "I've told you I was working out in the garage last night. I was upset about going to the execution and forgot to put on gloves in my haste. Check the punching bag for traces of blood."

The cop pursed his fleshy lips making him look like a blowfish.

"Lots of killers profess their undying love for others

before they go on to kill. In fact, it's become a cliché, it's been used so much. Statistically speaking, you're our most likely suspect. She was living with you at the time. Only thing that would make you more suspect is if you two were married. Anna Jane Hale. Three names that sound like the moniker for a killer if you ask me."

"What's your middle name?" she asked. "Because it sounds like you're saying that middle names make for a killer. If that's the case, who's not one?"

The cop leaned forward, tenting his hands on the table, his tone dripping sarcasm, his displeasure obvious. "So why don't we cut the crap here. Was it an argument that got out of control? Over her being pregnant? You weren't happy about her staying with you and now the added burden of a baby to help her with. Thought you'd be as piss poor at it as that murdering role model they put down in Texas? Or were you jealous?" His eyes lit up with an unholy light, his lips turning down. "You're gay, right? Never seen you with a guy in years. Upset about her boyfriend, maybe?"

"That's none of your goddamned business!" Relationships were hard, dangerous territory, difficult to navigate in her experience. Best to go it alone, it was much safer. Yeah, she had trust issues that ran a mile deep. But that was one thing she didn't think anyone could blame her for, considering her upbringing. Then she realized what else he had said.

"Tia was pregnant?"

"It was confirmed by a coworker. Said she'd been sworn to secrecy."

Why had she not told me? Probably because she was the kind of woman not to add any pressure to the already difficult situation she'd been dealing with down in Texas.

She had to hang on with all her strength to her wits

now, not let the asshole know how badly she was affected by the revelation. Why hadn't Tia shared the good news with her? Was she that lacking as a sister and friend that she couldn't tell her? She just had to go back to Texas. Stupid move. That asshole had ruined her life yet again. How could that be allowed to happen? Her mind whirled with the implications, her stomach roiling with despair. Once more, the universe had dropped a bomb on her not of her own making.

"Wanna come clean? Change your story and make things easier on yourself?" The slick words fell from lips with a couple of crumbs attached at one corner, adding visceral disgust to an intolerable situation.

Anna wanted to strike something. Her hands fisted at her sides; her vision narrowed.

"Did you have an accomplice?"

"What? No! For Christ's sake, I've told you everything I know over and over again, I had *nothing* to do with this. Why aren't you out looking for her abductor?" Frustrated, she silently repeated the words in an effort to stay sane and focused. *Death before dishonor.* No way would she let this pathetic excuse for a human being make her less than she was.

EIGHT

SIX MONTHS LATER—ANCHOR, ALASKA

The man slipped automatically to his knees on the low bench in the confines of the tiny booth, crossing himself as he did so. The odor of furniture polish assailed his nostrils while he waited for the little window to slide open. He held back a sneeze. The pain that instantly blew up his sinuses brought a wash of tears to his eyes that he blinked away, clearing his vision. The creaky sounds of the confessional door sliding open focused him. The opportunity for absolution was not to be taken lightly. Where else could he go and be given complete forgiveness for admitting his transgressions?

"Forgive me, Father, for I have sinned. It's been six months since my last confession." *Six months since she was given to me.* Her image filled his mind. Her rare beauty, her quiet charm, her patience especially with him, all had lifted him from the abyss. But it had ended and now he had a new love, waiting for him. Sudden anger slipped past his defenses, something that was happening more and more. *You said I would never be loved. That I was unlovable which is why you had to do the things you did. That I forced your hand. You were wrong, Mother.* Of course, they all left him, in the end. But not before giving him what he craved most: companionship to stave away the aching loneliness. And there was always the hope that one would stay.

A slight rustling on the other side of the privacy screen Followed by a clearing of the priest's throat. He'd been silent too long and that was not normal. *Normal is important.* His mother's commanding voice echoed in his mind. He must work harder to appear that way. She'd always reminded him he needed to copy other humans. Learn from them while keeping himself apart from their tainted behavior. He considered himself a master of disguise from years of practice, pious on the outside while watching and listening on the inside. Smarter than all of them.

"I accuse myself of the following sins." He started with the small stuff as always, weighing how soon to reveal what he needed most to be given absolution for. What he came for. Had to have.

"I self-pleasured and took the name of the Lord in vain two times. I drank spirits and practiced gluttony. I didn't give a full ten percent tithe to the church as promised, though I now see the error of my ways and intend to make up the missing monies."

The words began to spill off his tongue, easier and easier. *I should have been a priest. I have the oratory for it.* "I confessed in a letter but neglected to sign it in my hand." There, he'd admitted the worst sin. He quickly added. "I envied those with more money. Those who have a loving family and those who make friends easily. I shot at a skunk."

His mind wandered to the letter. The entry for crafting that perfection had been lifted right out of his journal. He'd been keeping the daily entries since he'd begun the journey of revelation, one woman at a time. It had come about in a moment of divine inspiration. An opportunity to let them know their loved one was chosen by a higher power, not himself. He only wished he'd thought of taking this route sooner.

And better to have done it with the precision his great-grandfather had demonstrated in Germany during the war, when he had been keeping track of all his medical experiments before he'd started the Circle of Friends in Alaska. COFA, the acronym for the survivalist group with many still living in a compound fifty miles due north of Anchor and in precise line with the North Pole. His exacting notes, careful attention to penmanship, so inspiring that they had spoken to his very soul. Allowed him to become what he was meant to be.

When he'd been away to college, his cravings had started. All he'd wanted was to get a woman to go out on a date with him. Take an interest in what he had to say. Maybe bestow a goodnight kiss or two. He became sick to death of watching other men hooking up while he was rejected at every turn. Laughed at, and not always behind his back. A terrible memory of a pair of females drunk at one particular house party not even bothering to hide their contempt when he'd approached them, trying to treat them like ladies while they mocked him. Snickered like dirty hyenas.

During a semester learning of the processes capable of giving a body a longer shelf life, an idea had appeared that took form over a matter of weeks. Then he'd read the precious diary uncovered in his mother's safe deposit box when she passed during spring break. She'd left him everything, the house, the business, the land, and he discovered a new plan had been sent from above. He'd understood then he'd been saved for a higher calling. The words came back to him now of what he'd written in each letter to the cops and the press, the words perfect in all their glory.

> *He found her in a desert land,*
> *And in the howling waste of a wilderness;*
> *He encircled her, He cared for her,*
> *He guarded her as the pupil of His eye.*
>   Deuteronomy 32:10.

Know that she has been chosen. Do not fear for her earthly presence, for a higher power is at work and controls all things.

Yours in death,

The Black Rose

He was suddenly aware that the priest had gone quiet. Nervous now, he swept his hand over his neatly combed hair, reminding himself to breathe normally. *In and out. In and out.*

"Do you have that letter with you now? Could you read it to me?"

The questions made the cold sweat increase. It caused the freshly ironed shirt to dampen as the perspiration slipped down his sides. He shuddered with the horror of it. He had to get home soon, shower, or go mad. He'd bathe every hour if he could. Spend his days immersed in cleansing waters and never come out. Images of the invisible bacteria a human body was covered in seared his brain, but obligations and responsibilities curtailed more than two or three full-body scrubs a day.

"No. Like I said, I gave it away." A copy had been published in the local rag, a fact that brought immense satisfaction in its wake. Now they saw *him*, after all those years of neglect. Just taking, taking, taking. People were so predictable. Did they think they were blessing him with their fake tears of grief? They were feeling sorry for themselves, it had nothing to do with the deceased. What could the dead feel, they were gone. *Dust to dust, ashes to ashes.*

"Was anything else left behind with the letter?"

The question surprised and worried him. He considered how to answer, knowing a falsehood was unacceptable to be granted full forgiveness. Now he would have to fly farther north. Find a new priest. One less curious.

"No, of course not. It was nothing of importance anyway." *Just the most perfect Ice Blink rose given the luster of a fresh drink in black dye.*

He swiped the sweat from his perspiring face with the back of one hand at another pregnant pause. His heartbeat quickened. *Hang on, it's almost over.* Running away now would only draw more unwanted attention.

"I'd advise you to consider revealing your writing of the letter to the proper authorities. May I have your permission to pursue this?"

Much as he hated to make light of his gesture turned into words and written down so succinctly, this speculation had to cease. "No. It was a letter written in jest. Short-sightedness on my part. It won't happen again. I apologize."

"Very poor judgment indeed. As penance, six Hail Marys and five acts of contrition. For harming one of God's creatures, no meat for a week. Go with God."

"Thank you, Father." Relieved, he made the sign of the cross and scurried from the cramped, claustrophobic space, desperate to wash away the stink of stale sweat. He snorted as he pulled on his thick wool overcoat, left abandoned on a pew, before stepping outside into the rawness of an Alaskan winter day that could freeze skin in less than a minute. He was a vegetarian—what did he care about consuming meat?

NINE

A loud crash came just as Officer Josh Pace opened the door of his parent's house. The chilling sound made him drop the bouquet of flowers and Valentine's candy he was carrying but had no use for other than the faint hope of making his mother feel better. She had mostly forgotten what had happened to her daughter Tia in these past weeks since she was stricken with the life-altering disorder. Dementia was good for one thing, and one thing only, helping the afflicted to avoid the pain of loss. Though he was more and more certain that it was the pain associated with his sister's abduction that had brought on his mom's condition. He raced full tilt now to his mom's bedroom, his heart in his throat. Out of breath, he looked around frantically for his mom. Not seeing her, he advanced into the bathroom, taking in the picture in a split second.

"Why are you trying to drown me? Let me go!"

His mother was wet and wrapped in a towel, screaming blue bloody murder, her face almost unrecognizable under the wet hair. Another woman was looming over her, her frustration obvious in her expression. Without thinking, Josh reacted, rushing to pull the woman away from his mom.

"Who are you? What's going on here?" he asked. He had the person under control, arms held behind her back. He kept a careful eye on his mom, not wanting her to fall.

"I'm Roberta Whyte. I'm here to look after Cindy. I was hired as caregiver for the night by Zoe Pace. Who are you?" The older woman asked, her expression even more annoyed now as she tried to jerk her arms away. "Would you kindly let go of me, please."

Josh let the woman go, experiencing a rush of adrenaline all too familiar. "Sorry, I'm her son. Josh."

"Well, fine thing it is when one sibling doesn't let the other know what's going on." The caregiver gave him a stern look of warning as she straightened her clothing. "Zoe went out and called the agency for some paid help."

"Where's Zoe? I don't want this woman to be here." His mom began to cry, her sobs tugging at him in the worst way.

"It's okay, Mom." Josh crouched down at the side of the tub. "It's Josh, your son. I'm here now."

"I want Zoe. Josh never comes home." Guilt replaced the adrenaline rush making his insides quake.

"Let's get that soap rinsed out of your hair, Cindy," Roberta said, gently pushing Josh aside. "We want to get you all pretty for bingo tomorrow. Maybe we can try putting your hair in curlers for a change? Then add a fancy hairband?"

His mom just looked at the woman, her eyes blank. But at least she appeared calmer now.

"I'll make some tea." Josh drifted down the hallway in shock. In the kitchen, he bent down and picked up his useless gifts. He should have been here more. Kept a closer eye on what Zoe was dealing with. It had come on so sudden and he'd been so caught up in leaving the military for training at the police academy, then gaining the new position with the Anchor Police Department, he hadn't spared more than a moment for what was going on here at home except for one thing. The drive to find out what happened to his sister burned brighter than anything else. And he wanted the badge to make that happen.

He made the tea, then waited for Roberta to finish up with his mom. The woman joined him at the table, her expression wary.

"I am sorry about that. I didn't realize how bad off she was getting," Josh said, pouring the woman a cup of tea. She must have needed it by the way the woman quickly drank it down.

"It's okay. She's resting now. Do you want me to stay?"

"No, I can spend the night. When's Zoe expected home?"

"She figured she'd be home before midnight." Roberta glanced at the kitchen clock. "Almost that now."

"Why were you giving my mother a bath so late at night? Seems an odd time."

"She soiled herself." The woman's face remained placid.

He closed his eyes briefly than opened them with a new determination. "Does my sister pay you each time?" he asked, reaching for his wallet.

"No need." The woman waved him off. "She pays the agency and they pay me."

"Okay. Thanks for not making a big deal of this. I'll see that you get a bonus for your trouble."

The woman nodded her head, her gray curls bobbing. "That would be appreciated. I look after two grandkids and they're at that expensive age. Always needing some-thing for school."

"I'll see to it." Josh saw the woman out, then went and sat down at his sleeping mother's bedside to wait for Zoe. The minutes ticked by slowly until the clock in the hall announced midnight, but still no sign of his sister.

By morning Josh was frantic, calling around to check with friends to see if anyone had seen her. One sister missing had nearly destroyed their family. What was Zoe thinking staying away so long?

The phone rang at eight o'clock and Josh rushed to pick it up.

"Zoe? Are you okay?" he asked.

"Josh, I'm afraid I have some bad news." The voice of Sergeant Jack Brown held deep sympathy, making her heart squeeze painfully.

"What is it? What's happened?"

"It's your sister. No easy way to say this, but she's been taken. Same as Tia. A rose and letter left in her vehicle."

TEN

Anna parked her truck, then walked over to the vendor side of O'Brien's, the ice and snow crunching like exploding popcorn under her boots. She slipped inside the small vestibule and pressed the button, then stepped back to wait for service, holding the cash at the ready in her fist. She prayed that the person who came through the door from the bar to answer her ring would not be Sam. The guy was well meaning, but he just couldn't shut up. Tonight, of all nights, she didn't want a long drawn-out discussion on life.

The old wooden door creaked opened and Sam's amiable face appeared beneath a halo of curly red hair. Anna inwardly cursed. Why should tonight be any different? No one ever answered any of her prayers, even the smallest ones.

She ran her hands through her tangled hair that had not seen a decent conditioning in recent weeks, trying to smooth the unruly waves.

"Evenin' Anna," Sam said, moving to the work area

behind the vendor area where all the beer and hard liquor was stashed. "Same as usual?"

"That'll work. Thank you kindly, sir." No matter the situation, her Southern training by her mother always won, making social interactions a high priority. She waited while Sam pulled the whiskey off the shelf.

"You doing okay?" Sam asked, ignoring the folded money that she thrust at him.

"Fine. Just need to get home is all. Appreciate the asking though."

"I don't think this is what Tia would have wanted," Sam said evenly, coming closer and looking her square in the eye. "She wasn't the kind of person that would see you stop looking after yourself."

The futileness of the discussion ate at her. "Who knows what she would have wanted? She's not here to have a say."

"There're people who still care about you in this town, me included. No one thinks you had anything to do with Tia's disappearance."

She had to look away from the earnest expression on Sam's face. She could not forgive herself for not being there, try as she might. To save Tia's life as her family had saved hers. "I'll be fine. Don't waste your life worrying about me. I'm getting by, planting one foot in front of the other." She placed the money on the counter and grabbed at the bottle, leaving Sam shaking his head as she clamored out the door. She was not paying attention and crashed into a huge body planted right in her path.

"Watch where you're going!" The man put up a hand to stop her, pushing her hard. Anna stumbled, then righted herself.

A familiar discordance of items jangled together for a couple of seconds on the man's wide belt, naming the source. Ah crap, a cop. And not just any cop, but Karloff. She'd never forget the man's name or his insinuations that she'd killed Tia. But she wished she could, along with everything else to do with the police department's bungling of the investigation. But drawing attention was ill-advised. *Risk assessment: moderate to high.*

"Well, if it isn't Anna Hale, failed PI." A tone riddled with scorn pierced through some of the mind fog.

Anna went to move around the rotund man, but the extra-wide body continued to block her way.

"Not so fast. Seems your vehicle is illegally parked. I only came in here to find the culprit, and low and behold, here she is. Figures. You do have a track record for obstruction of justice. If you weren't such a pathetic figure, I'd haul your ass in right now, knock the truth right out of you. Too bad the villain has more rights than the good guys."

The old Anna would have taken offense, fought back with the truth that she had nothing to do with Tia's disappearance. A part of her still felt the urge underneath all the heavy weariness. She'd become a house divided, unable to stand, torn apart by insinuations and outright lies.

"Why don't you leave her alone? Can't you see she's hurting?" Sam said, his voice wavering from anxiety. It had fallen to this. Disgust and shame filled her, her blood running hot and cold. *God, I need a drink.*

"Yeah, she ain't worth it." The cop stepped aside, his shoulder knocking against hers on his way by.

Her path clear, Anna stumbled outside in the cold air. How had it come to this?

ELEVEN

Zoe Pace parked her SUV halfway down the street, grateful to have found a vacant spot. It would have to be sleeting frozen snow, making the roadway a hazard. But what else could one expect in the dead of winter in Anchor, Alaska? If she wanted warmer weather, she'd have to move down south. Hmm, maybe back to where they'd started in Kentucky before what had happened to Anna had made their father move them as far away as possible? Or not. All her family resided in Anchor now. What little was left of it.

Tugging the collar of her blue parka closer around her face and neck, she hurried down the sidewalk through the partial whiteout before deciding to enter at the side of the red brick house. Her snow boots were thick with ice crystals and she didn't want to track up the formal living room rug going in the front door. Aaron was a stickler for keeping a nice place, one of his characteristics that surprised people at first meeting.

She was thankful for one night off from dealing with her mother's increasingly erratic behavior. She wasn't even bothered about the snow messing with her hair that she had taken the trouble to curl for the first time in months. *Have I done the right thing?* Yes, the sitter had her number and had promised to call if a problem developed. The woman had great references, but still, the guilt tugged at Zoe. She hated to let down Aaron too. He had been sweet enough to ask her to join him for the annual Valentine's Day party at the Bison Inn, knowing she'd be all alone once again. Not often she agreed to such a thing, but if not now, when? Her twin had been missing for six months now. And she grieved the loss every day. But she was close to the breaking point. Found herself wanting to scream at her mom when she wouldn't listen though she had managed to stop herself in time. She needed a night out, for her own sanity. And that would make her a better caregiver.

She was so caught up considering a catalog of *what ifs* and recriminations of failing her mom that she stumbled, catching herself from taking a tumble off the landing at the last second. Her foot twisted sideways. A groan of pain burst from her lips. Damn it, she'd half-broken the heel off her fancy new boots. *I should have worn my snow-packs.* But at least she had a pair of dress shoes waiting in the car.

Peeking in through the large window cut into the door as she leaned against it to deal with the offending boot, she caught sight of her friend Aaron Stone in profile, both hands raised in an odd gesture of surrender. Behind him, a thin attractive female in her late-twenties hid as best she could, her face a mask of pure terror. Zoe hesitated, distracted by the strange tableau, her damaged footwear long forgotten. *What the hell's going on?*

A muffled sound echoed inside the house. Aaron stood frozen for a second before collapsing to the floor in a tangle of limbs. The frightened woman appeared to be begging someone out of Zoe's sight, the words impossible to hear through bricks and insulation. *Oh-my-god, oh-my-god.* Silent screams echoed in her mind. *Aaron.*

A man suddenly came into view. *I know you.* She swallowed hard, fear restricting her throat, her breath short, raspy gasps. He held a long-barreled revolver he set aside before grabbing the defenseless woman around the neck, began choking her.

She gasped aloud, unable to stop herself. When he turned her way, she ducked, her heart slamming into her ribcage. *Did he see me?* Watching the murderous rage that consumed his face, she had no doubt he would harm her as well. No doubt at all.

She crouched low and crab-walked along the side of the house to the back alley, thinking no one would think to follow her back there, the iced bricks rough to the touch even through her leather gloves. Her ankle still supported her, though it throbbed incessantly. She began to run, though traction was a problem, causing her feet to slip and slide in the process. She ignored the piercing pain, focused only on getting away. What to do? *Josh. He'll come and help me right away.*

She'd reached the end of the alley. Double back for her car or keep going? Something told her it was best to get as far away as possible, even if it meant leaving her vehicle. Racing across the deserted street, she searched frantically for her cell phone in her bag. *Damn it, where was it?* The harsh glare of sudden headlights made it impossible to see. She tripped on the pavement, landing hard on the frozen surface. Her skinned knees exposed between the tops of her boots and her parka burned from the cold and abrasions. Terror gripped her. The sounds of a car door being opened. Then she was lifted and thrown roughly into the back seat. *You.* She locked eyes with the murderer. No, this couldn't be happening.

"What are you doing? I need to go to the hospital." Her voice was weak, raw. Impossible to speak over the hard lump in her throat. This man had killed Aaron and the woman.

The man said nothing, and roughly tied her hands together before yanking a hood over her head.

"Let me go!" Nothing left to lose. Words of her police officer brother came back to her. *Never let them take you to a second location. Fight it out where you are.* She struck out with her feet, trying hard to kick him.

Then something slammed into the side of her head and she fell into a deep, dark void that stole her every thought.

TWELVE

Anna slumped on the sofa. A long pull on the bottle burned as it went down, but she was seeking oblivion. Only way she could sleep these days. *What was freedom but nothing left to lose?* The songwriter had been right. Since Tia's disappearance, she'd been oscillating through a hellfire she'd never known existed, and she'd been to war. One minute so angry she felt she was about to drop to her knees with a coronary, the next taken over by a grief so powerful she was unable to move, her body frozen.

She picked up her favorite photo of her with the Pace family. Everyone smiling and happy. A fun day at the beach, the sun glinting off the water. Her gaze fell on Tia, so identical to her twin sister Zoe, with their long blonde hair and bright blue eyes. She hadn't shared this with a living soul, but three days after Tia went missing, she'd experienced her first visit by her ghost. Her appearance in corporal form convinced her she was gone and led her to where her head was at now. That, and being incapable of living with the blame and dishonor now associated with her name.

She didn't know if she believed in God anymore, for what divinity would allow such things to happen? Or maybe they were a benevolent being that did not judge, left it to mankind to work out as best they could? Hell, she had no idea. All she knew was she was losing her way. She stared at her Glock sitting so silently on the coffee table, her fingers itching to reach for it. It would be so easy.

A flicker of a memory forced its way in from the first time she'd cheated death. When her heart had stopped from the smoke that filled her lungs, squeezing the life from her. She'd been aware. Seen things. Had it been real, what she had experienced? She'd been so young. Maybe it had been nothing but a hallucination, caused by lack of oxygen.

She closed her eyes to dispel the images of another time and place. She took another swig of the liquor, remembering coming back to consciousness on the ground surrounded by firefighters and first responders.

A wolf howled nearby, drawing her attention. The call meant something. A short edict from a combat vet of native ancestry came unbidden and word-for-word: *Wolf is our protector. Your spirit animal, Anna, because in your heart you are part wolf. It is the burden you carry. Never throw away your pack. Claim your territory and destroy your enemies, just like they do.*

A loud pounding at the front door startled her into sitting upright on the sofa.

Damn it. Go away.

Another round of fist thudding on her front door drew her to her feet. She crossed the room in long strides and flung the door open, her body stiffened with outrage. The sunrise glinted in her eyes and she blinked, clearing her vision. Recognition froze her brain.

Stunned, she stared, unable to find the words. Josh Pace. The oldest sibling and only brother to Tia and Zoe, a boy she'd had a huge crush on as a teenager. The insignia of the Anchor Police Department displayed on his uniform was a surprise. Last she knew, he was stationed overseas. No, that wasn't right. Zoe had mentioned that he was taking training to be a police officer a few months back. But what in the hell was he doing here at this time of the morning?

"Josh. When did you get home?" Josh was the illusive older Pace sibling, always out of the house. It was the twins she'd spent most of her time with.

Then her eyes narrowed with suspicion. This was not a social call. The tenseness around his eyes gave him away. She crossed her arms over her chest, bile rising in her throat.

"You got questions for me, Officer? Still think I had something to do with your sister's disappearance?" Her anger and frustration boiled over, ashamed that she was a mess while he stood there all slick shined and polished. *Now he's one of them? When the hell did that happen?*

"No, Anna, you misunderstand. I'm so sorry. I should have been here for you. I have no excuse. I've been away finishing my training these past months. I didn't even get home on weekends, though I did keep in contact with Mom and Zoe. But I'm sorry I wasn't here for you. Can you forgive me? I thought my becoming an officer would help in finding my sister. Sorry, our sister."

Josh had removed his hat, holding it nervously by the brim between his hands, letting in a rush of frigid air from the door still being open. His words took all the fight out of her, her shoulders sagging. If there was one thing she understood, it was withdrawing from things. For the past few weeks, she'd shut down to the point she had no idea how Charlie was running the business all by herself.

She hesitated letting him in, not wanting the terrible reminder of their shared loss. What good could come of it? Say what he might, there was no doubt in her mind that he must blame her on some level for not being there to keep Tia safe. She did, so it stood to reason others did as well. She was certain that Zoe was too polite to say anything, but she'd caught her looking at her sometimes, and she felt Zoe was questioning how it could all have unfolded as it had. She'd once mentioned why had Tia chosen to come live with her instead of with Zoe and her mom. But Tia hadn't wanted to do that, said she needed a break from being smothered by her twin and her mom. Anna got it. She needed her space too and her house was larger than the downsized house Cindy Pace had moved into after her husband died.

"Please, I really need to speak with you. Can I come in? Just for a few minutes?" he begged. His voice was strained, making her wonder what was up.

A sense of owing him and the family made it difficult to turn away much as she wanted to. This night had been particularly bleak for her. The altercation at the vendor with Karloff had sent her into a bad spiral. But what if her adopted family had turned a cold shoulder to her that fateful night? She'd be long dead.

"You'd best come in out of the cold. I've been a recluse myself of late. Hell, I didn't even know you were back." Josh had been home on compassionate leave for a few days last time she saw him at the beginning of the investigation into Tia's abduction, but that had been months ago.

"I've been back in Anchor for a couple of weeks. I meant to call around, but it's been kind of crazy with

Mom and everything. I'm a cop now, joined the force. Well, I guess that's obvious by the uniform. Slowly getting the hang of things."

"I'm really sorry about Mom." The disease had come on so sudden, like the stress of Tia having been taken had brought it on. Cindy had gone from a vibrant woman to a shell of herself in a matter of weeks. But Josh joining the force wasn't a big surprise in hindsight, knowing his interest in justice as a teenager. Lots of lively debates about it around the dinner table once she'd joined them permanently. But why had Josh felt compelled to come by at this ungodly hour?

Josh swiped a hand over his face, his expression turning haggard. Now that she took a good look at him, she realized he was nearly as bad off as she imagined herself to look. It was just the shock of the uniform that had hid it before.

"Why are you here, Josh?" She knew she sounded brisk, less than hospitable, but the untimely interruption was playing on her. Something was amiss and much as part of her didn't want to know, another part wanted any bad news, if indeed it was bad news, to be gotten over with as fast as possible.

"There's no easy way to say this. It's Zoe. She's missing. Been taken."

"Zoe? Gone?" Tia's twin sister, a foster care case worker, left an indelible print on anyone's life she touched. She was one of the most caring and kind people Anna had met during her thirty-four years on earth. A sense of her world imploding again made her sway on her feet and she grabbed at the coatrack by the door to keep herself upright. Why was this happening again?

"Are you okay?" Josh frowned.

She stared at him. *No. I'll never be okay again.*

"It's like what happened to Tia." Josh's expression grew paler and more stained, if that was possible. "Her car was found abandoned last night with an identical letter and a black rose on the front seat."

"What the fuck! The words exploded, her entire body vibrating in anger. Everything horrible about that time came rushing back in a tidal wave of roiling pain. Not that it ever left, but now it was in searing technicolor. The suspicions of the detectives even after she'd explained where she'd been, at the execution of her stepfather. But over and over again they shoved in her face that she had to be involved in some way. Not all of them, mainly Karloff, who wouldn't leave his theory alone. Why he hated her so much was anyone's call. It was the argument between her and Tia before she'd left for Texas that was held most against her. The fresh traces of blood on the floor of the garage. Her damaged knuckles. And the fact there were no other suspects.

No body had been found, no proof anyone was dead for certain. But in her heart, she knew Tia was long gone. If she wasn't, she'd have gotten away. Contacted them somehow. She'd taught her special defensive techniques that should have kept her safe. She wanted to punch something, anything, to free herself of some of the destructive rage pulsing inside her like a nuclear reactor ready to detonate.

"I'm in a terrible state. The cops are out looking into it, but I need to ask you. Is there anything you know that might help us to find them? Anything at all that made you wonder? I'm desperate. You might know something and not realize it."

Anna shook her head. "I was kept in the dark so much. At first, everyone suspected me. The thinking was the apple doesn't fall far from the tree. That maybe I was

JANUARY BAIN

more like *him* than not. Karloff still does. But I did work
the case day and night for months. But there were no
leads. Not one shred of evidence found that led us to any
suspect. And a lot of the time I had to defend myself
instead of being free to work to find her. I felt stymied at
every turn."

His eyes filled with liquid sympathy. "I know, it's hard.
But too often someone close to them is the person
responsible. Statistics prove this to be true."

"Dumping more fuel on a person's pain isn't right."
She shook her head. "And they kept saying that it will
help us find her if you cooperate. They were just hoping
I'd slip up and implicate myself. But I had no idea what
had happened or even what was happening. I wasn't in
town when she disappeared. Eventually they had to
accept it, since I don't have a damn doppelgänger. Karloff
insinuated I must have had an accomplice and still
believes it. Still insists I had something to do with her
disappearance." She gave it to him straight, her guts
roiling.

She wasn't letting the way she was treated be taken
lightly. How many other innocents had been given the
third degree, pushed into a dark place with no escape?
She glanced at her gun still visible on the table. The
movement of her eyes caught Josh's attention and his
glance shot toward the weapon.

He nodded, looking her straight in the eyes. "No, I'm
sorry, I didn't know. You have every right to feel the way
you do. Sometimes this job sucks. And that's saying
something since I just started the long slog to pension."

"Now that's an attitude guaranteed to make the big
bosses sit up and take notice," she said, falling back into
the old pattern she'd often shared with the Pace family
growing up with the monster always close by. Letting out

60

frustration in dark humor kept her inner wolf at bay. The beasts never got hungrier than they did in the far north, a wild place so far from civilization it brought out strange happenings that occurred with some regularity. Something to do with the long, cold winter days and nights with little sunlight to free a person's soul from a sea of darkness.

"There are lots of good men and women on the force who care deeply about people and justice, and I intend to do my darndest to emulate them. I need to say, so you know how things stand with me, Anna. I may be jaded by war and life, but not in my belief that most police officers are good people first, wanting to serve justice."

"Yeah, I know. Most are good apples. You want a beer?" she asked, wondering if there were any left. She needed to quit talking about this, any distraction would do. She couldn't get her head around the fact that now a second Pace daughter was missing.

To his credit, Josh didn't mention the time, or the whiskey bottle abandoned on the coffee table. "I can't. I'm on the clock. I have to get back." His eyes turned bleak. "The first forty-eight hours are critical. Every second counts."

"I'm sorry you and me have to go through this. That it's happening all over again. I—I really don't know what to say, really. It's just so unbelievable." Maybe it was best Cindy's mind played tricks on her. At least she wouldn't be aware her other daughter had been taken.

"I shouldn't have bothered you—you've been through so much already—but I was thinking…" He paused and she knew he was hoping she'd resume the mantle of private investigator and use her hard-earned specialized skills to assist in whatever way she could. But her skills hadn't helped Tia. What good would they do now? The miasma of grief had hung over her completely after Tia's abduction and being blamed for it hurt worse than she could say, clouding her judgment toward the end, stopping her. The problem with life was it didn't come with an owner's manual. She'd had no idea how to cope. Then or now. How to move on. Stop the pain of living through one more fucking second mired in agonizing grief, feeling herself labeled with the burden of being tagged a suspect by some.

She shrugged, uncomfortable with the unspoken words hanging between them. It was so much easier to have a few drinks and fall into a stupor. No one could blame her. Her life was a desert filled with demons and shadows. But something else stirred way down deep inside. Maybe her sister was still alive? Maybe a tiny shred of hope still existed? It wasn't like she had anything pressing to do other than get drunk and pass out. If she could be of some value. Because now, there was nothing left in her life to stop her doing anything and everything, legal or not, to get to the truth. The thought riveted her, made the ground seem firmer beneath her feet. A fresh perspective maybe just what was needed. At least she could try. She felt the old drive stir inside herself, the one that took over and did the impossible if she let it.

"I can't promise—"

"Anything at all you can do, I'd appreciate." He'd jumped in before she could finish the thought.

She gave a nod. She owed the Pace family more than she could ever repay. "Just let me get cleaned up and I'll head out."

"Thank you."

"We'll find her." The hollow words sounded even worse spoken aloud, making her cringe. But Josh didn't seem to notice or was pretending not to.

"Yes, we will."

Unable to look him in the eye again, she opened the door for him to leave, letting in another freezing draft of icy air.

One day at a time seemed almost too much at the moment. One hour. She'd start with that.

THIRTEEN

The Buck pulled up his appointment calendar on his computer and checked the schedule, taking a moment to delete the weekend's main event. Now that his wife was gone, time for the cat to play with the little mousey. He shouted, "Elena, where's the entry for the Museum's Charity event? It's missing from the schedule."

His new office assistant came scurrying in, her large breasts bouncing under her frilly white blouse momentarily distracting him. Was she aware of why she'd been hired? She noticed the downward slant of his glance ogling her chest and blushed a becoming shade of rosy pink, avoiding looking him in the eye.

"It should be there. I updated the schedule this morning." Her tone was underscored with worry and rightly so, after all she had only held the position one week. She moved in closer to the computer when he didn't get out of the way. She grabbed the mouse and began to frantically scroll the screen. The action placed her right in his personal space where he wanted her situated. He breathed in her enticing fragrance. Nice, vanilla, easily controlled. He picked up a can of cola. Waited for his chance. Then made a precise, controlled hand movement at the exact second she turned back toward him. She jostled the pop tin, splashing some of the bubbly brown fluid on her pristine blouse.

"Darn it, so clumsy of me." He yanked a bunch of tissues from the box on his desk and patted at the growing stain on her blouse front. Very perky indeed. The now translucent material revealed a remarkable set of boobs, held firm in a low-cut push-up bra of white lace fabric. His mouth watered at the sight. Did her panties match? Maybe he could talk *The Man* into her becoming one of them, then he could do whatever he wanted to her without objection? The idea sent a rush of anticipation soaring through his system. "I'll buy you a new one to replace it. What size are you?"

She grabbed the tissue from his hand. "Let me. Please, don't worry. I'll take care of it."

"I think there's a T-shirt left over from my campaign. You can change while you rinse the stain out." He reached into the bottom drawer of his desk and pulled out a form-fitting shirt with the phrase "Save a Buck with Duffy!" prominently display on the front. "You don't want it to set. That's such a nice blouse and looks so pretty on you it would be a shame."

A deeper blush stained her cheeks. She reached for the article of clothing and he held onto it for an extra second, flashing dimples he knew women found charming. "Please, forgive my clumsiness."

"No worries." She smiled and ran away while he waited impatiently to see the reveal of the fit of the size small shirt on her well-endowed frame. He drilled his fingers on the desktop, pondering the upcoming election. Now that he had the doc in his back pocket, he had it all in hand. She'd never divulge his secret, she had too much to lose. But who could have guessed how dark the doc actually was? He snorted, feeling like a downright choirboy in comparison.

The phone rang, interrupting his thoughts and he answered it personally, something he often did to make himself appear a man of the people. *Phttt, people were so easily fooled.* The Buck was never going to be one of them, not by a country club mile.

FOURTEEN

Thirty minutes later, showered and feeling more herself after two huge mugs of coffee, Anna picked up the battered metal disk she'd laid aside on the coffee table. She ran her fingers over the discolored metal, feeling the imprint of the wolf's head image. It had been baptized by fire so many years ago. Then she took a deep breath and tied it around her neck, ready to do battle. She dressed in a parka rated for fifty-below-zero weather and exited the three-bedroom red-brick house on the outskirts of Anchor she'd purchased along with twenty acres of land, ignoring the burning pain the cold always caused her physical scars. It felt empty with Tia gone. She didn't bother to lock the door. What did it matter if a whole tribe of raccoons or a family of black bears moved in while she was absent? At least they'd be company.

Where to start? Her mind shot back to the few facts the cops had shared. The car left abandoned. The ominous letter and black rose. Thoughts of how kind the twins were to everyone they met even when they didn't deserve it rose to the surface, giving her an idea. It would have been so like either of them to stop and help another. Maybe the setup was someone pretending to break down on the highway? Had the asshole laid in wait? She needed to find out where Zoe's car was found. Because it was obvious now they had something bigger going on in Anchor. And in the dark winter of a lost soul, any cruelty to man or beast was possible.

She picked up her cell and punched in the number Josh had shared and without preamble asked, "Where was Zoe's car found?"

"Anna." His tone was one of surprise. "Right. Out on Cariboo Drive just before it connects with Gambell on that lonely stretch of road, about a quarter-mile from where Tia's was found."

"Are they looking into the situation of the unsub pretending to be stranded?"

"The department doesn't have the resources for a profiler, which is why I came to you. You're the best at deduction and tracking for a thousand miles. But it makes sense, knowing Tia and Zoe. They'd stop to help *anyone* in need." His tone of voice changed, became more somber. "You know, Zoe's been looking after our mom full time."

Guilt wrenched her body. The rest of the world had been moving on while she'd gone stagnant, needing her help or at least her attention. To think Alex was gone and the woman who had been so kind to Anna, taken her in, was losing her mind. Nothing fair about it, bad things happening to good people. "I'm truly sorry. I should have been there more." She had been by to visit, but she felt like an intruder. Cindy often forgot who she was, their long-shared history. She'd been angry at Anna a lot, as if she blamed her for the abduction. Or maybe it was all on her? No excuses acceptable though, for not visiting every day to give Zoe more breaks.

"No need to apologize. You've had more than enough going on these past few months."

"Thanks, but I'm guilty as charged and I do apologize for my neglect. I'll get over to see her soon as we find Zoe, I promise." She changed gears, pushing uncomfortable thoughts to the back of her mind. Right now, Zoe needed her more. "I'm guessing the department didn't want to cover overtime for a stakeout?"

"*Phttt.* With budget cuts, we don't even get partners anymore for routine patrols. Besides, with six months between events, it would be a lot of overtime, and that's knowing it was going to happen again, which they couldn't have foreseen."

"Events" didn't half cover it, but there was a human need for such strategies. Label it "kidnapping and murder" and all hope was lost. She could be circumspect, ease Josh's pain for now. But carry the coping mechanism too far, and dissociate identity disorder, or DID, could develop. It was always best to face the truth, even if it led to devastation for that too will pass. No, that wasn't quite right. It had not passed for her. She rubbed her head aching from the slight hangover, wishing she had not had anything to drink tonight, confusion worrying her brain before she pushed the conundrum aside.

"Well now they do. Most operators shorten their timeline. When it happens again, it will likely be sooner rather than later," she said. "And it will happen. He leaves a letter and a rose—he's a serious contender, not trying to hide completely in the shadows. He's marking his territory, leaving breadcrumbs to follow. Thinks he's smarter than anyone else too is my bet, hiding in plain sight."

It was obvious the unsub fell into the organized category. Both events had been planned, the location ideal to avoid detection. The perpetrator had a signature with the rose and letter. He had to be intelligent enough not to have been caught: most likely a sociopath, notwithstanding the religious quote, which might be deemed justification or just a prop to throw them off the trail. No bodies had been found, which was highly unusual in these cases and would hamper the investigation considerably.

Horrific as it was for the families, a body provided essential clues to the crime. It allowed the investigator to envision how the offender experienced it. Obviously, the unsub used cunning to lure the victims. Motive, the why of it, never mattered to her as much as results did, but it was important to consider it if she wanted to fully understand the crimes and solve them. A comprehensive picture was what was needed, not falling into the trap of narrowing the scope of things too soon. Not like that damn Karloff's way of solving crime, wanting an easy target rather than finding the real culprit. Tunnel vision was useless, detrimental to solving crime.

"We have to catch him, now, before it's too late," Josh said, interrupting her thoughts, his voice strangled by emotion.

"Yes, we do. My suggestion is for you to check records going back ten, fifteen years. Who as a teenager was caught being cruel to animals? Or was lighting fires around town? We're looking for a man in his mid-twenties to early forties, male, likely white, with no interpersonal relationships. Above-average intelligence who's either physically strong or has knowledge of how to control his victims. Tia was tough, I taught her a lot of defensive moves, so he might be drugging them to make the process of taking them easier. Maybe with a syringe filled with a powerful muscle relaxant." Her own words make her cringe, thinking of what the two women had been through. But no time for that now, she had to push back, or she'd be of no value to Zoe and Tia.

"I'm on it."

"I'll be in touch." She clicked off the call, shoving the cell phone into her jacket pocket. Between the searing cold of the morning and having Josh counting on her, her brain had finally cleared. Her training was giving her the edge now. When she'd been determined to get her private investigator's license, she'd already undertaken a degree in criminology and it included courses in criminal profiling and geo-tracking. She'd even studied using body language and lie detecting to aid in interrogating suspects. It didn't matter where a person lived, she could be the best at what she did, in her humble opinion.

Problem was, there had been no witnesses when Tia had been taken. There was no CCTV in that area of Anchor; so many details missing due to having no way to determine all the facts finding a body with its trace evidence would have provided. Instead, all they had were photos of an empty SUV, a black rose, and a letter typed on a keyboard, the easy-to-come-by paper clean of fingerprints or DNA. Would the cops find someone who'd seen something this time? Out on that stretch of deserted highway it was unlikely which was why it was chosen.

Maybe she'd head into the office first, find out how things stood with Charlie. She felt deep regret for how much she'd piled the running of things onto her slender shoulders these past few months. It hadn't been right, and her only excuse was her inability to function. But that was over for now. Or at least part of her believed it as she wished it into reality. Not that she'd ever be able to live as a whole human being again, but she'd get Tia's and Zoe's abductor, if it was the last thing she ever did.

FIFTEEN

To the strains of his namesake crooning in the background, the man added a sixteen-ounce bottle of embalming fluid to a two-gallon bucket of water. Then watched the blue liquid swirl and disappear while giving it a quick stir with a stainless-steel spoon. He knew so many death secrets others would never know, and that alone blessed him with a lovely sense of one-upmanship. As he prepared the liquid, he glanced over at Richard whose job it was to massage the body.

Vigorous actions were necessary to prepare the deceased to accept the fluid, preserving it long enough for it to be viewed by family. Though usually his cousin was quick in his massage movements, today he was sluggish and seemed not to be enjoying the job as much as he usually did. Maybe because the body was an old guy and not a young female?

They didn't get too many prime ones. Most of their work was with the elderly.

"Are you nearly ready?" he asked, unable to keep the growing impatience out of his tone.

His helpmate only grunted but then stepped up his manipulations to the body. A few minutes later, he announced, "Okay, hook him up."

"Could you at least put a towel over his private parts?" he said, his mouth firmly compressed at how casual the guy was around the bodies, like they had never been human.

Richard made a face at him, but he did casually throw a towel over the old man's withered genitals. "There, you happy?"

He went about his duties diligently, ignoring the dig, letting the calming music work its magic. There was always a peace about death that soothed him. A corpse has a beauty and a dignity which a living body could never hold. Cleaning the insertion site, he sliced into a vein near the base of the clavicle and pushed the tube in toward the heart. He carefully tied a ligature around the lower side of the tube. An artery would take the embalming fluid and he repeated the process, then hooked up the pump that would inject the substance into the man's body.

His instructor had drilled it into him that he must think the deceased's family could walk through the door at any time, stating all the dead must be treated as if they were a member of their own family. He tried to live up to the highest standard of care, but he couldn't say how many times he'd seen others do things that would have brought the teacher's wrath to bear on their foolish heads.

He watched the embalming fluid bulge the network of blue veins and made sure the drains continued functioning, occasionally needing to clear the entry ports of clogging blood and tissue. When only twenty percent of the mixture remained, he reversed the cannula to the other side of the artery, careful the eyes didn't pop from the pressure. An assistant, fired on the spot, had made the mistake once and it had taken all his skill to ensure the corpse looked natural after. Finally, he turned off the machine, tied off the injection sites and used sealing powder on the wounds to stop them from leaking.

Now he needed to use the trocar to aspirate the internal organs. He inserted the instrument two inches to the right and two inches superior to the umbilicus as he had been taught. It was necessary to clean out the hollow organs such as the stomach, pancreas, and small intestine to keep gasses from building up. He removed the trocar and turned it around and did the lower body, making sure to catch the large intestine and the bladder. The odor for this part of the procedure could not be contained by the vapor rub they had both dabbed on earlier on the outer rim of their nostrils in the futile attempt to avoid it. He gagged a couple of times as discreetly as possible but caught his assistant looking at him with unholy glee as he worked a lit cigar. Richard and his expensive cigars. He shook his head but said nothing.

Taking up the cannula once more, he inserted it into the body and began injecting the heavier cavity fluid that contained a larger abundance of formaldehyde. He didn't want to be the one responsible for having the body purge so he did a thorough job of it, finally removing the trocar and putting in a trocar screw to stop any leaking. He had previously stuffed the man's anus with cotton and was relieved he did not have to do it now. Richard watched the process with disinterested eyes, finishing the smoke, and then throwing the butt into the drain. Pig.

"You want to wash the body?" he asked though he knew the answer. His lazy ass cousin always had him do the majority of the work. It was a matter of principle with him to ask though.

"Nah, you're doing a bang-up job. After he's dressed, I'll help get him in the coffin." Richard somehow managed to sound magnanimous.

Big of you, he thought, but did not utter the words aloud. The final makeup touches to add life-likeness to the face would be done by a professional cosmetologist who worked at all the funeral homes in town on retainer. She'd taught him a trick or two, though she generally kept her distance since an incident that didn't bear remembering.

Turning his mind back to the job at hand, he stirred up the disinfectant and gave the body a thorough wash, being careful to get into all the crevices. Older people were more work, with their wrinkled bodies. After it was dry, he redressed it, trying not to give his lame-ass assistant a look of approach as he struggled with the clothes. Finally, he nodded at Richard and the two of them hefted the old man into the waiting coffin. He closed the lid. Bernadette wouldn't be by until the morning and he preferred not to leave a casket open to the night air.

"Decent job, little cos," Richard remarked.

He hated being called that, but swallowed his pride as he so often did. Richard had the dumb luck of being born first. Most people seemed to forget they were even related. He was well aware he was nothing to look at. Nondescript no-color hair and bad skin, too tall and thin by half though he kept himself fit by working out and had become strong enough to lift his own weight easily. His mother had mentioned more times than he could remember that he was unlovable. But she didn't live long enough to see the man he'd become, after she'd perished in the fire. His heart pumped louder, ringing in his ears with the memory of the roar of the beast as it consumed everything it touched. Dust to dust, ashes to ashes.

"Did you hear the news?"

"No, I've been busy." He itched for a shower to rid himself of the smoke and germs, wanting Richard to be long gone. He steeled the usual impulse to bash his cousin over the head, though the visual of his brains leaking out all over the floor gave him a surge of instant satisfaction.

"Another girl's gone missing. A black rose and letter left in the car at the crime scene again." Richard's smarmy expression swam before his eyes as dots of light danced across his vision.

"What?" A sliver of rage escaped him before he shut it down.

"Yeah, that's something all right. Now it looks like we have our very own serial killer right here in Anchor. I wonder what he does with them?" Richard's eyes gleamed with an unholy light, obviously imagining the unthinkable.

"Probably faked it."

Now his cousin looked confused. Then pissed off. He got off on delivering news first, always had to be right. "Why do you say that? The words were *exactly* the same as printed in the paper last time. Well, after the letter was leaked to the press. Of course, it's real. Has to be. The girl that was taken—Zoe Pace—did you know she has an identical twin sister and she disappeared six months ago? Bet you didn't know that either. Don't it beat all."

"*Phtt*, sounds like a copycat to me." Some asshole doing such a thing grated at him, flayed his skin. Made him want to strike out.

"Why do you care? Not like you don't impersonate

Elvis. You're not half bad at it." Richard gave him a speculative glance.

Now he was certain his cousin wanted a favor. The
guy never came close to a backhanded compliment unless
he needed something.

"Do you think you could manage a gig tonight? The
hockey team's having karaoke and they're hosting a farm
team from down south. It will make the town look good
Elvis showin' up. Since I know you won't help by offering
a billet for one of the players."

"I can't have people staying here. You know that." His
growing collection of old cars and trucks was taking up
more and more space. His newest toy, an old Cessna he'd
lovingly restored, promised freedom. One of these days
he'd have to cull them, though the thought sent anxiety
snaking through him. He did not like to give up on
anything he owned, though he was verging on becoming
a hoarder. He needed to be smart, not draw more attention to himself than the Elvis gigs already did. But it was
his passion, not his hobby, dressing up and becoming The
King. He could hide inside the man. Only then was he
respected.

He weighed his options now about helping out his
cousin, knowing the last dig was meant to sway him with
guilt. *Yeah, right.* Saying yes was the easier choice, but he
had something important to do. The pull of the stage
tugged at him hard as well. He never looked better than
when he was channeling The King. Beat John Wayne
Gacy all to hell with his stupid-ass clown face. Instead, he
would be splendid, outfitted in a black wig, spectacular
makeup, and fancy costume. Perhaps he could manage
both events.

"I promised a friend I'd help them move, but yeah, I
can do a number or two. If we don't get a call." An under-

taker's life was never their own. Somebody was always dying. And "we" meant him. He always took the summons by family, hospital, or personal care home.

Richard raised a skeptical eyebrow at the mention of his needing to help a friend move. Or maybe it was at his having a friend?

"I'll text you the deets. Later, cos." Richard stomped up the steep steps of the basement without a backward look. No help offered, of course, for moving the deceased over to the conveyance and hoisting it to the main floor.

He sighed, unlocking the wheels of the gurney with a shove of his boot before pushing it toward the elevator, reliving a favorite entry from his e-reader on the Zodiac killer. There was much to admire in the guy's MO, the genius far too clever to catch even with his taunting of the public and press. Following the exploits of serial killers had been an interest of his since his teen years, though he'd learned to keep the intel secret.

SIXTEEN

DAY ONE

Anna parked in the alley and opened the driver's side door, shivering from the blast of cold after the warmth of the heater. It took all she had in her to make the short walk up to the back entrance of Lone Wolf Investigations with its iconic signage of a white wolf against a black background. She intended to slip in the back door to avoid questions, but soon as she did, Charlie was there to greet her.

"Hey, good to see you. Good timing as well. Got a client who needs your special skills in hacking cooling her heels in the waiting room and she looks lower than a snake's belly in a wagon rut. Would you be up for it?"

Charlie gave her a bright fake smile, her eyes wary. She had the right. And the license to use her favorite Southern expressions during business hours or otherwise. A matter of fact, even after all these years, Tia, Zoe, Josh, herself, and especially Cindy as all spoke with some leftover traces of accent and speech pattern from living during their formative years in the Deep South. The last time she'd showed up here, she'd not made it more than half an hour before disappearing on Charlie. If she was disappointed in her, she didn't let on. She had a lot to make up for, best get right to it, though every fiber of her being wanted to jump on Zoe's abduction.

"I can always find some time for you, Charlie. I've got news for you, I'm about to begin working on another case. Unfortunately, a tough one."

"You are? That's great." Then her eyes clouded over. "Oh, right, Zoe Pace is missing."

"I've just met with Josh. He's a recent hire by the APD. I'm going to see what I can do to help out." She itched to get to her office computer. Begin a file and do some sleuthing for leads.

Charlie hesitated. "Maybe I should take the new client?"

"No. I can do it. Bless your heart, but you've done so much already, running things while I've been AWOL. I can't thank you enough for keeping things together. You're a good woman, Charlie Cameron."

She shrugged, a shadow passing over her face. "Least I could do. I needed to keep busy anyway. And chasing cheats has always been my specialty. Love finding me someone who's milking the system or a philandering spouse and catching them getting their rocks off. Especially since I've been living through the biggest drought since the Dirty Thirties."

TMI was Charlie's other MO. She and Charlie could not be more unalike in that regard. It was a good thing. She filled in the gaps of a conversation. Anna would most likely be in worse shape, if that were possible. *Why do people always say it could be worse?* Sometimes, people stumbled through experiencing the worst shit life could throw at them and didn't need to hear it could be worse or they'd pack it in. "Okay. Give me a minute to get settled and send in the client."

"Will do, boss." Charlie hurried away, the efficient aura surrounding her nearly as strong as her favorite perfume.

"You can really do that? Get rid of all those nasty pictures of me?" The young woman who'd introduced herself as Sadie Brown, with the sad eyes and jaded smile, sat up straighter in the office chair, her flagging energy seeming to revive in an instant.

"It's what you want, right?" Anna raised her eyebrows at the new client. It was a rare moment of victory in many months. The very reason she did this type of work, spending hundreds of hours learning how to hack into accounts. One more troll was going to bite the dust.

"Do I? It's all I've wanted since that scumbag accused me of cheating on him and then spreading all those slanderous lies and posting my private pics. I shouldn't have trusted him. It was stupid and I'll never forgive myself." Sadie began to chew on another ragged cuticle.

"What? Forgive yourself for loving him? You have nothing to forgive yourself for, Sadie. As my mother always said, 'men don't make it easy to love 'em, but the least they can do is keep from airing their dirty laundry in public.' She'd tell you to take the high road now and move on." Her mother had been an angel. The least she could do was pass along her wisdom, as much as it hurt to speak of her. Honoring her memory was more important than her pain.

"Yeah, I'm never going to take that chance ever again. From now on, no naked photos, no matter how much they beg." Sadie offered her first genuine smile since she'd arrived in her office.

"Good. Then I won't need to do this for you again."

"Say, you know who you look like?" she asked.

Sigh. "No idea."

"That actress. What's her name? She was in a Sean Connery movie. She was a great sleuth in that one, good thief too. Oops, sorry; didn't mean to imply you are. A thief, that is. Of course she isn't either. Just a part she played. God, time I shut up already."

"Okay then, is there anything else I can do for you, Sadie?"

"I do have two questions. How did you learn to do this? And can we turn the tables on him?"

"Anyone can learn how if they've got the patience and the inclination. It takes about ten thousand hours to master a new subject. The second question I can't help you with. I don't believe it's right to replace one wrong with another." She shrugged, keeping her expression neutral, wondering if she *really* believed it anymore. The words had come out rote, left over from a different era with no real meaning under the surface, for who would miss an abductor of women? Or children? Damn right, the herd needed to be culled. The memory of the person who had first planted the seed coming to mind, Sergeant Carter. Back then she had mostly rejected it. But now the idea fired a heat missel that raced through her blood-stream, energizing her in a good way.

"Well, thanks for your help." Sadie hesitated, glancing around her rather spartan office. No signs of personality existed except for a favorite photo of the Pace family taken before Alex had died.

"I'm sorry about what happened to your sister."

She pressed her lips together, managing a curt nod. At least the woman hadn't heard the latest, that her other sister had now disappeared as well. The reminder sent her wanting to run for cover. She pushed back at the sensation with all she had, remained seated at her desk. "Thank you. I'd appreciate it if you would check in with Charlie on the way out. She'll need your particulars for billing."

The time for innocence had passed. She couldn't afford to do pro bono work to the same extent anymore. The business was faltering and she needed to step back in the game if it was to continue. Did it matter if the business came to an end? But all the hard work of learning the trade and starting the enterprise had meant sacrifices. Time away from the family. If only she had known what was coming. But now she couldn't let all the sacrifice go to waste. Past time to step up and help if only for one more kick at the can.

Plus, she knew Charlie needed the job. She'd gotten into trouble in her teens and had found it difficult to find her place in life, a reason to clean up her act. Lone Wolf Investigations had done that for her. Hell, she'd even let her choose the sign that hung over the business on the street outside, remembering how she had insisted a white wolf being the best choice for representing the owner. Hmm, a gray one might actually be more appropriate now, considering her leanings of late. But how could she take that away from her now after all she's done keeping things together so she'd have a business to come back to? She couldn't.

SEVENTEEN

Zoe's head ached. A terrible throbbing pain that made it difficult for her to focus. What had happened? Where was she? She forced her eyes to open though they stung like someone had scraped sandpaper across the corneas. Blinking rapidly and painfully, she peered at a darkened room. A basement? A dugout? She was surrounded by dirt walls and a low ceiling, lying on a narrow cot, a smelly blanket covering her. She pushed it away in disgust and sat up.

Waves of vertigo made a hot wash of acid flood her mouth. She leaned over, retching and puked onto the packed-earth floor. Stones were visible here and there, poking up through the soil. The stench of musty soil annoyed her sinuses. She sneezed a few times in succession, adding to her misery.

Wiping her nose and mouth with the back of her hand, she pushed herself upright, getting her first good view of where she was: a small, rough room with a couple of wooden pallets for hauling freight piled haphazardly along one wall. But why was she here? Nothing. No inkling came through her scrambled brain. Scared now, she began shaking violently with fear and distress. *What the hell's wrong with me? Why can't I remember what happened? And to think her brother Josh had perfect recall of every day he'd lived since he was two years old.*

She got unsteadily to her feet, her vision still blurry, her limbs heavy. Stumbling over to the trapdoor in the low ceiling which seemed a mile away, she tried opening it, but it was stuck and she slammed her palms hard against it, rattling what sounded like an iron ring on the topside. "Hello, anybody home?"

Dead silence.

She tried pushing at the wooden boards harder, banging with her fists, screaming louder for assistance, but it made her head throb so badly she leaned over and was sick again.

She crawled back to the cot, pulled herself up and lay down. This was bad. She had no idea why she was locked in and unable to figure out where she was in the unfamiliar surroundings. *Who* could have done this to her? What was her last memory? *If only my head didn't hurt so much.* She searched through the messed-up puzzle that was her damaged brain and pressed her fingers to her temples, unable to figure anything out. Thirsty now but too sick to look for water, she fell back into a stupor, her legs drawn up tight to ward off the chill, tugging the musty, revolting blanket over her cold shoulders.

EIGHTEEN

The music was too loud, the crowd oppressive when Anna walked into the Yellowhead Arena. The odor of hot bodies and yeasty beer permeated the air, making her wrinkle her nose in dissatisfaction. But what better place to check on the current lines of chatter of Anchor with half the town in attendance? People talking and giving up secrets was a lifeline for her occupation. Between here and O'Brien's she had gotten most of the intel necessary over the years to find a lead to solve a case. Never knew who would spill what useful bit of information when they were deep in their cups. She'd insisted on the place, though Josh dithered, preferring the idea of a coffee shop. She appreciated his sensitivity, but she was a grown-ass woman and could set aside the bottle when necessary. Iron will was one of her strengths when she chose to reach for it.

She caught the supercilious glances. It had been months since anyone had seen her out in public, other than the liquor store, so they were entitled to wonder.

But being under the microscope of suspicion had tainted things. The suspicions were clear in some faces. It made her skin crawl. She wanted to turn right around and leave them to their silly fun. Didn't they understand there was a possible serial killer lose in Anchor and it wasn't her? Yes, she realized, she believed it now. And damn it, the clock was ticking down on whether they'd find Zoe if they didn't act soon. They had to figure out the puzzle and storm the place if she had any chance of making it out alive.

She glanced at the karaoke stage and wished she hadn't. An old schoolmate, drunk and off-key, was stumbling through an awful rendition about putting a ring on it. Singing like that, shambling about the stage, she'd lowered her chances considerably of having it ever happen. Lots of good time gals in town. Lots of good women too. She ignored the wrench of pain and headed for the bar. About to order a double whiskey shot and beer chaser, she stopped himself. She needed a clear head.

"Orange juice," she half-shouted at the waiter. The natural sugar and vitamins in oranges were at least a start in the right direction. She'd put in a full day at the agency. Had made sure Charlie had felt appreciated for all she had done to keep the business alive during her absence. Spent time learning what the police had to date on the case. Hacking into databases was one of her specialties. She wasn't going to feel one iota of guilt after law enforcement had tried breaking her in half, squeezing her dry for weeks on end. Sure, there were moments she had almost left the office today, but she'd hung in there, taking it a minute at a time. Tomorrow had to be easier, right? *Crap, I freakin' hope so*. She took a swig of orange juice and grimaced, taking a look around while she waited.

The usual suspects, from the eighteen-and-over gang, all gathered round rough-hewn wooden tables. She spotted Josh threading his way through the crowd in her direction. The sight of him out of uniform, appearing far more vulnerable, made her swallow hard. It was somehow worse, understanding what the pair of them were going through. The disbelief, the agony of not knowing, time ticking away like a bomb about to explode in her head. At first, she'd been so certain it had all been a big mistake, Tia was detained somewhere and would be coming in the door at any second, apologizing for being late. But it changed. Slowly the image faded along with her fragrance and she knew she was alone.

"Evening, Anna," he said, sitting down across from her.

"Hey, there. Want something to drink before we begin?"

He shook his head and leaned in. The music was too loud by half.

"Thank you for coming," he said. He indicated his clothing with a gesture. "I thought civies might make people more comfortable."

"Sure. We're an outlaw town. Ever collect any of those Alaska Outlaw playing cards?" she asked to lighten the load, underlining how out of practice she'd become interacting with other humans these past weeks. The fifty-two card decks were popular and demonstrated Alaskan history in an entertaining way, each card famous for one legendary person or event.

He snorted. "I got the rebel and cons versions. You?"

"Sold a few decks to help raise money for the arena in my day. Probably some kicking around somewhere." She gave a lopsided smile. "I may or may not have raided the

APD data bank today. I reckoned I was owed a level playing field this time around."

"You should have your own rebel card. Ace of Spades." He gave her a speculative look. "I don't care how it's done —what we have to do. I just want Tia and Zoe found. You gotta raid the White House? I don't care. Mom's in a terrible state, asking for her daughter. Zoe's the only one who can soothe her." He leaned forward, his expression strained from trying to speak over the caterwauling trying to pass for music. "I think we should drive out to the crime scene tomorrow and compare notes."

"Yes, that's exactly what I planned to do next. Reconnoiter the area so to speak, dig up what I can." She didn't mention the Ace of Spades was the death card and had been since Vietnam. Maybe he knew and was giving her carte blanche? No, it was a coincidence. Josh was far too law-abiding to understand the new needs of society she was only beginning to unravel. Culling the herd was looking better and better.

And it was actually the old way as well, when frontier justice reigned supreme. Who could protect the people if the hands of the law were tied up in red tape, taking decades to find justice? And that was only if some half-assed lawyer didn't get them off on a technicality, or because they whined about their client's terrible lot in life. Gosh, give them another chance and they'd turn their tenth-grade education into a university degree in no time, clean up the drug use and be a *huge* asset to society. Right. And if they believed it, then bless their foolish hearts. For if there was anyone in society that deserved the death card more, it was serial killers. She could get behind. Big-time.

They were certainly getting their fair share of speculative glances at the moment. By now everyone would know the deal, of course. Some did look on in sympathy. Others, well, they had their own agendas. Did she believe people were inherently good? Yes, most, but others were born evil. Easily twisted to the dark side and able to hide among good people who didn't suspect such monsters existed. Otherwise, how to explain some people going through hell and turning out decent human beings with their moral code intact, while others chose the pit of deepest depravity at the slightest push or excuse?

"Looks like Elvis is about to take the mic," Josh said, gesturing with a nod toward the stage.

"Time to make a getaway." She grimaced with distaste.

"What? You don't like impersonators?"

She shook his head and got to her feet. "No. I prefer the real deal. Let's meet early. You up for a sunrise visit?"

"Sure. If you're okay with the early hour, I am too. Not like I'll be sleeping anyway. But you know, if you wanted to be Catherine Zeta Jones's stunt double, you might find your way in Hollywood." He got to his feet as well, zipping up his jacket.

"Hollywood's not for me. I've always called it the city without a heart, chewing up all those actors in the grinding machine they call the casting call." She didn't have to fake the shudder. "But Mom, I couldn't be more sorry about it. It's a cruel disease, robbing people of who they are, and who they loved, before their time."

"Yeah, me too. She doesn't sleep at night. Wanders the halls mostly. Zoe had to bar the doors." They walked toward the exit in single file, weaving between the drunken revelers.

"You got any help? You can't go every night without sleep and figure this case out. You're not superman. Even if you do have the gift of perfect memory of every day you ever lived. What's the freaky ability called again?"

He opened the door for her and they made their way into the freezing cold and onto the sidewalk in front of the arena. The overhead lamplight's glare was softened by a halo of frosty air. The fresh air was welcomed.

"Hyperthymesia. HSAM. And it's rare, not freaky. No, Zoe was—*is* a superwoman." Josh's expression crumpled at what he had implied with the past tense.

She looked at him, then away. A swift hard squeeze to her chest announced itself uncomfortably. Her heart had required surgery to close a small hole as a baby had taken a huge beating the day of Tia's abduction, would probably never be as strong again, according to her doctor if she didn't get adequate rest. But today she was still alive, strong enough she could aid someone. That Southern expression, run with the big dogs or stay on the porch, about summed it up. She could destroy evil and never look back, if it was what she was called upon to do.

"You okay, Anna?" he asked, noting the gesture.

"Just indigestion."

A group of men slammed through the doorway behind them, the loud noise making both of them whirl around. Hackles fired on her neck.

Risk assessment: moderate.

"Well, if it isn't the killer's kid, the one who lost track of her own sister," the tallest one spoke out, his tongue fueled by booze. "And the rookie cop looking to give her some comfort."

Tommy Speck, a town bully who had drunk himself to oblivion after his family was killed in a DUI crash. All through high school he'd been a thorn for many of his fellow classmates and for her particularly once he'd discovered the link between her and the monster.

"They're not worth it, Josh."

Josh wasn't having any of it. "You apologize to the lady. Right now."

Silence.

Tommy threw down the stogie he was smoking, adding littering to his litany of crimes. The gleam in his eyes suggested he might not know it, but he was headed for the mats. The words of Anna's favorite hard-nosed drill sergeant who taught Krav MAGA and risk assessment came to mind. *If you finish your opponent, you finish the fight.*

"Yeah. I think it's *you* that needs to apologize for the harm your stepdaddy did. Oh, right, I heard he's been executed down in Texas, so he's already paid heavily for knowing your candy ass—"

Anna slammed her right fist into Tommy's face, the crunch of bone very, very satisfying. Her actions had caught the bully by surprise. *Superior fighting knowledge can end a fight sooner than expected, asshole.* She got in another solid right hook before the man crumpled to his knees, concussed and no longer a threat.

Then one of the other wannabes in the group jumped her from behind, taking them both to the ground. Anna rolled with it, jabbing an elbow into the man's ribs, making him lose his grip. Jumping to her feet, she realized the men were backing off. Why? She was just getting into it, needing some stress relief. Ah, the taser held by Josh, his feet splayed for proper balance.

"Back off unless you want to spend the night in the drunk tank. Though personally, I don't think any of you are worth the paperwork," he said, his voice filled with such cold conviction it sent a shudder down her spine. He was going to be a good cop, given some seasoning.

Though maybe he'd already achieved it having been tempered by fighting in a war zone.

The four men grumbled and postured, but finally lent a hand to their fallen lame-ass buddies and bore them away. They piled into an old pickup, racing the engine in a bid to appear bigger men as they squealed the tires on the pavement. *Sure, that works.*

"You haven't heard the last of this," Tommy shouted out of the passenger window as they sped off his face a mask of rage.

"You okay?" Josh asked, sliding the taser back into the holster under his unzipped parka.

"Right as rain. You didn't need to do that—I had it handled," she said, rubbing her side where the man had slammed a fist into her. "I reckon I might have a bruise or two tomorrow, but nothing's broken."

"Good. Let's not make this a habit," he said with a grimace.

"I won't if they don't. I never undertake violence lightly, but I won't step away from a fight either. Bullies need to be called out. Taken to task and made to see the error of their ways."

"I knew you were good, just not that good. Where did you learn to fight like that anyway? That kind of efficiency speaks to your knowing Krav MAGA. You didn't hesitate. Canceled the first threat in two blows."

"I must be rusty. Should have taken one. In battle, you only get one opportunity. Best make it count to my way of thinking." She straightened her clothing. "It was all thanks to Sergeant Carter. He was a firm believer in the method. You can't always count on your weapon not jamming at the wrong moment or some technology not working properly. He was big on every soldier learning hand to hand combat as well. I don't think he ever realized how much his efforts would save lives. Or keep assholes in line." If she ever got her hands on the bastard that took Tia and now Zoe, she'd tear him limb from limb. Would Carter have appreciated it? Damn right he would, always standing up for what was right, not what was politically or socially acceptable at the time. Fads fade, but truth never does.

NINETEEN

DAY TWO

False dawn, a hazy pyramid of light called the zodiacal, appeared to the east as Anna drove past the spot on the side of the highway where Tia had last been seen all those agonizing months ago. She continued on the short distance to where Zoe had recently vanished. This was the first time she'd driven down the road since the fateful day, always taking the longer route. But what good had it done? Not like she didn't live with it every moment anyway. Closure. The word was a joke.

She caught sight of Josh's SUV coming from the opposite direction. She eased up on the gas pedal, waiting to see where he would pull off the road. When he stopped, she pulled up in front of her. She checked the odometer reading on her vehicle: 49.017.0 Hmm, forty-nine was the number of days for a dead soul to be reborn for Tibetan Buddhists, seventeen was also associated with immortality, rebirth, and transformation. An auspicious beginning. Then she snorted. *Why do I still do that, look for patterns and significance in numbers? Not like it alerted me to what was coming down for us. And not for what was happening to Tia and Zoe.*

She gave up worrying about it and got out of her four-wheel-drive truck, the cold an affront to her exposed flesh while her breath instantly froze into a mist. The kind of cold that seeped into a person's bones and chilled the marrow. Skin could begin to freeze in less than a minute here, leaving a person damaged for life. No one with a lick of sense took it lightly, always carrying a survival kit in their vehicle.

"Morning. I brought coffee," Josh said, holding out a thermal cup for Anna to grab while he held on to a second one. He was bundled up as well, his face a white oval inside his hooded black wool parka.

"Thanks." She took a large gulp of the brew, appreciating the instant heat that warmed her belly. She needed bucking up for what was ahead.

"Get any sleep?" he asked. He worked the coffee like his life depended on it.

She shrugged. "Enough. How's mom?"

"Unsettled. I may have to look at hiring someone for night duty." Josh shrugged.

"I can help with that, or at least help you look for someone."

"Thanks, but I'll manage. I got some leads, just need time to follow them up." He finished the coffee and set it aside. "You probably already know this, knowing you, but Zoe was going to meet Aaron Stone, an old friend of hers, the night she was taken. He's missing as well. How her vehicle ended up way out here is anybody's guess."

She nodded. "Yeah, I know. Cops have any leads on finding him?"

"There's an APB out. If he's still in the area, he'll be found."

"Any indication of foul play at his house?" Anna had read all the reports filed so far, but there was always the scuttlebutt discussed between officers. Not the first time she wished she was invisible and able to enter anywhere at any time and gain the knowledge she required. Instead, she had to make do with being a ghost in the machine with her hacking skills.

"None. If anything, it was almost too clean. But forensics are looking into it further."

"He has a rep as being pretty fussy."

"That's a fact. Better take your shoes off in his house if you know what's good for you."

"Do you think he's the one that left the rose and letter?" she asked.

If Aaron Stone was involved, he'd certainly managed to hide in plain sight since Tia had gone missing. Though the coffee was warming her, the heat fired by thoughts of discovering who had taken Tia and Zoe burned a hole right through her mid-center. What would she do if she came upon Aaron by his lonesome? She'd learned EIT, enhanced interrogation techniques, while in the military, meaning she could pretty much guarantee getting the truth out of anyone. Reading body language was useful in certain situations, but getting to down to the dark and gritty, it really paid off. No hiding the truth when someone was prepared to go the distance to make a person talk. She recognized, then accepted a change was occurring in herself and her perspective on the world, perhaps not for the better, but one guaranteeing results when push came to shove. At least she'd been given and had learned the right tools in her life preparing her for this moment. It helped her make some sense of it all.

Josh shook his head. "I don't see it. And he wasn't a suspect in Tia's case. No priors, not even a parking ticket."

She didn't bother to mention the APD hadn't found any other suspects to torture in Tia's case either. "He'd be a real chameleon if he could pull that one off. Venturing into Doctor Jekyll and Mr. Hyde territory. Though that's exactly how sociopaths and psychopaths do it. Hide in plain sight behind the mask of normalcy. It's worked since the first known case of serial killers, the Poison Ring, recorded in ancient Rome in 331 BC. If it's to be believed, it was an all-female group who blamed it on the plague but died of their own concoctions when forced to drink them. That's taking the steel magnolia concept to a higher level."

Josh gave a faux shudder. "Interesting conversation for this time of the morning."

The near-silent swoop of a great horned owl overhead took her attention, its muffled hoots reminiscent of a distant foghorn. It landed on a stunted fir tree nearby, its yellow eyes unblinking in the twilight. She shuddered. Owls were harbingers of death in many cultures. She wanted to ignore the significance, preferring to believe they would bring Tia and Zoe home.

"Some serial killers and rapists do hide in plain view. Remember how personable Bundy was. And then Gacy actually played a clown. A church deacon, medical personnel, even a cop. The list goes on and on." He shook his head. "It's hard to imagine what kind of mind can do those kinds of things to fellow humans, and yet be so hard to spot. They should look different than us in a fair world."

"Not much fair in this world, Josh. Good people get hurt all the time—bad people get away with things.

Maybe people need to step up more. If I had my druthers, I'd have been born back in the day of reckoning when a man was hung for stealing another man's horse. At least the western frontier administered justice on the spot. Nothing too shabby about living by the Code of the West, making your own justice when push comes to shove."

"It's long gone. No point in going there." He turned away and stared at the bleak landscape. His profile stood out against the shadowed sun obscured by a thin layer of cloud that was announcing another day, rising over the tundra. A yellow ball in a gray world. "I know what's causing you to feel this way. But it won't help if you go off half-cocked and do your own thing. I don't want to see you hurt further by this."

"Way too late for that. There is no deeper hurt than losing the ones you love." Unfortunately, it was something they had in common. The twins. Zoe and Tia, being identical, had a tighter relationship than most siblings. She'd seen evidence over the years—they even finished each other's sentences. Sure, they'd fought as children, but it had always been obvious they had a deep unbreakable bond.

"I don't want to lose you too." Josh turned to stare her in the eyes. "I know you too well, Anna. Promise me you won't take it upon yourself."

She took a moment to debate it, but still came to the same conclusion. "Can't make promises I can't keep. All I can say is I never do anything without calculating the risk. Not in Afghanistan, not in Iraq. And not here in Alaska."

"Just come to me first, that's all I ask." He waited a beat then added, "Mom has been telling me a lot in the past year about how time is short. Don't make it any shorter, please, Anna. I need to know I can be there for you. Can you do that for me at least?"

"Time permitting, yes, I'll call on you first. Best offer I have in me."

He didn't look happy about her answer. "Do you remember the great debates we used to have in Mrs. Thompson's English class back in Lexington? Your stance on capital punishment? Even quoting from Francis Bacon's essay *On Revenge*. You impressed the hell out of all of us, taking the high moral ground. That, and knowing who Francis Bacon was."

"That was a long time ago, in a galaxy far far away before my mom was murdered, I was left for dead in a burning house, and our sister disappeared without a trace. I was fourteen years old for heaven's sake, altruistic, thinking sanctioned murder made it somehow worse than the original act." She was uncomfortable with the memory of her former self, knowing if time travel was possible, she'd not recognize the girl she'd once been. "Now, I'm more of the mind they can't murder again if they're not around to do it. Of course, there has to be rock-solid evidence the crime of murder actually happened. I guess I'm more a realist than a moralist these days. And it's a little early in the day for philosophy arguments."

Then she asked, surprising herself. "You still believe in the moral high road?"

He let out a deep breath, shooting a frozen mist that spread around his face, making him look almost other-worldly. "If *anything* bad happens to Zoe, ask me again."

"I hear you." They locked glances for a long moment, strangely connected by a moment in the past. Josh had even more depth than she remembered. Of course, he'd been in war. Now she'd discovered a new war at home, a personal one that was going to change him, more than he knew. She felt the sensation of things being in flux again, but this time it bothered her less.

Then Josh looked away. "Okay, let's head over. Her SUV's been towed, but we can check the ground, maybe get a feel for it or spot something."

Together they strode over to the area where it was obvious a vehicle had been parked. Scant snow was left over the length the compact would have taken up on the graveled edge of the road. She stood about where Zoe had sat in the driver's seat and took a look around.

The tall chimney of the town's crematorium stood out bleak against the landscape, belching thick smoke into the sky. It brought with it an old memory of a kid in grade school on Memorial Day, giving a very short speech about his great-grandfather from Germany who had been a medical doctor in the camps. And that was all Anna had learned before the teachers and administrator had quickly intervened and stopped the kid mid-sentence. Who was the kid? The name eluded her, and she gave it up, taking a closer look around. It was a lonely stretch of highway, built between two subdivisions. The ground was stirred up by too many footprints, leaving little evidence.

Following a hunch, she walked along the roadway, looking carefully at the graveled section. Sixty feet back, she found what he was looking for. The place where another vehicle had stopped. Maybe the driver had pretended to need assistance? *Good, less disruption here.* Se crouched down and stared at the frozen ground, tracking over it in a grid pattern with her eyes. The vehicle had been parked here longer. The snow was melted from the exhaust, turning it into a sheet of black ice. The most dangerous kind of ice, invisible until a vehicle's wheels hit it and slid.

"See anything?" Josh asked, joining her as she took a series of photos with her iPhone.

"I think someone waited right here. It could be connected to Zoe's disappearance." She pointed at the evidence, giving a brief scenario.

He nodded. "That's plausible."

Spotting what looked like a cigar butt, she bent and took a closeup photo then carefully retrieved what might be evidence from the ice holding it to the ground, using her Leatherman tool to dislodge it from the crusted frozen snow.

"Cuban." She sniffed it. "Smells expensive. Who sells these in town?"

"A new place just opened up on Front Street a couple of months ago. The Perfect Smoke. Bit exotic for Anchor, but at least it means the town's growing."

She tucked the cigar into a small paper bag and pressed the flap closed. Plastic destroyed DNA evidence, sealing in bacteria.

"I'll be needing that." He held out her hand to retrieve the evidence.

She thrust the bag into her parka pocket, ignoring his request.

"Anna, you're not a cop. I could lose my job over this. I can't afford any missteps, I just started there."

She nodded. "I'll give it back to you later. You have my word. I just want to check out the cigar store first. I'll be careful of the DNA."

The sounds of a vehicle made them both look up. An unmarked police car approached. Crap. Detective Sergeant Cecil Karloff sat in the driver's seat, his usual expression of annoyance more pronounced than usual. He hoisted his more than considerable bulk out from behind the wheel and stepped out of the vehicle. Was this the asshole in charge of the investigation? Anna narrowed her eyes while observing the man lumbering over to join them, remembering past interactions. She'd not given this situation a risk assessment rating, figuring the man wasn't worth the effort.

"Lousy morning for making house calls," Karloff said by way of greeting.

"No need. Could have saved yourself the trip," Anna said.

"Heard you two were out here snooping around."

Fake news. Only one vehicle had gone by since she and Josh had stopped, a hearse, and it had turned down the road to the crematorium not five minutes ago. A red flag advanced on the play. Karloff was lying through his beaver-sized teeth. Again. Of course, he'd say it was strategic for getting answers.

"Find anything, Officer?" he asked Josh, deliberately ignoring her.

Anna glanced at Josh, noting the slightly flushed skin that could be attributed to the cold. She thrust her hand into her pocket and was about to pull out the cigar remnant when he answered the query.

"No, nothing. Just having a look around."

His answer shocked her more than Karloff's sudden appearance. A newbie never went against the establishment if they wanted to keep their job. Maybe he didn't care about it as much as she thought? Yeah, maybe he cared more about solving cases? Though the Anchor detachment had been interested in her help before Tia had gone missing, often recommending her services to the prosecution, since then, she'd been shut out entirely. Persona non gratis.

"Well, if you do, you know the rules. I'm in charge of this case now and things will be done by the book. Hell of a thing. Another woman goes missing. Sorry about your sisters, Officer Pace. And where were you on Friday night?" Karloff turned on her, a mean look replacing the weak or perhaps fake sympathy he'd shown to Josh.

Anna shrugged. "Home."

"Can anyone verify it?"

"Am I a suspect?"

"You *do* want to help us, right? Find the abductor of your sisters? The very family who helped you growing up. Your stepdaddy, evil minds begat evil."

"I am *nothing* like that monster." The words shot out before she could hold them in. But being seen in the same light again as that man had caught her off guard. It struck at who she was, what she stood for. Her hands fisted at her sides inside the thick leather work gloves. She'd never wanted to strike a man more. But what would it earn her? Time in jail for assault on a police officer. And no help to Josh in finding the twins' abductor. Karloff was right about one thing: she did owe her family. A debt that could *never* be repaid. She had to suck it up, do the right thing and stay out of jail. Being raised in the south might have made her sound polite, but in her heart, she knew herself to be a true rebel. Perhaps she was broken. But at least it would be of some use if she wasn't tied to the same rules as others. She could go beyond the normal rules of society to get at the truth.

"You've been warned, don't leave town. And I expect your statement to be completed by the end of the day as to your whereabouts Friday night between the hours of five and midnight."

Neither of them said anything this time, instead

waited for the asshole representing the worst kind of law enforcement to leave.

Karloff grunted his displeasure, letting out a belch that suggested he'd had garlic in the past twenty-four hours.

"Officer," he said, giving Josh a final nod before getting back into his cruiser.

"Yup, going to be a long slog to retirement," Josh deadpanned. "I apologize on behalf of all us who don't think or act old-school. The department is changing, one retirement at a time. Same as any business or industry, I'd guess. But Karloff, he's a rarity. Most of us stay well clear of him. I was warned about him on my first day."

"Yeah, Karloff's definitely one of a kind and it's best you stay clear of him. You can be anything you want to be, you know that, right? If this job doesn't work out, you're young enough to try something else. You got a lot to offer the world."

"It might come to that. Thanks for helping. I know it can't be easy."

She wanted to hug him. "No worries." She cleared his throat. The sun was above the horizon. Time to move on.

"I can take your statement later, if it helps?"

"Yeah, I'd prefer it. Seems they might be looking for an easy patsy again."

"No, I'm not going to let that happen to you. And there are lots of other officers out there that wouldn't either, not without proof. I know without a shadow of doubt you had nothing whatsoever to do with what happened to them. You're a good person, Anna. Don't forget that."

The words were salve for her soul, hearing them aloud. This time she hugged him.

TWENTY

The Perfect Smoke looked deserted when she pulled in front and got out of her truck. The sun was now moving on its lowest orbit across the sky, meaning it was constantly in the face of drivers for months on end.

When Anna stepped through the doorway, the telltale sound of a chime overhead let her know the room was under surveillance. She took note of the display shelves laid out with a vast assortment of imported cigars lined up with military precision. An image of her own battered desk back at the agency came to mind. What did it matter? People who came to her for help didn't care about her furniture.

A middle-aged man appeared in the back doorway a couple of seconds later, his smile of welcome already in place. His salt and pepper hair was longish though more stylish than most, his clothing a simple white shirt and black dress pants, a cut above the usual dress of Anchorites. Sweats, canvas overalls, and jeans made up the majority of clothing choices with the ubiquitous camouflage jacket or parka. *What is everyone hiding from?*

"Good morning. How may I help you?"

"You own this place? Very nice setup you've got here." She'd grown rusty at the art of small talk these past few weeks, ignoring the job and staying the hell away from people. It actually felt good to be reconnecting with others, bringing up old mannerisms. She could thank her Southern upbringing for knowing how to get along with people. Well, most of them, that is.

"Thank you, yes. My business. My risk, eh."

"I'm Anna Hale, by the way." She held out his hand and the other man gave it the expected shake.

"Archie Goodman. Nice to meet you." The man gave her a closer look. "I hope you don't mind my saying so, but you sure do remind me of that actress, what's her name? Catherine something or other, I think? Sorry, I can't remember. Ever thought of taking on a part time job? I might sell a ton more cigars."

Inwardly, she groaned, then remembered why she was there. "I don't mind at all. It's an honor to be mentioned in the same breath as the actress. She's a terrific actor. So, Archie, I was wondering if I could check a cigar stub with you and if you could tell me if you sold it here?"

The man's face fell slightly when he realized Anna wasn't there to buy his goods.

"And if you could suggest a good smooth middle-priced smoke?"

"Ah, yes, we have many choices in the mid-range that are popular this season." His smile had been upped a notch, nearly stretching his lips to the far edges of his face. "Would you prefer domestic or imported?"

"Not given it much thought. What do you recommend? An acquaintance of mine was smoking the one I wanted to check to see if you sold it here?" She dug the paper bag out of her pocket.

"Why not ask your friend?"

"An acquaintance. And they've left town already. I thought you might know? Save me looking a bit silly making a point of asking him, especially since I kind of chastised him for smoking around my dog." The white lie slipped easily off her tongue, meaning she was back on point. And to her mind, it wasn't a crime, when it was for the greater good.

"Of course. May I see it?"

"This might seem a bit odd, but can you check it out without actually touching it?"

A raised eyebrow or two, but the man nodded at the strange request. "Of course. Tweezers."

Anna handed it over and the man opened the top flap of the baggie and held it to his nose, sniffing it. "Aw, the fine aroma of an expensive Cuban. Always earthier. I fancy it's due to the process of being hand-rolled on warm fem—human thighs." The man smiled, obviously long used to using the phrase to lure customers.

"Could you narrow it down?"

"I'd need to check the leaves carefully under a magnifying glass, you understand. There's not much left of the butt and no markings, but the leaves, the composition, and how they are assembled may yet tell the tale. A little side note, back in 1887, when Arthur Conan Doyle wrote *A Study in Anna* he had Sherlock Holmes identify cigar ash as being unique. It led to Edmund Locard, who is responsible for the Locard's Exchange Principle which states every contact leaves a trace, publishing a paper on identifying tobacco by studying ashes found at a crime scene in the paper, *The Analysis of Dust Traces*."

"Interesting bit of history, Archie." She actually did know those facts, but she found it easy to give credit to others. She was way past needing to compete in such a trivial way.

Archie beamed like a graduate student excelling before an awards committee. "I'm an aficionado of assorted facts. No need to be less than just because we're living above the forty-ninth parallel."

Anna nodded. She was beginning to like Archie Goodman, too bad she had to trick him to get the intel she required. "I couldn't agree more. Would you have the time now, to use that expertise to help me out of a bind?"

The man hesitated. "I don't like to leave the store unattended during working hours."

"I'd really appreciate it. I'd also want a box to smoke myself if you can identify it. And another for my friend to make up for our differences over smoking around animals."

"Well, then, if you could hang around? It will take a few minutes."

"Of course. Thank you, sir."

"Perhaps you'd like to try a sample in our glassed-in smoking area while you wait?"

"No, I'm fine." Indulging herself in an old vice did not sit right at the moment.

"Okay, I'll be back directly."

The memory of Tommy Speck throwing a stogie on the ground a split second before their fight last night came back to her, giving her an adrenaline surge. Now there was a possible suspect. If she could prove Tommy had dropped a cigar at the scene of a crime, it would be a beginning.

Archie came back a couple of minutes later, a smug smile suggesting he had information.

"You've figured out the brand?" she asked.

"Indeed, I have. It is one of the Partagas family of fine

cigars that began manufacturing the cigars in 1827. Specifically, Partagas Serie P No. 2, 6 1/8 in length with a ring gauge of 52."

"Impressive."

"Not so much. The fact it had a bit more of a pointy end helped." Archie gave a self-depreciating chuckle which caused her to appreciate the cigar man even more.

"How much do they cost?"

"Not cheap by anyone's standard, but more than worth it. The cigar has a strong and unique robust flavor, stronger than the one you've just finished, which was our house brand. That particular Partagas is meant for the higher-end market."

"I'll take two boxes to start."

"Perfect. Do you have a cutter, a personal humidor?" Archie was elated.

"No, load me up."

She watched the man pull a few choice items off the well-stocked shelves. She agreed to each choice with a courteous nod, figuring she didn't need to worry over-much about smoking prematurely shortening her life. The way it was going, a long, extended life didn't have the same allure it once might have had. When this was over, she'd need to start therapy again, depending on what unfolded. Beyond that, she wasn't going to dwell on things.

"So you have other patrons asking for that particular brand of Partagas? Maybe been in here recently?"

"Hmm, it's higher end, but yes, a few clients enjoy the Partagas. I'd have to check my records for specifics?"

"Would it be a possibility? I just had a bit of inspiration you might appreciate. Thinking of starting an exclusive club where everyone smokes the same brand of cigars and drinks whiskey. You know, like those clubs where everyone in a small town with the same name starts one. Trendy. There's one in town now for everyone called Linda. The Linda Club."

"I love the idea! And I would enjoy helping you chose the perfect name. Maybe the Alaskan Cigar & Whiskey Club? Let me check for you. Don't go anywhere. I'll be right back." ,

By the time Anna left the store, her wallet was fifteen hundred dollars lighter, and the shopping bag housed everything from a semi-airtight storage tube for individual cigars to a double guillotine-style cutter to nip the ends. The business owner had even slipped in a free ashtray containing a small bag of silica sand for safety's sake, along with several boxes of free matches with his store's logo prominently displayed.

The best part? She had the names of the four men who appreciated the cigar brand.

And Tommy Speck was top of the list.

TWENTY-ONE

The man sat down at his antique desk and drew out the well-worn black journal from the hidey-hole. He'd only found the secret compartment by accident a year ago. Before that he'd hidden it under a floorboard, but this was so much more convenient, not having to pry up the hardwood and replacing the dresser and rug every single time he wanted to write in it.

He picked up the fountain pen and dated the entry on a piece of looseleaf he used as his rough draft, making sure to check he had the information correct. So many times he'd done this, he needed to number them. And no one had an inkling. Not a clue.

The Black Rose Log: Wife thirteen. February sixteenth. He then enjoyed changing the information to code, enjoying the process that would one day guarantee his legend: 6NAS 3ON13SSW ASL14E18 2N73SSW3O.

He'd chosen an ancient method called the Cesar Shift, thrown in a unique twist by adding a few numbers for good measure, shifting everything two spaces forward though sometime at random to spice it up, before renaming it the Elvis Code. Let the historians figure out his method. He wished he'd be around to witness those future anthropologists scratching their collective heads over it, like the Zodiac killer had managed for decades. He'd be the enabler of many conspiracy theories, a thought that brought him intense satisfaction.

He paused, thinking of the exact wording to use, the nib of the old-fashioned pen hovering above the page. He'd also turn certain passages that held clues to his identity into precise code, then re-enter it all in the journal. It didn't matter how long it took, how many times until he had perfected the final wording and code, he didn't need much sleep, a few hours a night being sufficient. He'd gotten long used to be disturbed as a child for long sermons so often called at the darkest hour of the night.

Tonight, I did what I do best. So far, the new proportions of drugs are working perfectly. She looks like she did before, maybe even better. A light touch with the cosmetics works best, at least at first.

I've acquired a number of warmer items including animal furs to wear for when we are together. Keeping her chilled an extra degree seems the better way to help preserve her. To that end, I have been keeping a scientific record of what exactly it is I do. It may be of use one day.

She seems happier, more angelic than in her previous life. Like all women, she's a bit enigmatic, like the famed Mona Lisa painting I've viewed online. Trust me, virtual galleries are the wave of the future.

I hope this time around to spend more quality time with her. I will write more when I have the opportunity. Running a business takes up far too much energy. There is a lot of competition between the businesses operating in the area. Not enough people are dying to support us. Ha-ha.

He enjoyed his moment of dark wit before his

thoughts drifted. The one that had recently left him had lasted so long before her perfection began to wane. He'd been certain for a time she was the one. To stay with him. But it was not meant to be. He closed the journal, slipping it back into its hiding place.

And if she wasn't the one, he'd pin his hopes on his first love. He was ready now for her having learned from the mistakes of the past. Suddenly, an idea arrived fully formed, like an epiphany directed from above. His heart fluttered with excitement. *Yes*, why had he not thought of it before? He didn't have to wait. Two women to comfort him, listen to his day, see to his needs.

Then he sighed. Such a busy day awaited him before he could plan for the event. And no doubt his cousin would be of little help. He'd gotten in late last night after a night of partying, by the state he was in on the video monitors. Richard had moved into the guest cottage a few years back, promising to make up the rent by doing more around the place. *Right*. It had been a fiasco. The only reason he let Richard stay was that he was his last living relative.

He grew more pensive, drilling his fingers on the desktop and staring into the middle distance. Something hadn't been quite right this last day or two between them. The strange look from Richard. One that defied explanation. Like he knew something and was considering when to share it.

Had his cousin stumbled upon something incriminating? He'd been extremely careful, timing his movements to precision. No way was he exposed. And if he was, well, he could live without a living relative as well as not.

TWENTY-TWO

Striding through the doorway of the Anchor Police Station, Anna kept her chin up and her expression on lock down. Every past interaction in the place belonged under the SFB file: shit-for-brains. Sure, some wanted an easy wrap up to a crime they were unprepared to deal with, but the extent one of the lawmen had come after her suggested something more nefarious. Parking tickets and rousing drunks on Saturday night were more Karloff's comfort zone. *Risk assessment: high.*

Every fiber in her being wanted to turn right around and head back out the door. Never darken those pain-ridden, antiseptic-stinking hallways that did such a piss-poor job of covering the smell of vomit and urine. She probably would have if Josh hadn't come hurrying over.

"Anna. Glad you're here." Josh licked his lips, a sure sign he was worried or nervous. "I wanted to take your statement, but, ah, it has to be someone actively working the case. I'm sorry. My supervisor insisted."

"I have the evidence on me. And one you need to test it against." She'd gone and located the cigar left outside the Yellowhead by Tommy Speck during the fight and photographed. Bagged it. Made sure to keep a sample of each to send in for separate verification. She no longer trusted things couldn't be tampered with. If someone could trap her, they might chance it. Just because she was a bit paranoid these days after her experiences, didn't mean she didn't have something to be paranoid about, remembering the wildest accusation thrown at her during the earliest stages of the investigation. But they had found nothing on her and had to finally admit defeat, though not before her reputation was ruined.

Josh took a quick look around, probably feeling as many eyes on him as Anna was currently seething under. Her paranoia rose to its highest level since she'd begun attempting to drink herself into oblivion.

"We can't talk here."

"I'll call you later," Josh half-whispered.

She handed him the paper bag with both samples carefully wrapped separately and away from the food bought to make the transaction easier. "I brought you some lunch, if you're interested?"

"My favorite sandwich joint. Thank you, that's very thoughtful of you, Anna."

Anna strode out the front door of the police station two hours later, her head threatening to explode. It had gone about like she'd expected with Karloff. The power posturing of an angry man dissatisfied with his lot in life, the ominous accusations of what he knew or would know soon, the warning to not leave town again. Well, crap, who didn't live a life of quiet desperation in these harrowing times? Maybe she needed to cut him a little slack. Or not.

She squinted her eyes against the sleet that had begun to whip around during her sojourn inside. Ice storms blew up quick in Anchor, launched across the Bering Sea from moisture-laden clouds. But at least the gun range was inside, offering protection against the elements.

"Good to see you, Anna," Evan Swan, the owner of the firing range and gun club, greeted her. He was standing behind the counter and searching through the contents of a shipping box. "It's been a while."

"You as well. I've been meaning to get some practice in, but you know how it goes. Never enough time in the day." She shrugged. Though in reality it wasn't the ability to shoot with excellence that caused a person to miss their target when it counted the most, but instead it was the chemical adrenaline that got in their way, interrupting fine motor skills to the point their vision and hearing were adversely affected. Not that keeping the skill up didn't help with displaying confidence when it mattered. But what a person had to do in adverse situations was remain calm, something she worked on a lot thanks to Sergeant Carter's mentorship. She pointed at the display of ammunition behind the counter. "I'll take a box of those. My supplies need topping up."

Evan reached behind him and nabbed a box of shells before handing it over.

She pulled out a few bills from her pocket and handed them over. "Keep the change."

An hour of intense practice later and Anna was satisfied she could still hit a target with a weapon other than her hands. She exited the front door of the gun range, thoughts of where Aaron had vanished remained topmost in her mind. Find him and most likely the mystery or part of the mystery behind Zoe's disappearance would be answered.

The storm had increased in intensity since she'd been cocooned inside the windowless warehouse that comprised the shooting range. Once upon a time in its former glory, it had been a railway roundhouse, according to Evan who was a railway enthusiast. She tugged the hood on her parka up to keep the ice crystals at bay while she marched across the parking space. His car was the last one on the lot, leaving only Evan's red Ford in sight. Wary of the isolation, she kept a sharp eye out for any activity. But it remained quiet, other than the droning of ice crystals bouncing off the tin roof of the long, squat building.

When she finally made it back home after driving down slippery streets, it wasn't raccoons or bears who awaited her, but a huge dog that might be part wolf who lay huddled in a tight ball and shivering on the tattered welcome mat of her front stoop.

When the dog spotted her, the poor creature shambled to its feet, his tail wagging slowly side to side as if to say a desperate hello. The action dislodged a rain of sleet from the animal's fur, turning it from ashy gray to brownish black in patches.

"What are you doing here, boy? You lost?" She set the shopping bag on the ground and leaned over to pat the dog's broad head. Something deep and wounded in the dog's whiskey-brown eyes, liquid pools of longing, hit her hard in the solar plexus. Anna swallowed at the reflection of such intense emotion in those sad eyes and had to look away, checking around the dog's neck for a collar or anything to identify him. She'd been hearing sporadic gunfire of late. And there had been talk of a dog culling due to a person being badly bitten a few days ago. The poor creature might be a refuge escaping the event.

She shuddered again at the horrific image deemed necessary to protect citizens and felt equally bad for the experience of the person bitten. Both sides had a right to a decent life, free of fear of only trying to get through another day. An urgent idea took hold of her. She needed to figure out a way to raise some serious cash. Build a dog sanctuary in Tia's name to honor her memory. She loved animals and often fed the birds and deer that flocked to their property. Almost like they could read the No Hunting signs she'd posted.

"You'd best come in. You're half-frozen, bud."

She opened the front door, then waited until the poor creature slipped through the doorway ahead of her. She picked up her shopping bag and followed the dog inside.

She covered the sudden lump that had appeared in her throat with a short cough. "You hungry, boy?"

The dog chuffed like he understood, wagging his tail quicker as confirmation.

"Duh. Of course, you are. Let's see what I got in the fridge that's still fresh."

The dog obediently followed her down the hallway to the back of the dwelling which housed a huge country kitchen. It had been love at first sight and she'd immediately bought the house. Now, instead of being a bright space filled with the warm fragrance of a meal cooking spiced with spontaneous laughter between family and friends, it had become a silent tomb, seldom entered but always missed.

After opening the refrigerator door and looking around, she pulled out a container of takeout and gave it the sniff test. "Not sure when I ordered this, but it smells okay. You want some? Though on second thought, I might have a tin or two of beef stew in the pantry that might be better for you. Taste better too."

She retrieved a large shallow aluminum bowl from a cupboard and filled it with tap water. She opened the tins of beef stew, then dumped them both into a second bowl and lay it on the floor beside the new water dish.

"There you go. All set."

Soft slurps were all the thanks Anna required. She retrieved a can of beer and sat down at the kitchen table that was covered with a skiff of dust. She drank the beer slowly while watching the dog eat his supper. The first signs of life in the house had taken her by surprise, but at the moment they were welcomed.

"What should I call you? I know I have to put a notice in the local rag, but I can't just be calling you boy or dog in the meantime, right? I had a black lab when I was a kid, you know, but crap, that's a bad memory."

She swiped her hand down her face as if to wipe it away. So much of her life was tainted by childhood memories that didn't bear remembering. "Hell, it has to go better this time to have a dog around with that asshole dead and gone. So, let's see. How about you wag your tail when I get it right?"

The lab finished eating and moved over to sit down directly in front of Anna, as if he was totally invested in the subject at hand.

"My first dog's name was Blackie because he was a black lab, but that don't fit and I think something new would be better, right? You look like you might even have some wolf in you. Though don't take this as meaning you will be staying for certain. I'm almost never home and when I get on the case—well, sufficient to say I tend to get obsessed." It felt good to fill the silent void of her life with words. And even better to be on the track of a killer.

The dog slanted his head to the right, his expression somewhat quizzical.

"If only you could talk. Well, I've always been partial to the name Friday. Once had a friend who called their owl by the name because he found the lost owlet on a Friday morning. I know it's not that particular day of the week, but it's rather cool, right? Are you a Friday? My man Friday? At least for now?"

A soft chuff persuaded Anna the name passed muster.

"Okay, until we settle this thing, you can come with me to the office. Charlie's in most of the day—paperwork and the like—and can offer you some companionship. That work for you? And probably more treats than anybody deserves."

An affirmative bark settled the matter.

She checked the digital clock over the stove. "Okay. I need to go out again. Got an important meeting with a friend. But you're welcomed to stay here. Find a place to sleep in the meantime. You good with that?"

Friday looked less than certain, his head poised sideways as he listened to the tone of the speech, but there was nothing else for it. The house might be destroyed by the time she got back for the night, but at least another living creature would be there.

TWENTY-THREE

Twenty minutes later, Anna walked into O'Brien's, needing intel and something to eat. It was five minutes until seven and happy hour was just ending. The press of heated bodies was not unexpected and she shed her thick parka, laying it over the back of a barstool.

"Good to see you out, Anna. I was missing my Catherine Zeta-Jones fix. And selling to you at vendor's not quite the same as having you join us. What can I get you tonight?" Sheila asked, a wide smile accompanying the question. Sheila Watson was an old school classmate who had landed squarely in her corner after Tia was taken so she could get away with the poke about her resembling the actress. Guilt at not appreciating more those who had spoken up for her during the darkest period of her life struck her. She pushed back, willing it away. She had to believe it was never too late to make amends, otherwise, why go on?

"It's good to see you as well. A light beer with a water chaser. And one of Floyd's famous chili cheeseburgers."

She nodded as she wiped the small round table with a

clean cloth. "The scuttlebutt is you're working the Zoe Pace case?"

"Yeah, looks like it."

She leaned in closer, her shoulder nearing touching hers. The strawberry fragrance of shampoo or perfume wafted over her.

"I heard something. Might be important. My brother Sheamus works with Aaron Stone over at Powell Motors in the sales department—the guy who's missing—and he mentioned Aaron had been acting different. All hush-hush over an affair he was having with some woman he was head-over-heels for."

"This fellow got a name?"

Sheila grimaced and fiddled with a lock of errant hair, tucking it behind an ear. "Sorry, everything but. Aaron wasn't slow to spread the details of their trysts between the sheets, but he never divulged a name. Just that they had to be careful a jealous husband didn't find out or there'd be hell to pay. Sheamus got the impression the man was a high-visibility figure and wouldn't take kindly to be made to look a goat to the entire community."

She grimaced. "No, no one enjoys that. Share this with anyone else?"

"No. I don't trust the cops—especially after the way they treated you. Unforgivable."

"Right. Tunnel vision's epidemic over at the station among a chosen few. Is Sheamus around tonight?"

"He should be in soon. He's been working a lot of overtime lately. You know him and Joanne have a kid on the way?"

"I hadn't heard. Finally going to be an aunt, eh. Congratulations."

"Yeah, since it doesn't look likely I'll get the experience firsthand." Sheila added a rueful look, shaking her head.

DEATH SECRETS

"Don't despair. A good-looking woman like you—you can call the shots."

"Phttt, for a quick jump in the hay. Seems all the good guys leave the community or are already taken. I'll get those drinks for you and one of Floyd's famous chili cheeseburgers *platters* to boot—no extra charge. You need fattening up."

Sheila left, her hips swaying a bit more than necessary. She was back in short order, drink and burger platter in hand.

"Here we go. Enjoy."

Anna was making quick work of the tasty burger and crispy fries when Sheila stopped by again. "By the way, Sheamus is here. I told him you wanted a word. You can use the office if you like."

"Thanks. I'll take you up on it." She threw down some bills that included a generous tip and picked up her jacket, making her way to the back of the bar and down the short hallway that led past the storeroom. Footsteps resounded behind her and she whirled around, her hands instinctively coming up into combat stance, before recognizing it was Sheamus advancing toward her.

"Hey, Sheamus." She relaxed her shoulders though she kept her guard up. She didn't know Sheila's brother well...except that he was hardened by combat like herself.

The well-built, dark-haired man nodded. His expression was open and friendly, further defusing the situation. "Anna."

They shook hands, then stepped into the manager's office.

Grabbing one of the chairs that littered the space, she sat down and waited for Sheamus to pull up a seat.

"Sheila said you wanted to speak with me? About Aaron?"

"Yes. She said you had some intel on him about his having a torrid affair with a married woman?"

"Bad idea, I know. I warned him about it, but he was like a man obsessed."

"If it helps, lots of that going on around here. Blame it on the isolation. Or the long cold winter nights."

"I'm sorry about your sisters."

"I appreciate it." Odd, she was beginning to feel numb now. Disconnected. What was that about? A grief expert would probably have a field day with the intel. She pushed her focus to watching Sheamus for any tells. People lied all the time. Four times a day was average, men more often than women, and she wanted to be certain the information she got out of the man was correct. "So, this woman who was having the trysts with Aaron. Any idea who she is?"

Sheamus continued to look him in the eye, a good sign. "I don't know her name, but Aaron let drop that they often met up at the Yellowbird Motel. Should be able to suss it out from that."

"Yeah, that's helpful. Thank you kindly."

"For my two cents, I don't think Aaron had anything to do with Zoe's disappearance. He was too busy chasing tail. But they were friends, I know. Just might be a coincidence. A red herring."

"But it might tell us who the husband is. And if he's the jealous type, no telling how far he went with it. Maybe Zoe got caught in the crossfire?"

"Shoot, never thought of that. Hope they're okay. Aaron always showed up for work in the past. Of course, until he didn't."

"So why haven't you gone to the cops with this?"

Sheamus stiffened, his expression shifting to one of wariness. "Not a fan of being a snitch and I'd prefer to keep my name out of this. I guess I hoped Aaron would show up and things would go back to normal. Besides, now you know, you can take care of it. You got a good reputation in this town for sleuthing out the truth, Anna. A certain cop—not so much. Well, not telling you something you don't already know."

"Don't you think it's strange the cops haven't interviewed you? You being a friend of Aaron's?" Unease stirred again. The APD might have its dissenters but there were lots of good people there as well. This seemed well beyond the pale.

"Yeah, now that you mention it, no one's questioned me from the force at all. Maybe they haven't gotten around to me yet? Not like I made a federal case of Aaron being missing."

"Yeah, maybe. I promise you. I'll look into this."

"Good. Let's me off the hook." Sheamus pushed himself to his feet. "I got an opportunity to not be so lonely tonight, so if that's all, I'll leave you to it."

She nodded, her mind far away. Something was niggling at her about who this celebrity might be. In Anchor there wasn't many people high viz. Especially with possible jealousy issues. God, she hoped she was wrong.

"Yeah, thanks for the lead."

"Anytime, buddy."

Sheamus strode from the room, his footfalls softened by the carpet on the office floor.

Anna got up. Time to visit the Yellowbird and see what intel she could squeeze out of Stubbs.

TWENTY-FOUR

The Yellowbird Motel, known locally for its strict adherence to turning a blind eye to public shenanigans, was set well back from the highway, protected by a privacy screen of thick foliage and ancient fir trees. It was really nothing but a series of old log cabins, refurbished and brought in from around the countryside and given new life. Lots of small buildings littered the area from gold rush days, the town's main claim to fame. They were meant to add a nostalgic flavor to the motel, but instead looked rather sad to Anna as she pulled up in front of the motel's office. However, the business did a fair trade in people wanting a bit of privacy for their chosen activities.

George Stubbs, the owner and operator of the establishment, sat on his usual perch by the till, nodded as she walked in, the unnecessary bell ringing over the doorway. George kept a sharp eye on the place even if said eyes were of the crossed type that flitted back and forth like ping pong balls, confusing customers as to which eye to watch. In Anna's opinion, it was best to watch both—the man was slicker than used motor oil. Charlie was directly responsible for the metaphor coming to mind.

"Howdy Anna, surprised to see you here," George said, his lips barely moving, seeming stuck to his teeth. He was a short fleshy man, which gave him the appearance of a puffer fish, fully puffed.

"Yeah, it's been a while. You look like you're standing up fine to the competition. I noticed lots of traffic in and out of the parking lot."

George ignored her reference to the quick turnover of visitors to his fine establishment. "I don't think I've seen you outside of town in months. Sorry about Tia. I've been expecting news of a memorial for her."

"She's missing—abducted, George, not declared anything else." She knew one day the family would need to do something official. But not now. A slim thread of hope still blindsided her at times, thinking she saw her blonde head across the street or moving through the tree line near their property. Mostly the last one.

"Right. Right. Well, if anything changes—"

"Yes, you'll be the first to know, bless your heart." She always felt closest to her mom with the bless your heart saying, still hearing her mom say it to her friends.

"Now you're just being facetious. No need, we're all friends here. What can I do you for?"

"It's come to my attention that Aaron Stone frequented the Yellowbird with a certain young lady." She hauled a few twenties from her pocket, let George see what she held between her fingers. "I was wondering if anyone saw them together? Recognized the woman? Put a name to her?"

George's eyes darted between Anna's fingers and the ceiling, hedging. Maybe for more cash? "Don't know nothin' about it. None of my business. People come to my establishment for anonymity. They have a right to expect their privacy be respected."

She put her hand back in her pocket and pulled out a few more similar bills. "Of course, but with Aaron missing, the situation has changed. Cops will be all over this once they know about it. Not much privacy then."

George's expression turned petulant. "Yeah, bastards will be all over this place like flies on dung."

Maybe the fact she appreciated the simile meant she was getting far too jaded. "Well, share anything you know and I'll see to it doesn't come back on you. I'll owe you one. Since I'm the only private eye within at least five hundred square miles, it may be of some use to you one day, like a get-out-of-jail-free card."

George scratched at his scraggly half-gray beard. "I got a nephew lookin' to get himself in trouble. I may need help tracking him and his friends down soon enough. Plus the cash you have in your hand?"

She nodded, though it pained her. The guy was beyond incorrigible. And his nephew, Jason Stubbs, also known about town as an instigator of petty crimes with his small gang of thieves.

"Okay. Hand it over and I'll fill you in."

"I'll need a name." She warned as she held onto the twenties when George reached out for them with a pudgy hand.

"Yeah, sure, I saw her, even though Aaron tried to hide her being here." George gave a cackle, pointing two fingers at his own face. "But I'm the all-seeing-eye. No one can hide secrets from me."

She handed George the cash, not bothering to ask how George learned all he did about his customers. Best not to know. In-room cameras were prohibited though not out of range of possibilities, the minuscule size of those suckers these days. And George was one of the most likely candidates to use the devices if there ever was someone up for the dubious job.

George rocked backward on his stool, the seat creaking from the uneven weight distribution. "And without further ado, the lady in question is—"

She waited impatiently, ready to straighten out those ping-ponging eyes with a good shake as George enjoyed his moment in the sun, pausing for emphasis like he expected a bloody drumroll.

"Mrs. 'The Buck' Duffy. Teresa to her friends."

"The mayor's wife? You're certain?" Her heart rate jacked up. *This* was big news. A powerful lead. And not entirely unexpected.

"Dead certain."

"You have proof?"

George's eyes began bouncing quicker and quicker, making her dizzy. She couldn't begin to imagine what it must be like for the man to be on the other side of such vision problems. "No, you'll have to take my word for it." He was lying, of course, confirming he did have the whole thing on camera and didn't want to divulge what he'd been up to.

"Fine."

"And we'll keep this between us?"

"Won't come from me. I don't owe anybody anything. Well, except a future favor to you, sir," she amended her statement.

The man grunted, satisfied. "How you use the information is up to you. Out of my hands now." He made the fast swipe across one fat palm with the other to cement it. "But if this blows back my way, I'll be holding you accountable."

Anna ignored the dig. "Good seeing you again, George."

"Yeah, you too. Come back when ya got more green to give away." The man made the sign of money by rubbing his thumb and finger together.

Her step brisker than when she walked in, Anna exited the motel. This was big news. News that could tear Anchor apart. She had to be careful not let on she knew just yet. George wouldn't be disclosing this to the police any time soon. They'd look too closely at his operation and he had too much to lose if they discovered he was filming customers. No, this would give her time. Leverage. All important aspects of the PI business. And most importantly of all, maybe help bring Zoe home safely.

But something chewed at her. Few of her profiling points seemed to fit Mayor Buck Duffy. He wasn't in his twenties or thirties, being fifty if he was a day. Married to a much younger, very attractive woman. No record of "The Buck," as he enjoyed calling himself and being called by others, in trouble as an adolescent to his knowledge. Full of himself, maybe, but he didn't strike Anna as a serial killer.

Every serial killer had a reason for the kill, some unable to handle their violent impulses, others enjoying each death like a meal. Sociopaths see people as dispensable. They don't grieve or feel regret. Then there are the attention seekers. Assholes who think of it as a game, smug in their ability to outsmart everyone else. The Buck was more like a man who could be pushed to sudden passion. So why on earth would he take Zoe? A shocking thought struck her. Was Tia still alive? Did that blow-dried perfection hide a man capable of abducting women? Keeping them hidden somewhere? He did have an ego big enough to rival any bigshot politician who referenced himself in the third person.

It was all she could do to keep herself from racing out and finding The Buck. Waterboard him if necessary for answers. Her fists clenched tight at her sides at the satisfying image. Had Buck found out about the affair? She knew he hadn't fessed up or the intel would have made it into a digital file at APD headquarters. Maybe the mayor wasn't the serial abductor, but he had to know something of importance. Something he wasn't sharing with authorities. And that made him vulnerable. Dangerous even.

TWENTY-FIVE

Anna jumped into the driver's seat of his truck, the leather seat crackling from the cold beneath her. She rushed to turn the motor over, sparking it to life. On second thought, she didn't want to alert The Buck she was onto him if he was the unsub. Best to do some sleuthing first. Not give the egomaniac time to hide his crimes. Thoughts of what could mean to Tia and Zoe if they were indeed still alive shook her to the core. To be this close and lose it all again would be too much. Oh, but it was a promising lead. *Thank you, Sheila and Sheamus.*

First order of business, find out what Buck's wife Teresa had to say about Aaron's disappearance. She checked the time. Yes, just before nine p.m.—the office might still be open. She cranked the wheel of the truck in a tight U-turn and headed back to town. Teresa Duffy worked for Anchor Realities and should be easy to track down.

But when she pulled up in front of the business, it was dark with a closed sign in the front window.

Damn it. Now what? She couldn't very well head over

to The Buck's house and barge in without an excuse. She had just put the truck into reverse when the front door of the reality office swung open, alerting her to company.

She quickly put the truck back in park and jumped out to confront the person.

"Hey, Sandi, sorry to bother you this late. But I was wondering if Teresa was about?"

Sandi Banks looked harried as she pushed back her parka hood to get a good look at him. "Hi, Anna, no, Teresa's been MIA these past two days. Which is why I'm holding down the fort all on my lonesome. Good thing we don't have any open houses this week. I'm swamped looking after everything."

"Yes, ma'am, that's a lot for you to handle alone." It was easy to sympathize with her plight. Not that the real estate market was booming in Anchor. Far from it. More like stagnant for decades.

"What did you want her for? Thinking of selling out?" A spark of life gleamed into Sandi's eyes at the thought of a nice commission for her house. It might not be a home anymore, but it was her last connection to Tia. A rush of sensation accompanied the thought of that maybe, just maybe she would come home again? *No, you've seen her spirit. Stay calm. The chance of her still being alive is slim to none. Don't let emotion interfere with what needs doing.*

And no way would she be selling anytime soon, though the house was in the mid-price range with acres of surrounding land and would have a better chance at selling than other locations in town.

"I wanted to have a quick word. You know, see what the property is worth?"

"Good time to sell. Things have taken an upswing of late. Sold the Anderson farm last week."

"Great. Who bought it?" Farming wasn't exactly a paying proposition in Anchor.

"A newcomer. Jimmy Short. Wants the outbuildings and shop to start a business. Didn't say what business he had in mind."

Most likely a grow-op. She didn't voice the suspicion aloud but smiled at the woman. Sandi was a decade at least older than Teresa and had started selling real estate ten years ago. Teresa was more the eye candy, there to bring in customers with her looks and her connections through Buck and city hall, including the entire police force. Buck and the police chief went way back.

"Did she say when she'd be back? Do you have any idea where she went?"

"Buck said she needed some time off. Apparently, she headed to her sister's down south for a while. She comes from Seattle. Married well. But I have to work for a living so if this is going to drag on, I'm going to need to know when she'll be back."

"I would think it would only be fair she share her intentions with you." *Hardly suspicious, Teresa vanishing so conveniently.* What the hell was going on? "Well, if you hear anything?"

"Sure. But in the meantime, I can handle it for you."

"No, that's fine, I'm okay waiting until Teresa gets back. I spoke with her about the house a while ago, and promised if anything changed, I'd talk to her first. A promise is a promise."

"Yes, it is," she said with a sigh. "If there's nothing else, I got a meeting I've got to dash off to. Book club night."

"What are you reading?"

"We've been on a poetry kick. Came up in the draw-of-the-week. Not sure it's for me. I'd rather read a book of cocktail recipes personally. More useful around our house after a long, hard day."

"I hear you. Let's stay in touch."

"Will do. I should say I was very sorry to hear about your sister Tia, and now Zoe. It's crazy, how could both of them have been taken? I have no idea how you're coping." Sandi's dark eyes expressed an honest sympathy.

"Thank you kindly." At least it was getting easier now to hear the condolences. And getting out in the community was having a decent effect. Getting a sense of being in control, doing something, that helped the most.

She strode back and got into the truck. Then sat and stared at the front of the reality office, pondering events. She had a bad feeling Teresa Duffy was long gone, and not to her sister's. Had Buck come across Aaron and Teresa together? It was likely if they were going at it hot and heavy and taking chances, the first hot throes of passion being the most intense. But how did Zoe enter into it? She'd gone missing the same night. Had she seen something, been a witness Buck had to silence? It wasn't a big leap. He had motive. If that was the case, where was Zoe now? She couldn't see Buck killing her, more like he would stash her somewhere, though if he killed two people that night, a third might not be much of a stretch. But she saw the man more of a crime of passion type, not the kind to kill someone in cold blood.

It was all subjective, of course. But nothing else fit quite as well as this tragic solution. Though it didn't explain Tia's disappearance. Was the mayor possibly copycatting the original crime? Was there another perp out there? *Crap*. Her head spun with it. Now what to do? Josh needed to know. Holding it back any longer and she would make him look like the bad guy. Something she couldn't do to a man she thought so highly of. Sat beside at the dinner table year in and year out. He'd treated her as just another sister during the early years in Anchor before he left the nest for the military.

After deciding to call Josh soon as she got home, she started the truck and drove down Main Street. She stopped at a convenience store and bought a few tins of dog food, a couple of chew toys and more beef stew. Ten minutes later, she pulled up in front of her house.

Parking in the garage this time, she entered the house through the side door. The sounds of scraping nails on floorboards drew her attention and suddenly Friday was there to greet her with a loud chuff, his tail waving like a banner in a Thanksgiving Parade.

"Hey, boy. Got you some eats. You hungry again?"

A loud whoof settled the deal.

She stood by the door as she let Friday out for a quick use of the yard, then fed the dog before pouring a light beer and settling down on the couch for a difficult conversation. She punched in Josh's phone number and drummed her fingers on the armrest waiting for him to answer.

"Hey, Anna. I was about to call you."

"Oh yeah. Anything happen?"

"No, I wish. But I wanted to touch base. You learn anything?" His voice held a trace of hope.

"Yes, a lot actually." She went on to succinctly lay out all the facts she'd learned in the past few hours.

"You really think our mayor is the one? That he would do all that?"

"The facts can certainly be read that way. What you do with them now is your decision, Josh."

"No, we're still in this together. You know, this could lead to some information on Tia?"

"Maybe." Not if this was a copycat case. She'd be back at square one. But Zoe still had the best chance of being alive of the pair.

"Where do you think he could be hiding her?"

"That's the sixty-four-thousand-dollar question. He owns a lot of property. Comes from a well-off family and they got a lot of clout in this town. Cozy with the chief of police from what I've seen. If you go in with guns blazing, he's going to lawyer up. Pull in political favors," she said.

"Damn it! I feel so freakin' helpless. You've gotten to what I think could be the truth or at least part of it, but how in the world can we prove it right now? The Buck is not going to be easy to handle. And God help him, if he's harmed a hair on either of their heads, he will wish he'd never been born."

"I hear your frustration. Your sense of an uneven playing field. But we need to be smart about this. Gain some hard evidence."

Friday let out a series of quick barks, taking Anna's attention.

"Was that a dog barking? Did you get a dog?" Josh asked.

"More like he found me. I'd best check out what he's barking at."

"Okay. I'm coming right over. We need to discuss how we're going to handle this. I need your input."

"Sure."

She hung up the phone. "What is it, Friday? You hear something, boy?"

Friday went to stand in the doorway leading into the kitchen and the back of the house. He growled in the back of his throat before turning and vanishing.

Anna got to her feet, all senses on high alert. She pulled her gun, sensing Friday was warning her of imminent danger. Holding her gun steady in both hands, she followed the dog she'd already begun to trust down the hallway, switching lights off as she went. The curtains were drawn in the kitchen. No point in being an easy target.

When she got to the kitchen, Friday was by the back door. The huge dog stood still, a canine sentinel, whining softly, his ears high. A muffled sound echoed outside. Was that a gunshot? Or the backfire of a vehicle? The neighborhood was notorious for shooting at skunks.

"What is it, Friday?" She kept her voice low, addressing him. "You think maybe someone's up to no good?" Property crime was also a problem in Anchor. Home invasions happened. But not usually in a house that held an arsenal of guns like she was known to have. Sure, the cops had confiscated a few when Tia had gone missing, but she'd since replaced them.

A wolf howled nearby, making the hair rise on her neck. Her early warning system. Wolf, *pathfinder*.

Anna pulled back the curtain and peered out the small window cut in the metal door, scanning the spacious backyard. It led to a shadowy forest of fifty-year-old jack pine and poplar trees. Ah, the lights of a large vehicle shone through the trees in sporadic shots of light. The front-end loader used by the Anchor Cemetery workers for digging graves. The town's largest cemetery butted up against the back of her property, far enough away to avoid it being creepy, but when they dug graves in the winter months it was more obvious without the thick foliage to hide their activities.

She waited a few more minutes, but the backyard proper remained quiet and empty. If there had been another threat, it had passed.

"Well, whoever it was is gone now or you were

spooked by the operation of machinery." She lowered his gun. Then scratched Friday's head. "But feel free to alert me anytime you hear or sense something amiss. I trust you more than most people."

A chuff of agreement followed.

TWENTY-SIX

The front doorbell chimed.

Anna hurried back down the hallway, and checked through the peephole it was Josh before letting him in.

"Everything okay?" he asked with concern, peering around. "You hung up so quick, I was worried." He caught sight of Friday and gave Anna an inquiring look. "Who do we have here?"

"This is Friday. Showed up and made himself at home. He thought we had an unwanted visitor in the backyard. I did hear something, but it's quiet now. Sound carries so well in the cold. But I think it might have been the front-end loader working in the cemetery."

"Friday, eh, good name." Josh unwound his scarf and slipped off his coat, leaving it on a chair in the hall. "We need to plan. Got any coffee?"

"Yeah."

The three of them made their way to the kitchen, with Friday plopping down near his food bowl to demonstrate it was once again empty. Anna measured out the coffee grounds and filled the carafe with tap water, turning on the machine. Laying out two cups, cream, and sugar, she joined Josh at the table.

"I know I shouldn't be drinking caffeine this late, but I need the boost. Been a long day. But thankfully, yours was very productive. A lot better than mine. Nothing was found by any of the volunteers. Everyone went home at dark and most will be back again tomorrow first light. No new leads by any of the officers working the case either. It was looking dismal until your call."

"The police department is not going to like this intel. You know that, right? It would be better if we did this alone. I'd like to put a tail on The Buck, watch his every movement. Might be the best way to get a lead as to where he might be hiding Zoe."

"I disagree. We need more boots on the ground, more eyes. How can two people possibly keep track of all his movements and check out locations?"

"But if we share what I've learned, he might go ahead and do something, something I don't even want to think about. Get rid of any proof he did any wrongdoing. He has too much to lose not to tie up loose ends."

Josh's face grew more strained with her stark words. She couldn't sugar coat this. It was too important. "But with his wife missing? And Aaron? Surely the facts are adding up against him."

"Yes, but his wife isn't officially missing, only off visiting a sister. Or maybe it will be suggested there were problems in the marriage and she struck out on her own. Aaron's case can also be downplayed, or at least long enough to not do Zoe any good. I wish there was someone else we could trust." She snapped her fingers. "I can ask Charlie to help. You know anyone that would keep this all quiet? Not betray a confidence?"

"Other than you, no one. I've only been on the force

such a short while. I don't know who to trust or ask. I just want Tia and Zoe back."

Anna got to her feet. She retrieved the coffee pot, pouring the steaming brew into the mugs, then pushing the cream and sugar toward Josh, remembering he took it loaded.

"Nah, black now." He took a sip, nodding appreciatively.

"I reckon we should go with only the three of us for a couple of days. Give it a shot first. Keep a lid on what we know." She pressed her case. She'd seen too much not to be worried that calling the cops on this could cause havoc. Cause enough interference that Zoe and maybe Tia if there was still hope for her could be lost in the flurry of activity. Bad things happened oftener than people cared to admit from people setting out to do good as those setting out to do bad.

"There are lots of good cops in Anchor and just a bad apple or two. You know that, right?"

"Yeah, but how do we know which is which? You willing to bet their lives on it, Josh?"

He looked undecided still. Maybe she was overreacting after what she'd been through. Was she reading the facts incorrectly? Doubts assailed her. Hell, she didn't even know who her own father was. She'd tried to keep the thought squashed down flat to the bottom of her mind these past few months, hoping never to have to deal with it. But it was like the proverbial elephant had pushed up through the floorboards in that moment, pressing its case. Who the hell had provided the sperm that had led to her? To this odd jumble of thoughts and paranoia. Was it inherited? She had tried to be a good person, help others, and serve her country, but somehow fate hadn't bestowed any further blessings on her. Had even taken away all she held dear. Not once, but twice in her lifetime.

"I know I'm messed up. I freely admit it."

"Anyone would be, given what you've been through." He laid a hand on her arm, squeezed it with sympathy before withdrawing it and locking both his hands together in a prayer motion on the tabletop. "I need this job, Anna, I can't muck this up. I've worked too hard for the opportunity, gave up too much to throw it all away now. I even let Zoe take most of the burden with Mom while I trained to become top of my class, in efforts to learn how to find Tia. But hell, with both of them missing now, I have no idea what to think. How could this have happened?"

"One day. That's all I ask. I beg you. You came to me, remember, and I know this is the right thing to do. I'll take any and all flak if it comes to it."

"I may regret this later, but okay." He hissed out a deep breath, his eyes darkened by emotion. "But you have to promise me if we have no further leads, we take all of this to my boss."

She could tell by his expression it wasn't what he wanted right now and guilt struck for placing his job in jeopardy. Josh had always been special and deserved the opportunity to make a difference to the community. He had the smarts, the loyalty and the drive to make it to the top of any profession he chose. Her asking this of him was a lot. "I guess you must ask yourself if you really want to work with a gal who only sees the bad in people?"

"You're too hard on yourself. I'd prefer to see it more as balancing my too-optimistic view, only seeing the good in people. We need the yin and the yang in this world, so I've been told."

Anna downed her coffee, setting aside her guilt.

"Okay. I'll give Charlie a heads-up. Get things in play. You okay with getting time to do what needs to be done?"

"I'll sleep when I'm dead. Until Tia's home safe and sound, I'll just take drugs if I have to. Keep going."

She picked up his phone to check messages, sending a quick text to Charlie to see if she was still up, then thought to ask. "You want more coffee?"

"No. I'd better get going. I'm on the midnight to eight shift. It will make it easier to stake out *The Buck*." He said his name with extreme prejudice, adding a grimace. "I'll head to his house soon as I've clocked in. Pray everything stays quiet in town."

"Don't worry, *The Buck stops here.*" A look of agreement passed between them, his eyes dark and intense. "And text me at the top of each hour. And if you get pulled out on another call. I want to know you're safe. If Buck suspects we're onto him, he might get desperate. I'll be driving around to his other properties, checking things out. Less you know about it, the better."

"Right, I'm off." He jumped up and rinsed his cup, placing it in the sink.

Anna watched him leave, then called Charlie to fill her in. She was a night owl too. Her partner agreed to the new schedule in a split second, her voice tinged with hope that maybe, just maybe, they might find out something out about what happened, first to Tia and now her twin Zoe. After ending the call, she gave Friday a good rubdown, who blessed her with looks of what she took to be caring and keen interest. She felt somewhat renewed, ready for the fight again.

She offered Friday a chew toy before heading out. "Use this instead of a shoe or slipper, buddy. Okay?"

A skeptical look supplied the answer.

The weather had acquired an even bitterer note

and she was glad for a good block heater on her truck as she drove away from the house, the engine purring. With the clock already ticking on the twenty-four-hour deadline, she decided on her first location: Buck's office. She'd taken her laptop with her, intending to break in the modern way while she considered floor plans and watched any coming and going.

The mayoral floor of the building was in the process of being cleaned by the night crew when Anna pulled up, being careful to keep a discreet distance away. She had barely plugged into their file server when her cell phone buzzed.

"Hey, Josh. What's up?" She tucked the phone under her chin while she clicked away on the keyboard, looking for answers.

"This is bad. There's been another abduction. Tonight. Joy Evans, a nurse at the hospital. Same MO. But this makes no sense. Too soon."

"It does if Buck's the copycat and the first killer is acting again."

"Right. But we need to report what we know *now*."

"It doesn't change anything. They could be two very different and distinct cases if what we know pans out. And if we aren't careful, what we suspect could jeopardize getting Zoe back."

"But what if Buck *is* the guy? Not a copycat like you think is going on? Just because he doesn't fit your profile doesn't mean he's not involved in some way with the twins, and now Joy's disappearances. We can't be sure. The sooner we officially question him, the better."

"I'm at the office right now. I'll check his appointment book, see where he was during the times of the other disappearances. It might tell us what we need to know. I need a few minutes, then I'll call you right back. Don't do anything until then. Please."

"Okay. But I can't wait long on this powder keg. I have a terrible feeling it's going to blow up at any second."

"I'll get back to you directly, I promise. Hold on a minute."

Anna dropped the phone on the seat, her fingers flying across the laptop. She'd hacked into the government server before and had firsthand knowledge it wasn't as protected as everyone assumed it was, at least, not from her. Pulling up the computer file that allowed her to view the mayor's daily appointment ledger, she checked first where the man had been on the day of Tia's abduction, six months back.

The guy had a decent alibi, being the host of the local business awards night at the Anchor Bar & Grill. Anna needed proof he had attended. The local rag should have reported on it. And there it was, the photo of Buck Duffy shaking hands with a local proprietor as he was being recognized for his service to the community. One down, two to go.

Sweat was dripping in her eyes by the time she had the proof she needed to call Josh back.

"We can rule out the mayor as the original Black Rose killer. He has an air-tight alibi for Tia's abduction and for Joy's. Tonight, he's been officiating at the arena for the figure-skating production of *Guys and Dolls*. When Tia went missing, he was at the local business awards dinner. However, when Zoe went missing, he had the night off."

"Unless he had someone else's help? We can't be totally certain he's not involved."

"No. But he really doesn't fit the profile." Inspiration hit, making her blood pound through her veins. "*Here's the thing!* He probably killed Teresa and Aaron in a fit of passion, then decided to cover it up by using the Black Rose Killer's MO because Zoe was there that night and saw it happen." The more Anna thought about the more her gut agreed she was on the right track. The idea riveted er, seeing the whole thing unfold in her mind's eye. "Also explains a second abduction so soon. The original killer is either pissed at someone else taking credit for his crimes or it's just time for him to do it again."

"I'm not sure about all this. Zoe's phone is missing, obviously. She took it with her or I would check. I've tried calling her, of course, but there's no answer. It goes to voice mail. And no answer to my gazillion texts. It was a brand-new phone, damn it, and she hadn't gotten around to downloading any apps that would help me or the investigators find it. The department's working on getting the company to allow them access."

"Her phone! I could hack into it right now. Then, if it still has power, we can check her messages. What's her cell number?" She shook her head in dismay. She'd dropped the ball on that one. She wasn't as sharp as she'd been before Tia's disappearance. Grief had affected her more than she'd even realized. *Get it together, Anna. People are counting on you.*

Josh read off the numbers.

"Good. Also, the roses can help prove two separate cases are in progress if they are different. They need to be compared. The two from Tia's and Joy's against the one left in Zoe's car."

"Right. They would help prove your theory. No one's looking into it far as I know, everyone's assuming the perp is the same guy." A tinge of excitement entered Josh's voice. "Even the letters could maybe show differences in spacing or the like?"

"Good. Can you look into that as well?"

"Not until someone relieves me."

"Okay. Hang tight. I want to check on a few things, then I'll head straight over."

Forty-five minutes later, armed with a clearer mental picture of all Buck's family properties, and having narrowed the choices considerably to include only good places with little to no traffic to stash someone, she headed over to the mayor's ancestral home and Josh's stakeout to relieve him. And fill him in about what she learned about Zoe from her phone. She was more and more certain the mayor was the copycat killer. Her gut agreed. A seething excitement filled her, every instinct telling her she was on the right track, making her feel truly alive for the first time in months.

TWENTY-SEVEN

"I dare you! Jump in or be forever known as a dirty coward," Jason Stubbs, a.k.a. Dirty Boy, said with a practiced leer. He pointed at the prospect, Mikey Duffy. Jason grinned, enjoying himself immensely. Any dweeb thinking of joining their crew needed to step it up, even if he was the mayor's son. He liked the challenge he'd chosen for the guy, daring the skinny bastard to jump into the open grave. It was already prepared to receive a body in the morning. The graveyard was no stranger to them, him, Moose and Cutter all being aficionados of isolated locations to enjoy their homebrew and fat doobies.

"If you want to hang with us, gotta prove you got balls, Mikey."

"I'd rather take a pot shot at someone," Mikey whined, his face paler than a ghost in the light from the flashlight Jason held pointed at the gravesite. "You can have all my money." Mikey held out a few bills and a fistful of coins. *What a pathetic piece of shit.*

"I'll take that. But you still got to do it if you want to

hang with us." Ever since they'd binge-watched the Netflix series about zombies, Jason had known this moment was coming. Mikey had made the mistake of shuddering during certain scenes, giving away his aversion. Jason was good at reading people, judging their weaknesses, waiting for the right moment to unleash horror on them. He lived for it. Loved the sense of control he got from watching others squirm.

Mikey backed up a few steps, knocking into Cutter, who shoved at him. The action knocked the prospect off balance and he stumbled a couple of steps, teetering on the edge of the graveside.

A slight push from Jason and the petrified idiot fell face first, landing hard on his yellow belly seven or eight feet below.

"And don't come out until we say. You got that, Mikey?"

The stupid idiot starting screaming just then, his arms pinwheeling like he was trying to swim out of the grave or create a snow angel.

"Shut up! Or we'll shut you up," Jason threatened.

"He's going to draw heat. We need to leave. Now!" Cutter said, his voice tight with anger. "I don't want to spend the night in juvie."

"Get me out! There's somebody else down here! I beg you, please! Don't leave me!"

"What are you talking about, Mikey? There's no one else down there." Jason peered over the edge, wanting to slug the guy for being such a pill. The flashlight picked up the white gleam of a slender limb and part of a feminine face. He nearly dropped the flashlight in shock.

"Holy crap! Look at that. Mikey's right. What's a body doing buried in the dirt?" Cutter said.

"We need to go," Moose said, crossing himself. "This is

wrong. Something's going on and I don't want any part of it."

"You suddenly religious?" Jason scoffed, trying to slow down his jacked-up heart rate and pretend he was fine with what was going on. He studied the corpse. Damn, it was a woman, judging by the boobs pushing out the dingy white dress. The parts he could see appeared like a marble statue, beyond surreal. Too lifelike. He shuddered with distaste.

The terrified screams continued as Mikey scrambled to his feet. He held his arms outstretched, begging for assistance. "Help me out! I can't stand it. This is crazy, man. Please, don't leave me here." When no hands were offered to lift him out, Mikey began scratching frantically at the crystalized soil that lined the top half of the grave, trying to find purchase to haul himself out. The ground was frozen over four feet down, permafrost having set in deep.

"We can't just leave him here," Moose said. "What if whoever did this comes back? He could do Mikey in."

"You want to haul his ass out? Fine with me, but he owes us a different challenge to make up full membership."

"Anything else! Whatever you want! Just get me out!"

Jason used his cellphone to send a text while Moose and Cutter struggled to pull Mikey out of the hole.

"What are you kids doing here?" The gruff voice was followed by the sudden arrival of Richard, the slimeball that worked with an even slimier guy, the freak who pretended to be Elvis. Lame shit.

"Nothing," Jason said, his thumbs still working his phone, daring Richard to make a big deal of it. "Just having a bit of fun."

"The cemetery is closed. Can't you read?"

Jason stood up straighter, glaring at the man who was a head taller than himself. Richard went closer to the graveside and took a long look down, standing on the small mound of piled soil. "Is that what I think it is? You guys plant a body here?"

The twisted-gut feeling of fear hit Jason hard, tightening his muscles. No way was he getting blamed for something someone else had done.

"It wasn't us. Body was here we got here. Ask my crew."

"That right, fellows?" Richard looked over at the other three teenagers huddled pathetically together.

"Yeah, that's right," Cutter said, his voice dripping with scorn, stepping away from the other two. He took out his phone, pretending indifference as he fiddled with it.

"Can you prove it?"

"We don't have to. We didn't do it." Jason reacted with far more bravado than he was feeling.

"You think, just because *you* say so, they'll not put you under the spotlight? The cops are going to be all over this. And you four"—Richard stabbed a finger at each of them in turn—"you're all going to be suspects. Let's just say you don't exactly have spotless reps in this town, always getting into trouble."

"That ain't right. Shit, man, we had *nothing* to do with it," Moose said.

"Maybe, maybe not. But this mess—going to take some time to straighten out. By then, the stench of this will stay with you all your lives. Never going to get away from it. Just sayin'."

"What are we going to do, Jason? He's right. This is bad," Moose said, shaking his head.

Jason glanced over at Mikey. The coward was still quaking in his boots.

"You got to cover for us, man. We can pay you. You know we have the best moonshine in the whole county courtesy of Uncle George, right?" he said, deciding in the moment that bribery was a likely option.

"Well, I do love me some quality moonshine—say about two quarts a week of the Peach Thunder. And I know y'all got access to some decent weed. Add in an ounce of sweet grass and that should keep my lips zipped for now."

Jason managed to keep his game face on while Richard gave his lousy rendition of a Southern redneck. Bastard drove a hard bargain. Then he remembered some sage advice from his uncle while he had helped tend the still after school and on weekends. *Always be prepared to bargain for what you want.*

"Okay. But you got to give us something to hold over you."

Richard gave a nasty laugh. "You dun lost your mind, kid, if you think I'm going to do that."

Out of the corner of his eye, he observed Cutter giving him a discreet thumbs-up while coughing into his elbow. Smart. He'd bet Cutter had recorded the entire conversation. He could always count on Cutter to see the big picture. To catch the wave. Jason was a big fan of surfer movies, wanting to head to the sunny beaches of California soon as he had the money saved. And finished high school. His uncle was an idiot for not doing it years ago. Instead, he sat on his cash, pretending to be poor, making Cutter do all the heavy lifting. Well, at least the guy shared his best pics of female guests with him now. But he wanted them to be of California girls, tan and gorgeous, not white and pasty like most Alaskan females.

"Well, it was worth a try." He held out his hand.

Richard shook it, his grip less powerful than Jason had expected for a guy built like a linebacker.

"I'll expect my first delivery tomorrow," Richard said, thudding him on the back far harder than necessary.

"Yeah, sure, just got to clear it with my uncle first."

"You don't be telling him about any of this—you hear me. Not if you want things to stay quiet," Richard threatened.

"I have no intention of telling that old fart anything about this. But I gotta make sure we got the goods available."

"Whether you do or you don't, I will expect my order. Don't disappointment me, boy, that's all I'm saying."

TWENTY-EIGHT

Anna jumped out of her truck and strode over to Josh's cruiser, her breath a misty fog enveloping her face. Slipping into the front passenger seat, she gave him a look.

"He's at home. Drove into the garage about a half hour ago. So?" he prompted her. "What have you learned?"

"I tapped into her phone messages. She was headed to Aaron Stone's that night and happy about it. Then nothing more. Something happened right then, at his house. I'm close to dead certain Buck's behind her abduction, piggybacking it on the Black Rose crimes. Being made to look the goat would have driven a vain man like him to distraction. He'd want his day of reckoning. And he has that election to think about come spring. My bet's he would prefer her dead to causing harm to his chances —you know how he fawns on his father and what a bastard the old man can be. I've narrowed the places he could easily hide her down to half a dozen. All but the hunting cabin are close by. We check those out and my bet is she could be at one of those locations."

"I want him brought in for questioning. Right now!

No more delays. We lay this out before the chief. He has to listen to what we have to say, we've got some pretty damning evidence."

"You do know that the chief and the mayor are far too cozy? There's no telling how this will go down once we expose what we know. And if you think for one second they want to hear anything from me, well, sorry, that isn't going to happen. Karloff still pegs me for the crime, for heaven's sake! Right now, we have the upper hand. Let's not lose it." She had to convince him of the tactical error.

"Doesn't matter. Davis can't deny facts staring him right in the face. He'll have to bring him in for questioning at very least."

Chief Lloyd Davis was not Anna's favorite person. But to give the man credit, he did tend to listen better than some, but just not yet until Anna had her chance to end this with undeniable proof in hand. "I can get more out of Buck in ten minutes than any cop can get out of him in a week of Sundays. Leave it to me, I'm not hampered by law and order."

"And if word of it gets out about it? Your butt will be in jail in a flash. You think you're a pariah now? They'll throw the key away on this one. Holding back crucial evidence to a crime is a felony."

She had to get through to her, make him see reason. "How can I explain this to you?"

"There's nothing to explain—"

"No. You need to listen, Josh. You know what I was thinking of doing the night you came to ask for help with Zoe?" Nothing to be done but get right into it now. State the facts as best she knew how. Try to get him to see reason. Zoe's life depended on it.

"Drinking and feeling sorry for yourself?" He had the

grace to look horrified by his words. "I'm sorry. That came out all wrong."

"No, you're not wrong. I was about to hold a gun to my temple when you knocked. I'd had enough. I wanted out. I couldn't take it anymore. Not knowing what happened to Tia, if she was out there hurt or dying, it was eating me alive. It drove me crazy. My world had imploded, I felt unable to move, especially when others thought I did it or was involved some way."

Josh laid a hand on her arm, his expression one of total sorrow. She swallowed and looked away, needing to persuade him of his cause more than elicit his sympathy. "Then you came along and I realized I still had value. That someone needed my help. That maybe, just maybe, I could be there for somebody. So, you see, I need this. I need to make the bastard tell me where Zoe is or what he's done with her. I need to bring her home safe and sound."

"Okay." Josh's voice sounded tight. He cleared her throat. "I'll give you until the end of my shift." He glanced at the dashboard of the cruiser. "You got six hours to find out where our sister is. Then I have to take this to the chief, end of discussion."

"Fine. A few hours are all I need." She hoped she was right. She hedged her next words, giving him an out if he was questioned. "While I may or may not see about inter-rogating Buck, you could check out a few locations?" She raised her eyebrows, keeping her expression skeptical, like they used to do as teenagers when buying each other a Christmas present the other wanted, pretending they were not going to buy it right then and there. The memory of then versus now hit her hard. She had to work to keep her game face on.

"Fine. Give me the list."

She dug out an address list from her parka pocket, handing it over. "I'll head to the cabin myself later. It's the only one out of town. That way, if you get a call, you're here to answer it."

"Okay."

Josh checked the list using a discrete penlight to avoid drawing attention.

"I'm going to head over to the warehouse on Inkster first. It's a quiet area and looks promising."

"You be careful. Call it in if you see or sense anything suspicious. Don't go barreling in. That will only hurt Zoe in the long run."

"Anna, *you* be careful. Buck's dangerous, if he did it. Don't take chances and don't go overboard. He'll have you arrested if he can. Even shoot you as an intruder. Blame everything on you. You know that, right? I wouldn't even put it past him to plant evidence if what we suspect is true."

"Don't worry about me. Okay, I'm putting my phone on vibrate. Text me when you get the chance." She moved forward in her seat, preparing to exit the police car.

"Will do. And don't be a hero, okay?" He leaned in and kissed her chastely on the cheek, surprising her in a good way.

She shook her head, needing to put the idea to bed. "I'm no one's hero, Josh; just a gal trying to find our sister, to make up for not finding Tia."

"What you've done—what you're trying to do—that is the definition of a hero in my opinion. You got back up after all that happened to you. Do you know how many people would have given up? Instead, you're out here trying to help and you've already dug up more facts that my entire department has managed in months."

160

"I just about did give up until you knocked on my door."

"My point exactly. You didn't. And here you are. You're stronger than you think, Anna, and you got some heavy lifting ahead of you. A reason to go on. Help others. Lots of missing people. You can help with those cases once we come out the other side."

"I know what you're doing. Let's just finish this one, okay, then see what the deal is. I don't need a pep talk, Josh. I'm prepared to go to the limit for Zoe. When I bring her home, then we'll see."

She got out and strode back to her truck. She needed a few things before she entered the mayor's residence. Things that would likely guarantee the end result required. She knew better than to say it was a sure bet—there was always an unexpected element that might come into play. All she could do was plan as best she could, hope to get where she needed to be. And that was with intel that could help Zoe.

TWENTY-NINE

Anna rang the mayor's front doorbell, keeping her finger pressed on the lighted knob, listening to it ring endlessly and quite satisfactorily inside the silent house. The porch light came on after a few minutes, and she felt himself being observed through the peep hole before the door opened.

"Anna, I'm surprised to see you on my doorstep this time of night. It's two-thirty in the morning, for heaven's sake! What on earth is going on that you need to wake up my entire household?"

She knew The Buck was alone because she'd checked for other heat sources in the residence, meaning the mayor was trying to suggest he had people at his beck and call.

"Can I come in? It's cold out here." She rubbed her hands together to punctuate the point.

"Okay." Buck moved a step back to let her but stayed in front of her to keep her from coming in any farther. The guy was dressed in his bathrobe, though his hair was as perfectly coiffured as usual. "Couldn't this have waited until a decent hour?"

"Afraid not."

"What is it?" The mayor narrowed his eyes at her, his expression neutral. He waved vaguely with one hand. "I'd offer you a drink, but—"

"And I'll take it," she said before the man could finish his excuse for not being hospitable.

"Okay." Buck sighed like a man put upon and led the way to his study, the first room on the right of the hallway. She knew the floorplan well, having studied it previously. This would suit her needs just fine.

Without asking what Anna wanted, Buck poured two small measures of whiskey into two flat-bottomed crystal glasses. Shoved one across the desk at her.

"So?" Buck asked, his expression fueled by impatience.

She sat down, crossing her legs, then sipped at the liquor, meaning Buck had to do the same or be seen as a poor host. The guy needed voters. She glanced briefly at the desktop, confirming the brand of cigars.

Placing the glass down on the edge of the desk, she rested one hand in her jacket pocket. "It's come to my attention during my investigation that Zoe Pace was going to meet with Aaron Stone at his house the night that Aaron, your wife, Teresa, and Zoe all disappeared."

Buck sat back in his office chair, making the chair squeal in protest, his expression frozen. "And what has this to do with me? And Teresa's not missing. She's down visiting her sister in Seattle. You need to get your facts straight." The guy was lying through his teeth. All the tells were on high alert. Unable to look her in the eyes, his leg vibrating, perspiring though the room was cool.

"Can you tell me where you were on Friday night, the

night Zoe was taken? Shouldn't be hard to recall: it was Valentine's Day."

"I don't have to tell you anything. I'm not a suspect in this case. More likely that you are involved than not. Your sister, Zoe's twin, disappeared first and is still missing. You should direct your energies there, go after the facts in that case. Or is it you can't, being involved up to your eyeballs?"

The asshole was baiting her now, looking to regain his edge. *Risk assessment: moderate.* "Do you know something about Tia's disappearance?"

"Where are you going with this, Anna? What are you basing all these accusations on? You need to get a grip. This is a dead end. I know nothing about Zoe's case other than what I read in the papers. I can share that I've heard Aaron Stone's been hitting the meth hard. He's probably holed-up out there somewhere, drugged out of his mind."

"Or dead along with Teresa. I know all about it. How the pair of them were going at it hot and heavy down at the Yellowbird."

Buck moved, but Anna was faster. She had her gun drawn and held on the mayor before he could push one of the alarms hidden under his desk. Not that it would do him much good. They'd already been disabled.

"What's this? You do know that it can't end well for you, right? I've got you dead to rights on camera, coming in my front door at two in the morning. You'll never pull this off." The mayor pressed a hand on his upper chest, like he was having physical distress.

"You think so? You might want to check your home security system. I suspect it's out of order at the moment. You know—glitches in the system are a common hazard in this modern era. Things work—until they don't." She enjoyed the look of concern her words brought. "I got nothing left to lose and I don't care overly much if I walk out of here alive. Not much left to lose in my world," Anna kept her tone deliberately deadpan, her gun aimed at Buck's heart. "Someone killed my mother, left me for dead, and now my sisters are both gone. Maybe deceased. You're the one who needs to worry, Buck. I want answers and I want them now. What happened the night Zoe was taken? Did she come across a crime in progress? Then you decide to piggyback on the Black Rose Killer's MO?"

"I've no intention of answering any more questions. I want you to leave. Now. Before this gets any uglier. I don't want to see a war hero get hurt."

He was lying again. "Move." Anna waved her gun toward the bathroom she knew was off the side of the study. "Into the bathroom. That's if you want to live to see another sunrise."

Buck eyed her, seeming to consider the alternatives. "What are you going to do? Tie me up? Shoot me? That's not going to bring the answers you're seeking, now, is it?"

"Did you know I've been to war and learned things you can't imagine?"

"Yes, of course. I just said—"

"Move it." She cut him off by jerking the gun. "I won't tell you again."

The mayor turned and walked slowly toward the closed door of the bathroom. Anna thrust her hand back into her pocket to leave the gun and leaped at him from behind, quickly securing his hands with a white plastic tie designed for the job. Her movements were so sudden that the mayor was her helpless victim in a matter of seconds. Very satisfying indeed.

"I can also tell when someone is lying. And you, Mr. Mayor, are full of it. You know a lot more about what happened. And I intend to find out every last detail before

I leave here. A woman's life is at stake, so I don't care what happens to you or me. All I care about is finding Tia and Zoe Pace. Then they can try me for murder if they want. The old adage is true, *never* push a person who has nothing left to lose. Especially when she's on a mission and knows interrogation techniques the government doesn't admit to. Well, maybe in wartime and for the CIA."

This time the man was silent for a moment. "How are you going to arrange that if I refuse to speak? I don't have to tell you anything, but I imagine you're very good at your job. Otherwise, you wouldn't be here. The cops would be. Well, if Lloyd Davis and I weren't such good buddies, that is. You know he likes to keep a lid on things for the good of the town. Instead of all this rigmarole, how about we make a deal?"

"What kind of deal?"

Buck looked stronger now, thinking he had taken back the upper hand. "I tell you something I know about a certain business owner in town who knows something about Tia's case, and you let me go and I'll keep quiet about this little fiasco. We'll chalk it up to PTSD."

At the mention of Tia, Anna had all she could do not to knock the man's too white teeth out. Had he been holding back crucial evidence all along? "What about Zoe?"

The mayor ignored her question, his mind obviously focused on Zoe. "I know you don't believe me, but I know nothing about how Zoe is faring. If she's alive or not."

The mayor looked her directly in the eyes. Anna could see he wasn't lying about this one fact. Was she wrong? Did the man really not know anything about Zoe? Or was this some kind of ruse? Doublespeak to hide the truth?

"How was she faring on the night she was taken? Did you kill her at the scene or stash her away some place?"

Surprisingly, The Buck did not like the question. His eyes shifted to the left as he considered possible answers, which meant his next words were suspect. "I told you, I know nothing about it."

She pushed Buck into the bathroom, pleased to see the tub she was expecting. "Where is she? You have thirty seconds to answer before we begin stage two."

"For Christ's sake, Anna, stop this right now! You're just going to get yourself arrested or worse and then it's out of my hands. You can't do this and get away with it. No way."

"Oh really. I already have."

She secured the tub stopper, picked up a loose hair lying near the drain and tucked it in her shirt pocket while still bent over so Buck couldn't see her actions, then turned on both taps to fill it with water. She hummed during the actions, as odd as she found it to do. It would add an additional creep factor. Nothing scarier than a contented-sounding criminal, at least according to intel located on page one-ninety-five, subsection eight, appendix C in the *Secrets of Interrogation* she'd been lucky enough to lay her hands on. There were few if any of those out in the civilian population. For good reason—the book was a no-holds-barred manual in how to get answers from anyone. And totally classified.

Sirens in the distance surprised her. Had she missed something? *Risk assessment: high.*

"Bet you didn't know I have a medical alert device I wear around my neck under my clothes? It notifies authorities if a sudden movement is detected. You jerked me around pretty good there tying me up. Help will be here momentarily."

Anna's heart rate jacked up. The guy was middle-aged, not elderly. She'd only considered alarms connected to the police station, not an outside agency. "Why would you have one of those?"

"Ticker. Second heart attack last year. Teresa bought it for me. Said it brought her comfort. I took to wearing it to keep the family peace."

Having something in common with the mayor grated. Her jaw ached from gritting her teeth as she considered her options.

"You'd better untie me now. Otherwise, it's going to look rather unfortunate to the security personal that will arrive in under three minutes as the brochure promised. With your ass in jail, how are you going to find Zoe in time?"

Anna's fists clenched tight. The urge to slug the bastard nearly overwhelmed her. "You are a piece of work, Buck. I have no idea how you live with yourself." She put every bit of scorn and disgust she was experiencing into her tone of voice.

The mayor slitted his eyes, hiding his thoughts. "So, you going to be smart and cut these off me?"

"I'm going to be spending the night in jail either way," she said, itching to hold the man's perfectly coiffured head under water.

THIRTY

Officer Josh Pace disembarked his cruiser, watching for any movement around the gray aluminum-clad warehouse with the huge sliding doors and a large picture window on the front office side. One solo streetlight made it appear abandoned, snow drifts piled against the building and entrance. No footprints marred the pristine surface.

He pushed through the knee-high drifts to the main door in his sturdy, fur-lined work boots, putting his face to the glass and peering inside. It was too dim to see much, a frustrating turn of events.

He'd have to risk using his flashlight and pray that no one would call the cops spotting the light, though he could say he was just checking the area. It was preferable to not be answering questions at the moment, avoid spilling something about what he knew about the mayor.

How was Anna doing—really? And he didn't mean right now over at the mayor's residence. Worry about her was keeping him on edge. To think the very night their other sister disappeared she was considering killing herself. It hurt that he hadn't realized her state of mind. He should have, but his mother's problems, proving himself on the new job, and worst of all one twin and then the other being abducted kept him busy 24/7, though it was no excuse.

He would try to make up for it going forward. Keep in closer contact, like a good friend should.

Directing the heavy-duty flashlight against the thick glass of the small window cut into the door, he focused it on what he could see. Not nearly enough. He itched to get inside, take a proper look around. He prayed Zoe wasn't here—it had to be barely above zero if the heaters were turned on low.

His heart squeezed painfully at thoughts of Zoe. What horrors was she suffering? Was she even still alive? She had to be. Their family was shrinking, so quickly it defied reason. If only they hadn't come to Anchor. It had been to give Anna a fresh start, which made sense considering the horrors of her early life, but at the cost of his family, the reasoning was looking thin to him in hindsight. Perhaps that was why Anna blamed herself so much? He'd have to consider that, moving forward, if this nightmare ever ended.

How was he going to get inside? He felt along the top ledge of the main door just in case someone had left a key there. Stranger things had happened.

His phone rang as he fumbled with the flashlight under one arm and checked under the window ledge to his right. *Was this it?* A slim case was attached by magnetism to the metal window casement. He held one glove between his teeth and pulled it off, using his bare fingers to pry the case open. Its frigid, subzero surface instantly chilled his hands to the bone, but inside lay a sturdy metal key. Nice.

Balancing the flashlight and inserting the key into the lock to free one hand, he reached into his pocket to answer his cell phone.

"What's up, Jeannie?" he asked, recognizing the sitter's number. His next-door neighbor was helping his mom this week while Josh worked the late shift, until he could find a permanent solution.

"It's your mom. I'm sorry to tell you this. She's been taken by ambulance to the hospital. They had to revive her, Josh, the paramedics were still working on her as they took her out the door. It was…so hard to see." Jeannie's voice was tightened by worry and strain, the words nearly running together as she rushed to speak. "I don't know anything more. I'm going to head over there right now. She's at St. Boniface. You'll need to meet us there. She doesn't look too good, hun. Hurry, okay?"

The phone went dead, leaving Josh staring at it in disbelief. Operating on automatic pilot, he had the presence of mind to remove the key from the door, placing it back in its hiding place before racing back to his police vehicle. He barely kept his footing on the deadly ice.

Once inside the cruiser, he turned on the siren, jerked the vehicle into gear, and roared off down the street, headed for St. B. At the emergency entrance, he parked as close as possible, making the quick dash through the automatic doorway in record time.

"Where's my mom?" he half-shouted at the receptionist who looked up from her computer board as he approached. Realizing the woman's expression had gone blank, he filled in the particulars. "Mrs. Cindy Pace. She was just brought in with cardiac arrest. I'm her son, Josh, Officer Pace. I need to see her doctor. I have facts about her condition he needs to know."

"Hang on. I'll check."

Josh counted off the seconds while he waited for answers. The nurse picked up the house phone and spoke to someone then hung up.

"She's in the ER being attended to right now. You'll need to wait until she's stabilized before—"

"I know. Thank you."

He ran down the hallway, taking a sharp righthand turn, and barreled into the ER, scanning for his mother. Nothing or nobody could possibly have talked him into sitting in the waiting room, worried out of his skull.

A team of specialists were hovering over a bed nearby, at the point they were using paddles in efforts to restart a heart. It had to be her. He moved forward as if in a dream, unable to feel his body.

He swallowed against the sudden restriction in the back of his throat. His mom looked so tiny, so vulnerable, her body violated by machines and medical personal. She hadn't wanted that. His mom had asked not to be resuscitated, but he couldn't seem to say it out loud, much as his mom would have wished it. He wanted everything possible done to save her. *Please, God, let her be all right.*

He watched in horror and hope as the nurses and doctors kept up their frantic pace. He should have intervened, but no one paid him any attention, too focused on their patient. Then, as if on cue, they all stopped working, their expressions sad and defeated. Death had won.

"I call it at 4:18 a.m.," a masked doctor said.

No.

He about fell to his knees, no strength left to support his body, needing to use the wall to stay upright. He was a terrible son. He should have been with her at the end. His mom had deserved to go peacefully, not like this, being punched and prodded by a crew of strangers. Why hadn't they known? Where was her doctor?

"You shouldn't be here, Officer." Someone had noticed his plight. Hands reached out to help him. The person guided him away from the room and his mother laying there so still, directing him back to the hallway.

"I need to say goodbye. Please," he begged, holding back the tears with great difficulty.

"We need to do a few things for her first. Let's get you a cup of coffee."

THIRTY-ONE

DAY THREE

"Give him, O Lord, your peace, and let your eternal light shine upon him," the priest said from rote, raising his hands for the final blessing, the sleeves of his white robe widening as he did so. The vestment gave him the appearance of an angel descended to earth.

He pictured her, that beautiful glow. She'd been the best to date. So perfect, her beauty so eternal.

He bowed his head along with the flock of mourners and prayed for them all, each and every one. He made the sign of the cross now, then stepped forward to shake the priest's hand and see to the mourners. It had been a well-attended funeral. Giles Larson had been a popular man who'd lived a long time.

He caught Richard watching him, his attention annoying and concerning. What was up with his cousin? Unease stirred in his gut and sweat broke out under his armpits. He shuddered, barely able to concentrate as he waited for the mourners to leave so he could get on with things. Like get the coffin lowered into the ground. The backhoe waited just out of sight, ready to replace the mound of dirt back into the hole. Then he could wash off the stench of fear. The touch of other people. That was the worst part. And it was why he had to scrub his hands in plenty of bleach, to get rid of the horror of it. He could never understand why others objected to the fresh fragrance of ammonia when it promised so much.

"Hey, Elvis, how's it hanging?" Richard said casually, sidling up next to him.

"Have some respect for the dead," he hissed back, annoyed, worried someone might have overheard. He took a quick look around, but the crowd was lining up to shake the priest's hand or say something to the relatives that stood nearby. Nobody was paying them any attention.

"Maybe *you* need to have more respect for them," Richard said, his voice sounding far too smug.

"What's that supposed to mean?" He squinted at Richard, the piercing wind making his eyes water. He didn't like the new picture his cousin presented, of a man who knew too much. Of a person who had acquired the upper hand in the current situation.

"I think you know. We'll talk later, in private, after the mourners have gone. You're right, this is not the place or time for the great reveal."

He swallowed against the bile that surged up from his gut. Richard calling the shots made him want to lash out, squeeze the life from something. Or someone. Who did Richard think he was? He didn't have a business and know how to run it. Hell, he didn't even own the house he was living in. What could have happened to cause this? Did his cousin come across some information that had made him suspicious? If so, he had the solution for that kind of nosiness. The bastard better watch his step if he knew what was good for him.

He stirred himself to action. A few hours of work remained before he and his cousin could have that talk. He waded in to take care of it, keeping busy planning for any outcome every step of the way.

Finally, the last cup of tea or coffee had been drunk, the last sandwich consumed, and the last fake sympathy speech had been delivered. The mortuary emptied out except for the pair of them. The time had arrived to have the talk.

"You want to move this conversation to my office," he prompted with a jerk of his thumb in the general direction, not asking it as a question.

"Why not?" Richard said with a nonchalant shrug as he looked up from his phone he'd spent the better part of clean-up time tending.

He was careful to sit behind his desk with his fingers tented, leaving a lower-legged chair for Richard to claim. Even then, they sat at about the same height. He waited for Richard to speak, hoping to draw him out, make him feel a need to fill the silence first. But Richard just waited him out, checking his phone every few seconds.

"What did I tell you about disrespect? Checking messages and texting while someone else is in the room is inappropriate, Richard."

"Oh, is it? I would have thought your indiscretions would rate a much higher number on the inappropriate scale, cos. Say, a thirteen out of ten." He chuckled at his own lame humor.

"What are you talking about? What indiscretion?"

"Really? We're going to play *that* game?" Richard gave him a look, his eyes narrowed with derision. "Did you know that some kids have been using the local graveyard for gang initiations?"

"What? Did you call the cops on them? Who was it?"

"Doesn't matter. But the part that interested me was they like to put someone in a freshly dug hole as part of the initiation process. Then make them wait it out. Spooked the hell out of Mikey Duffy last night. He began to move around like a total jerkoff, disturbing the soil and pissing in his pants. Funny shit. But what he uncovered was not quite so funny."

"What's all that got to do with me?" *Damn it. Isn't Michael Duffy The Buck's son?* Major complication.

Richard gave him a sideways glance, his lips quirked upward. "I'm thinking to keep this intel on the QT, I need a partnership in this nice little business you're running here. You have the papers drawn up or what I know goes to the cops."

Judas wanted his thirty pieces of silver. He had a solution for that. "How do you know the boys won't talk?"

"No worries. I told them if they reported the body, they'd be under the microscope by the cops. That their dirty reputations would take them down before anyone else. Stupid asses fell for it."

His cousin had the gall to think that would be enough to keep a lid on this thing. He was dumber than he looked. How could they possibly be related? Well, he could use ignorance to his advantage.

"Fine. I always intended to bring you into the business anyway. Your help is invaluable around here."

Richard gave him a sharper look, probably looking to see if he was messing with him. He managed to keep a straight face with some difficulty when all he wanted to do was scream bloody murder at the imbecile, and choke the life out of him. *Leaving those boys alive to spread the word*. What was he thinking when he'd had the perfect opportunity to toss them all in the grave, cover them up with the backhoe, and no one would have been the wiser? He'd dug that grave deep—plenty of room for them. This was a disaster of epic proportions. This could actually end all he'd worked so hard for. But no, he couldn't let it happen. *Calm down*. He could fix this with a little planning, make this all go away. He just had to be smarter, and considering who sat in front of him, that would be an easy task.

"I'll have the papers drawn up by my lawyer right away. Cut you in fair and square. So, who were these hooligans? Jason Stubbs and…?" he asked casually, giving his version of a lifelike smile though it made his face hurt, like it was just a bit of information between cousins.

Richard visibly relaxed, pulling a cigar from his pocket and lighting it with a flourish, that smug smile back and plastered all over his ugly, conniving mug. "The leader, Jason Stubbs, he's the nephew of the creep that runs the Yellowbird, George Stubbs. Mathew Ferguson, calls himself Moose, and Sean Cutter are his pathetic minions. Hard to believe the mayor's son is wanting to get involved with those idiots. Mikey deserved to be thrown in the hole. Shit-for-brains if you ask me."

"Lot of that going around," he said amiably, eyeing his cousin with interest. How much did he weigh?

THIRTY-TWO

Anna felt a wintry breath brush her cheek as cold fingers slipped past her jaw. It was about to happen. Every hair on her body rose as the spectral formed and grew more solid. She lay on the bunk in the dimness, eyes unblinking. It was the vulnerable time just before dawn when the dark and the light collided. Then she appeared in the jail cell, holding a blanketed child against her breast making it impossible to see its tiny face. *Tia.* She came to her more and more often now. In the vulnerable time between sleep and waking, she'd see her form taking shape in the darkness, her eyes pleading with her to find her, to come to them. And for a moment she was no longer alone.

"Grab your coat, Anna. Someone's bailed your sorry ass out for some unknown reason," Desk Sergeant Jack Browne joked, adding a wry grin.

She gave her head a shake now, dispelling the recent image with difficulty, and focused on the conversation that was a lifeline to lead her away from the maudlin. For the most part, the guys on duty had been fairly decent to

Anna, considering she'd finally been arrested like some of those in charge had been wanting for months. Maybe no one who worked the actual streets of Anchor liked the mayor any more than she did? In fact, it was almost like some of the officers applauded her decision, making jokes to pass the time.

She jammed her arms into the sleeves of her parka. "That's good news. I was beginning to think my ass was never going to recover from the hardness of that bench." At least she'd had the cell to herself. Though on second thought, a cellmate might have been a good idea. Maybe keep things at bay she couldn't explain.

"Have you seen the asses around this joint? More like your eyes won't recover."

"Ass blind is best, in my opinion," she said, finding her ready wit in time, making the sergeant snort a laugh.

"And nose blind doesn't hurt." Jack held his nostrils pinched together for a second, making his point.

"So, who posted bail?"

"Charlie. She's waiting for you in reception." Jack handed her some items in a clear plastic bag, her belt, phone, and wallet.

She wondered where Josh was at and why he hadn't bailed her out. Like she'd heard the mental question clear as a bell, Jack said, "Officer Pace lost his mom last night."

"What? I'm just hearing about this now?"

"Not that you could do much about it. Knowing wouldn't have helped, Anna. I'm sorry for your loss. I know you thought of her as your mother too."

She swallowed, using the awkward pause to remove the items from the bag and suit up, ignoring the sympathy. *I was stuck in here when I should have been there with them.* Zoe and Cindy needed her, Josh needed her. Her heart squeezed with grief all over again and she rubbed her chest to relieve the pain.

"You know, we're not all bad guys. Most of us really care about serving the public's best interests. However, don't get me started on Cecil Karloff—they should have retired his sorry ass long ago. But most of us are here for the right reasons. Scout's honor."

Something needed saying. After all, the guy had been decent to her. "Thanks for your words of sympathy, sir. Cindy Pace was one in a million. She took me in at a bad time and helped make the best of things for me. I reckon I wouldn't have made it without her and Alex, Josh, Zoe, and Tia."

Jack nodded. "I hope Josh stays on with us. He's got a lot of potential. Good instincts too. Hard to be a rookie and then get slammed with all the shit that's come down for the family in the last six months."

"He deserves a break. I gotta hope you'll help him with that going forward. Well, time I hit the road, Jack." Running on instinct alone, she stuck her arm out at the officer.

They clasped hands, giving a firm shake. It left Anna feeling better. Not that it would last, she had to face Charlie next. Then Josh.

"What were you thinking, Anna? Taking a chance like that? You know the department is looking for any reason to nail your ass to the barn door and tan it to rawhide," Charlie said as they walked side-by-side out of the police station, proving yet once again she could make up a good Southern expression along with the best of them. She missed her old stomping grounds in the moment, the jovial camaraderie of a people who knew who they were to the core and relished it. They had a warmth of spirit she'd not found any place else. A way of looking at things that gave a person ease and helped with life's inevitable curve balls. "Or maybe the point is you're *not* thinking?" She slanted a look her. "Taking chances when you need to step back and clear your mind."

"The time for stepping back and clearing my head has long passed. The time for action has arrived. Thank you for bailing me out, Charlie. I do appreciate it."

"What else have I got to do? By the way, Jim called."

Anna stopped walking. "What did he say? Were they a match?"

She sighed. "Sorry, no. Jim was definitive."

"Then I need to get DNA from the others on the cigar list." She unzipped her parka and felt in her shirt pocket for the hair, praying it was still there. It was and she pulled the short strand out, handing it to Charlie. "Have Jim test this for DNA against the cigar sample from the crime scene. It belongs to The Buck. It will at least help prove my theory to the authorities."

Charlie tugged a plastic baggie from her pocket and carefully deposited the hair inside, zipping it closed. "That should be fun, along with staying away from the cops' radar, finding Zoe and, well, you get my drift. I'll take care of trying to obtain other samples if this one doesn't pan out. You got enough on your plate to choke a herd of cows as it is."

"That would help. But please be smart and stay safe." She began to speak her thoughts aloud. "So much is in flux. I can't quite grasp it all. Who's the other player running this thing? No way the mayor did the original crimes—he just piggybacked his crime of passion on the unsub."

"You'll figure it out. You always do."

"No, I don't."

Charlie turned beet red at what she'd said as they both remembered Tia.

"Okay. Clock's ticking. I have some locations to check out ASAP. Zoe is still out there, all my senses say so, but now that the mayor knows I'm onto him, he might finish her if he hasn't already. Take care of Friday for me?"

"I'll take care of Friday. I made sure he was fed last night and he's already watching things for me at the agency this morning. I do believe that dog is half-wolf the way he's so territorial." She handed her car keys. "Go. I'll take an Uber. But watch your back. They'll be gunning for you, now more than ever."

Charlie gave her a hug, then watched her drive away in her Beetle. She looked lonely and cold standing there as she observed her through the rear-view mirror. She didn't deserve her being so patient, jumping in to help her whenever and wherever she could, but she'd take it anyway. She had no choice if she wanted to finish this. Find Tia and Zoe. That was all that mattered now.

THIRTY-THREE

Josh reached down to pick up the piece of paper that had fallen out of his locker when he opened the metal door. He picked the eight-by-ten page off the floor, glanced at it, then crumpled it up in disgust. A photo of Anna with the caption, *time to look closer to home?*

"That the best you assholes can come up with?" he muttered, tossing the paper into a wastebin. Then changed his mind, digging it out and smoothing it down. It was time to get this all out in the open. He'd had enough of the culture of silence and intimidation in the department. Today, of all days, was not the day to muck around with Officer Josh Pace. Taking a couple of minutes to turn the page into a proper paper airplane, he stomped into the squad room and sailed it through the air toward the solid group of all-male faces that stared at him, lined up for the morning briefing.

"Right back at y'all," he said, his expression grim. Focused. A few of the officers appeared uncomfortable, shying away from looking him in the eyes as he took the time to look at each face above the blue uniform collar.

Desk Sergeant Jack Browne picked it up, checked what it contained, then crumpled it in his big meaty fist, his face turning red with anger. "Sorry, Josh, we unfortunately have an idiot posing as a lawman in this room. And right now, I call them out. You're on short notice. None of the rest of us appreciates this crap. Cease and desist or we will have you out. Hiding behind this shit just makes you a coward lurking in the shadows, as bad as some we look to arrest." His expression shifted. "And I want to say I'm very sorry to hear of your mom's passing. I'm sure that I can speak for all of us when I say you have our heartfelt condolences."

Josh nodded curtly. Then a few of the men in blue came forward and shook his hand, offering their own words of sympathy. He swallowed against the sudden lump in his throat, grateful for their actions. Maybe things at work would get better now. His home life had fallen to ruin. His parents dead. His sisters missing. All he might be left with soon was his career if he didn't fuck that up too. At least that was something to focus on.

He'd come into work today because it would be what his mom would have wanted. Find Zoe. The rest could wait.

"You should have taken the day off. No one expects you here with what happened last night," Jack said as they left the briefing together. Everyone had been brought up to date on what was happening with Zoe Pace's case. It was painfully obvious that without Anna working on it as well, things would not have progressed nearly as far. Of course, that was due to her not being hampered by law and having a skill set that went well beyond the norm. He was torn between telling them what he knew and racing around trying find Zoe at the locations Anna deemed likely.

"I have to find my sister. She's been missing for days now. Time is not on my side. I'll be fine, Jack. I'm alive and kicking."

"Did you know Anna Hale was arrested last night?"

"No." He'd missed the first part of the meeting.

"We talked about it earlier, before you came sailing in. Good on you. One or two of these guys need to be taken to task about how they've been treating Anna. I'm a firm believer that things need to be brought into the open instead of being hidden away. But further to Anna, she's already made bail. Her sister-in-law, Charlie. No biggie. Just had our beloved mayor in her sights last night at his residence."

He pursed his lips, considering things.

"I can see you already knew something about it. Be careful, Josh. I know she's a friend of yours—your adopted sister—but she's a maverick and that can make her dangerous."

"It makes her want to get things done. And I need that right now. Zoe's not some unknown victim I'm trying to find, but my sister. Anna and I have the most to lose," he said.

A sudden flurry of activity erupted all around the squad room, people moving quicker and scurrying for their outdoor gear.

"What's up?" Jack asked in a loud tone, his attention immediately diverted.

"A body's been found in pretty bad shape," one of the officers shouted out to be heard over the din. "Out on that barren stretch of Caribou Drive past the hospital. Teenage boy, by the looks of it."

Josh shook his head in disbelief. It was either a hit and run or a body dump. Someone's child, brother, or friend was lying on the frigid pavement while their loved ones waited for them to come home. Waited for someone who would *never* get to grow up, leave home or have a family. His lungs squeezed with the effort to take a full breath. Memories of his childhood asthma surfaced, furthering a sense of things spinning out of control.

"I'll catch up with you later. Get some rest, Josh," Jack advised before rushing away and joining the other lawmen forming a huddle in the middle of the room.

But he couldn't leave. He had to know who it was and what was known to date. He strode over to the others and listened intently to the conversation.

"The officers on the scene, Quinn and Bear, are saying it's looking more like a hit and run and that the vehicle had to have been speeding. Major head trauma when the victim hit the windshield, badly mangled legs broken in multiple places. They'll know more after examining the clothing and the autopsy, but Quinn said he could see glass sparkling on the kid's parka hood. Let's pray there was a witness or the perp comes forward."

"Who was it?" Josh asked.

"The Ferguson boy. Mathew. Everyone knows him as Moose. Hangs around with that crew that's always getting into trouble around town," Jack said, scratching his head. "Yeah, Jason Stubbs and Sean Cutter."

"I recently saw the mayor's kid, Michael, hanging around them too. Bet The Buck appreciates that. Doesn't look good for the mayor's re-election campaign if his son is seen hanging with those juvenile delinquents," Officer Williams quipped, his expression full of meaning.

Police Chief Lloyd Davis strode into the room. All the officers went dead silent.

THIRTY-FOUR

The skull of the body burning inside the cremator cracked wide open, shooting red-hot fire out of the eye sockets and jawbone, releasing Richard's soul to fly up to join his ancestors. Or at least according to the Hindu Vedas.

Every time he'd experienced this precise moment, it brought immense satisfaction. If it wasn't for the thin layer of dust and soot settling on his body, even collecting on the inner lining of his nostrils making him want to run screaming into the yard and immerse himself in the purity of snow, he'd have worshipped the process. "Breathing people." It meant absorbing their essence. That was power. But physically, he loathed the process.

He'd once thought of the finality that burning would have brought for his beauties, but had opted instead for regular burial. There were too many for him to stand the processes of cremation. But it would have saved the worry he now was left with. What if one of those boys talked before he could dispose of them?

He needed to stay calm. Believe. He recited the words,

"Thus says the Lord, your Redeemer, the Holy One of Israel: I am the Lord your God, who teaches you to profit, who leads you in the way you should go. Isaiah 48:17."

He'd taken a divinely sent opportunity, spotting one of them on the roadside last night. At least he was driving a vehicle not registered in his name at the time, or under anyone else's, for that matter. But first thing before implementing the day's plan, he was going to spend a glorious hour scrubbing himself to a germfree state in the shower. Of course, he could have opted for water cremation, saved all the annoyance, but time was of the essence and that option took up more hours he didn't have. All evidence needed to be destroyed, *now*, crushed to dust by another machine, the pulverizing cremulator before that nosey asshole Chad turned up for his shift.

He waited impatiently for the temperature to reduce to five hundred degrees inside the machine before opening the heavy metal door. He was careful to have donned the industrial goggles, thinking safety first. His mind went back to the copycat killer operating in his territory. His own crimes could be easily attributed to the bastard. At least it was an option if he didn't cover up Richard's mess in time. Maybe start fresh, somewhere else? The possibilities were endless for a man of his abilities.

He was in the process of raking the dregs of what had been his cousin Richard through the grate and into a container when he heard the outside door open. Damn, Chad was running early, interrupting the Zen-like moment of raking the leftovers. He hadn't even had the time to remove any metal bits from the remains before turning the small bone fragments to dust in the cremulator for twenty seconds of intensive grinding.

He moved quicker now, not wasting any movements,

hoping to finish up before he fell under the scrutiny of good old boy Chad. Chad knew he avoided this place like the plague. That he hated the fine dust that make anyone look like a Charles Dickens character.

Sweat broke out on his body and he shuddered, sensing rivers of black soot sliding down his face and body. The horror of it did not escape him but was his penance to bear. *Stay calm. You can do this. Just a little while longer.*

Sifting through the lumpy sections of the debris, he discovered his cousin's metal retainer from when he'd had his teeth straightened. He slipped it into his pocket. Too incriminating. All he needed was a dentist to recognize his own work. He'd dispose of it in a ditch somewhere.

He placed the bits and pieces that had been Richard in the industrial blender and set the timer for twenty seconds. While it worked, he noted movement out of the corner of his eyes. Chad had arrived at the scene of the crime. Except Chad didn't know and would never know.

He dumped the fine ashes into a metal box and shut the lid, tucking it under his arm. Then turned and gave the middle-aged man with the generous pot belly what he hoped was a satisfactory smile.

"Morning, Chad. Just had to get a body cremated earlier than normal this morning. Hope you don't mind. The family wants to bury them at sunrise and I knew you wouldn't have time to complete it before the ceremony."

Chad frowned. "Morning, Elvis. Strange, I didn't know anything about it."

"Last-minute call. Apparently, the grandmother's going into a home later today and they wanted this over and done with beforehand. I took care of it instead of calling you in so early. I'm not much for sleeping."

"Could have used the overtime," Chad grumbled, rubbing one hand over his thick bushy gray whiskers. How the hell could the man stand those *things* on his face, trapping germs? Furthermore, how could he possibly get all the soot and ash he was covered with on a daily basis washed out completely? It defied explanation. He kept his expression neutral as he was long used to when dealing with the vulgarities of the human race, not allowing his disgust to interfere with the business at hand.

"You do a lot of hard work around here. Maybe it's time for a raise?"

Chad's eyes narrowed in speculation. "Past time. I work my butt off around here. Day in and day out at the constant beck and call of seven funeral homes. Population's getting older. Lots more bodies stacking up."

Though Elvis had set up the business himself seven years ago, he allowed all the other funeral homes in the area to use the facilities. At cost. Goodwill was a magical thing, keeping others from looking at him too closely. Not that any one of them had the imagination to understand a keen mind like his.

"Expect a dollar an hour extra on your next paycheck."

Chad rubbed his beard again. "I got a lot of expenses. Shayla's needing braces, cost of groceries has risen alarmingly this winter—a buck's not going to go far."

"Fine." Maybe it really was time to move on? Was this the sign he needed? Having to deal with humans beneath him more often than not? He'd had to deal with Richard and his stupidity, and now Chad and his greed? The idiot was holding him up. Thankfully there were no funerals planned today. By tonight he should be close to finishing what needed to be done to keep him safe from exposure. "Make that a dollar fifty and a nice bonus in six months. That work for you?"

Chad considered, his beady eyes appearing somewhat satisfied with his bargaining. "How nice?"

The guy really must think he had something on him or he was a moron. *Be careful Chad, you're pushing my patience.*

"Say five percent."

The man had the audacity to grunt his acceptance, belching in the process and proving he was a big fan of letting nature have her way when it came to dental hygiene.

"I have to go," he said, restraining himself from the immediate satisfaction of grabbing the metal rake and knocking the man to the floor before disposing of his remains in the oven. He didn't have the time right now. Maybe later.

THIRTY-FIVE

"Time to wake up, Honey Bear. You have to wake up now."

Zoe wanted to sleep and sleep and sleep. For her mom to leave her alone. Didn't teenagers need more rest than anyone except maybe babies? She groaned, annoyed her mother wasn't going to take no for an answer when she shook her by the shoulders.

But when she opened her eyes, gritty and sore as they were, she was once again alone. Disoriented, she swallowed against the harsh dryness of her mouth and throat. She picked up the water bottle and opened the lid with difficulty, her hands raw from trying to make a dent in the trapdoor with a piece of wood she'd broken off from one of the pallets. She'd pounded away for what seemed hours, barely making process. At least the activity had warmed her up some. The longer she was down here, without food, the colder she became.

She tilted the small container upside down, trying to find one last drop to quench the terrible thirst that had assailed her since yesterday morning. But her tongue found nothing, just a stale plastic dryness.

Sighing, she sat upright, albeit very slowly, but still the dizziness the motion caused made her work hard against the need to throw up again. She couldn't afford to lose any more moisture. Maybe she should pee in the bottle? Recycle? It might come to that at this rate. What she wouldn't give for a hot cup of coffee with thick cream. The thought made her stomach growl. The image of a plate of bacon and eggs, with jam and toast, her favorite meal for breakfast, lunch, or dinner, only added to the nightmare. Maybe she was clogging her arteries, but she needed the fuel for looking after her mom's needs.

Oh, god, Mom, how are you doing?

Her mother would be in terrible shape by now. The thought brought a flood of tears to her eyes. She was the only one who could calm her down. Get her to eat. And Josh, he'd be a crazy person moving heaven and earth to find her. The reassuring thought was the only one sustaining her now. Josh led the calvary straight to her. Any second, her brother would come pounding down the stairs, gun drawn, ready to take on the world to save her. It was the only thing keeping her from sinking into the abyss of despair.

I have to hang on. He will find me.

Anna's image rose in her mind in all her Southern charisma. She'd been so depressed last time she saw her, so sunk into desire over being a suspect and wanting revenge for their sister, all her charms had been sadly missing. She understood. No way had she had anything to do with it which had to have make it much more painful. But maybe by now she was able to get herself into a state to help Josh find her? Her brother would go to her, she was certain of it. Josh cared for Anna more than she knew. And with her special skills, and his perseverance, they would be an unstoppable team.

A terrible reality crept in, overrode the idea of being rescued soon, making her shiver uncontrollably. Was the person who had put her here just going to let nature take its course? Let her die alone in the dark? She still couldn't remember their face. They must have caused some damage to her brain—the wound was seeping still, tender to the touch on the right side of her temple. It would be better to have put a bullet in her right then and there then to suffer for days on end like this. The bottle of water would soon be gone. How long could one survive without it? A few days? She'd read once it wasn't nearly as long as a person could survive without food.

A loud thud grabbed her attention. She froze, all senses directed toward listening. Yes. Footsteps resounded overhead, making dust pools shower down from the ceiling. Had someone found her? Or was it the bad guy back to finish her off? Didn't matter, she needed to call out, if there was the slimmest of hopes that someone was here to rescue her.

But when she tried, all she could manage was a hoarse whisper. *Try harder, Zoe,* she chastised herself.

"Help," she said, a bit louder. The noise stopped. Had they left? *No. God, please no!* She would die for certain. She knew she had little time—the lack of food and water, the insidious cold creeping into her veins and muscles, all spelled certain disaster.

"I'm down here!" she managed a half-scream, her rusty throat hurting so badly she had to hold her arms around herself in an effort to soothe the intense wave of pain.

Then someone was lifting the trapdoor up, the hinges squeezing in protest. But who was it? Help or death?

THIRTY-SIX

The man followed discreetly behind the pair of slouching teenagers before they veered off the sidewalk. They were skipping school today, making his job all the easier. He walked on by, watching them scurry up the snow-covered path toward a rundown trailer out of the periphery of his vision. Perfect. The place looked like a firetrap and was situated out of the beaten path. Kind of place where a meth operation could blow up, turning it into an inferno in mere seconds. And if that didn't work, there was always the tried-and-true drive-by shooting.

He just needed the proper supplies, easily come by in his vast storeroom. Sliding into the seat of the old half-ton that was lost in a sea of trucks so common to Anchor, he turned over the motor, enjoying the way the vehicle sprung to life under his fingertips. He kept his fleet of vehicles in top running order.

He never knew when he might need the use of one for a few hours to keep the scent off him and his known vehicle of hearse or black SUV. Many others were stored in old granaries around his property, ready and able when the time was right. *You can never be too prepared.* That had been his favorite motto over the years and now it was going to pay huge dividends.

He thought with supreme satisfaction at what the copycat would think of his expert preparations against him over the past few years. The smug bastard had no idea of what he'd planned to do if things took a twist. And in his experience, things *always* took an unforeseen twist. And not just in the crime thrillers and mysteries he loved to indulge in, but in real life as well. Otherwise, how to explain the human propensity to come up with such things? Had to have happened somewhere, sometime. Nothing new under the sun in his opinion. Just knowing history so you can take advantage of it, that was what mattered.

Okay, time to refocus. One to go and he'd have taken care of Richard's mess. Where was Jason Stubbs hiding? Most likely the kid's uncle knew something. Large-flaked snow began to fall as he drove through the nearly deserted streets of Anchor, the promised storm coming to blanket the area in pristine whiteness. Good. It would provide more than enough cover. Gotta love the north. The closest thing to a frontier the world had left. He'd miss it when he moved down south. But facts were facts. He was no longer secure in his position in Anchor. That idiot Richard had seen to it.

He turned left on Caribou Drive, heading for the Yellowbird Motel. The storm had finally let up, and the snowplows were out in full force, aiding him in his endeavors to finish the job. Tonight.

The last member of that punk gang who could expose him had to be worried by now, all his pals gone in a single day. Serendipity's divine hand. Had to be, right? What with all the good fortune to his cause happening so quickly? Hell, they'd been handed to him on a silver platter. It gave him confidence, letting him know he was on the right track. Still in God's graces. So much so, he was revising his exit plan. There was still time to go after the one he'd been dreaming of for years since his crush on her in high school. The only one who'd been nice to him, the reason he'd spent so many endless hours perfecting his technique. Time spent learning the secrets of the Egyptians, following every scientific discovery that might lead to the promised land of a body lasting for years, if not decades. It was a shame the experience would silence forever that contagious laugh she'd had. The one that could brighten anyone's day. Pain hit, a sharp knife blade cutting deep into his skull, blurring his vision.

An idea struck like an epiphany sent direct from heaven's gate, in a blast of pure light that always accompanied the pain. He rubbed his head at the suddenness of the idea, the enormity of it all. Maybe I can change it up this time? Keep her alive for as long as she promised to be his girlfriend? She was young, like him, and had a few good years with minimal wrinkles, barring any unforeseen disaster. What were a few smile lines between friends?

He stared out the SUV's side window at the movement of the door opening to the office. Low and behold, a few minutes after he thought the delinquent's less than inspiring name, the skinny male appeared in the doorway, a mulish look marring his face.

And then there were none...

When he had accomplished this last test of his resolve, there would be nothing left to stop him moving on to having his dream girl. Tonight.

He'd prepared his kit already and had stowed it under the spare wheel compartment for safe keeping. He was free to swing by her apartment as soon as he'd disposed of Stubbs. She'd unwisely chosen the first floor in the back of a fourplex. Easy-peasy to jimmy the lock and gain entry or cut the glass. Anchor might not be a metropolis like New York or LA, but it was large enough to have inhabitants who were less than savory, like that Dirty Boy.

There! Creepy Jason Stubbs was just now worming his way down the motel's sidewalk, trying to see if he could see anything in the mostly curtain-drawn windows. His very presence tainted the world.

Town riffraff. Like that pompous jackass who sickened him, wanting time alone with the women to keep his damn mouth shut. It took a lot of bleach to wash the stench away. He bet Dirty Boy didn't know how to treat a lady either. How to keep her safe from other men. A man's number one responsibility was to keep his wife hidden away from the dirt of other men's base intentions. His mother had drilled it into him and his sister Molly from such a young age that he couldn't remember when it had started. Men, she'd always said, were disgusting in their functional bodies without one ounce of grace. Their one job was to worship a woman, give her everything she needed. She was one of three sister wives, the eldest, and wise in ways he wished he better understood. He wondered for a moment where his real sister was? She'd up and vanished one day, never to be heard from again.

But he could give his dream gal what she needed most: a perfect life away from the evils of the world. A woman like her should not be in regular society. It was beneath her. The job would cover her in filth until she would wake up one day unrecognizable. He couldn't let that happen. He had to step in, make sure her fine beauty wasn't sullied further by him.

Ah, Dirty Boy was turning the corner and heading out back. Time to move.

THIRTY-SEVEN

Anna prayed like she'd never prayed before. *Please be there, Zoe.* She hadn't heard from Josh all day, assuming his mom's death was keeping him out of commission. She needed something good to happen and she wanted to be the person that made it happen. She kept her mind off the tragic circumstances enfolding around her by moving, searching, keeping so busy she had no time to think. It was something she hadn't managed to do when Tia went missing, too heartbroken to do much of anything at being a suspect. But now she was stronger, not willing to succumb to disabling grief and crippling depression. She had one last location to check. She'd exchanged Charlie's vehicle for her own, feeling safer driving in the country with a four-wheel drive.

So far, her search of the mayor's properties had come up with nothing. There'd been a couple of close calls, but she'd come away unscathed. She was headed out of town now, driving to the old hunting cabin thirty miles north of Anchor. It was located off the main highway, traffic being almost non-existent on the sideroad. She hadn't passed another car in ten miles. Perhaps word of the blizzard fast approaching was keeping people at home.

She caught sight of the lodge through the fir trees. It was built of solid logs, sturdy enough to last for generations. Picture-postcard perfect. She had to hand it to The Buck, he took care of his things. All his properties appeared in good repair.

Pulling up in front of the cabin, she took a careful look around, not wanting to be ambushed if someone was already there waiting. But no tracks marred the three-day-old snow. If Zoe was here, she'd been alone all this time. What would she find? Apprehension kept her wide awake. Had she always been like this? Waiting for the other shoe to drop? Always assessing the threat level?

She cranked her neck and looked up at the sky through the truck's windshield. Dark clouds were gathering overhead, forewarning of the storm building to the northeast. She had to hurry to do a thorough recon then head right back to Anchor before the storm hit, hopefully with Zoe in tow. A few flakes began to fall as she disembarked her vehicle, striding toward the front steps of the log structure through the already knee-deep snow that had fallen in the past weeks.

Surprisingly, the door was locked. So often, in the country, a cabin was left open in case of emergency. But there should be a key someplace. She felt along the top of the doorframe, her hands finding what she needed to save having to break in. Twisting the key in the lock, she pushed open the door, finding it as cold inside as out. She began praying again, shutting down her tormented thoughts, prepared to find what was there to be found.

She walked the length of the open concept structure, discovering nothing amiss on the main floor. Damn, and she'd been so certain. She turned to leave, her spirits sinking lower with each footstep. Where else was there to look? In that instant the door slammed shut right in her face! *What the hell?* An even colder sensation overcame her and she stopped dead in her tracks, knowing *she* was there. Tia. All senses on high alert, she turned around and looked about.

Maybe there was a cellar of sorts, though she had seen no evidence of stairs?

Was that a noise?

She froze. Listened. Another muffled sound. It was coming from below! Sizing up the floor, she pushed aside a large oval rug, finding what she'd expected.

Her heart pounding, she drew back the wooden bolt and opened the trapdoor. It was but a short drop from the main floor to the dirt basement below, but she'd need a ladder to get anyone back out. She crouched down on the freezing floor on her knees, catching sight of a cot with a woman lying prone on it. *Zoe.*

She jumped down through the opening in the floor, landing with her knees bent, figuring she'd worry about a ladder later. She dashed to her side, supporting her, looking into her eyes to see if she was okay.

"Thank God you found me," she croaked, her eyes filling with pain as she tried to speak,

She pulled a plastic container from her parka pocket. "Don't talk. Here, drink this."

She let her hold the water bottle to her lips, drinking it down in desperate gulps. Some spilled on the thin blanket she was clutching to her chest. When the bottle was half gone, she pulled it away.

"Not too much now. You'll cramp up."

She nodded, though her desperate eyes told another story.

"How did you find me?" Her voice sounded a bit stronger. She helped her sit up.

"Long story. It can wait until we get you to the hospital."

"How's Mom doing?"

She needed to change the subject. "Did you see who put you down here?"

"I don't remember." She rubbed her forehead in dismay. It was then she noticed the blood plastering her hair to her scalp. Did she have amnesia? She'd been hit pretty hard by the looks of things.

"We should get you out of here. Can you walk?" Her every instinct told her to get out. Now. But she couldn't rush the confused, sick woman. She was in a bad way, but at least she was alive. *Threat assessment: high.*

"I think so."

She carefully pulled her to her feet, supporting her as they made their way slowly over to the yawning hole in the floor above their heads.

"I'll need to find a ladder. Can you stand here while I search above?"

Her words were interrupted by the loud crash of the trapdoor falling back into place. *What the hell?*

Was someone in the cabin? Had they followed her? Or was it just a bit of bad luck?

The sound of receding footsteps overhead told the awful truth. Someone had locked them in the basement. Damn it, but that asshole wasn't going to get away with it!

"I need to sit you back down so I can open it up again. Okay?" She helped Zoe back to the cot, trying to sound more certain of the outcome than she felt. *The Buck* must have followed her, for who else could it be? The man had been careful. Anna hadn't spotted any surveillance. But then Buck would know where she was headed and could stay well behind, waiting for the perfect opportunity.

Well, she had a phone. She'd call for help. But when she tried, she found no signal, no cell service. It was likely due to the heavy cloud cover from the converging storm interfering with the satellite feed.

"Okay, I'm going to try to pry open the door."

"I was using a piece of wood from a pallet earlier." Zoe pointed at the thick board scarred from use, her eyes expressing her fear and concern. But at least she didn't say it aloud. Talking about it wasn't going to change it. Only action would.

"I have something a bit more useful," she quipped, pulling her trusty Leatherman tool off her belt. "I never go anywhere without it. It will take a bit of time, but I can promise to get us out of here. Just relax and sip the water when you need to."

She went to work, using the sharp-bladed tool to saw through the wooden draw bolt fastening the trapdoor to the floor. Thankfully it wasn't made of metal. It was slow going, though, taking time she wasn't certain Zoe had.

Sweat dripping in her eyes, she kept up the pressure on the inch-thick dowel for what seemed hours, sawing back and forth until she felt her arm was about to drop off. She rested every once in a while. The bolt was tough, not wanting to give up its job without a fight.

Finally, it broke free. They were halfway home.

She scrambled out of the hole, swinging herself up and in high pursuit of a ladder to help her sister climb out being in no condition to help herself. It took a few minutes, but she found one in an attached shed.

"Move out of the way. I'm throwing down a stepladder." She waited until she was certain she'd moved back far enough, then leaned over the edge and lowered the awkward device down into the cellar.

She jumped down the hole after the ladder, then helped Zoe onto the first rung, waiting until she had a grip of the sides. She was shaky. They would have to take their time. One step, then another, until she was finally on the main floor. Anna hurried the final few steps and took hold of her arm, needing to assist her when she saw Zoe swaying on her feet.

"Almost there. We just need to get you out to the truck."

It took longer than she would have liked, but slowly they made the way to her vehicle. She helped Zoe into the passenger seat, buckled her in, then raced around to the driver's side. She turned the motor over, the sense of getting away burning bright within him.

Nothing happened. Not the sound of a motor springing to life, but the dead sound of a starter grinding as it tried to turn over. *Damn it*. Buck must have disabled the truck, tearing away the distributer and destroying essential cables. Snow fell heavily all around them as Zoe looked to her for answers, her condition more obvious in the light of day. A quick look under the hood confirmed it.

"Let's go back inside. I'll see if I can rustle us some food. Get you warmed up." Surely there was firewood and canned food available? No self-respecting person would keep a cabin unstocked in the dead of winter. Of course, there was nothing redeeming about The Buck, soon to be stripped of the title and his freedom with any luck. But Anna's worst worry was Zoe's head injury. Her dizziness and lack of memory were bad signs.

But when she checked, she wasn't impressed by the amount of food Buck had seen fit to stock the place with.

Only a few packs of crackers and peanut butter remained in the near-empty cupboards. At least she could start a fire, warm them up. And she always carried protein bars in her emergency kit that could sustain them for a few days if it came to it. The snow was falling heavier now. Most pressing problem, could she wait out the storm to get Zoe medical attention?

"First things first. Let's warm you up." She tried to sound as cheerful as she could, watching her closely out of the corner of her eye. What if she had rescued her only to have her die from her injuries? She was far too pale, too disoriented, though she had asked about her mother, so that was something, right? She wished she hadn't jinxed it by thinking about things with the next words that came out of Zoe's mouth.

"Has something happened to Mom? Something you're not telling me?"

"Let me get the fire started then we can talk. Okay?" She didn't look at her, but continued bustling around getting an armful of wood stacked into the woodstove. Then lighting the kindling and bit of newspaper with the fire striker hanging alongside the black stovepipe.

Zoe had tugged a colorful log-cabin-style quilt from the back of the couch onto herself, only her face visible through the blanket as she sipped at the water.

"Eat some crackers. It'll help."

She shook her head. "Not hungry. I need to know about my mom."

She sighed. This was not going to go well. Zoe had enough on her plate—she didn't need to be involved with the acute grief that was going to follow her announcement.

"It's okay. I just need to know. Is she gone?"

"I'm so sorry. I wish I had better news." Anna winced

at the raw pain visible in her reddened eyes. She should have taken the hospital up on the offer of a grief counselor when Tia went missing. Maybe then she would know what to say, handled things better, not ended up with thinking of pointing a gun at her own head. But she hadn't actually done it, right, just visualized it. Lots of people do, doesn't mean they act on it. Maybe it was a way of coping, seeking control over things. Anyway, that time has passed.

Tears were flooding down Zoe's face and pooling on the blanket. She moved to her, put her arm around her thin shoulders, hugging her sideways.

"The bastard who trapped me down there, he's to blame for Mom's death. If I get my hands on him, he'd better watch out." Her hands tightened into fists, digging into her thighs.

"You don't remember anything about what happened to you?"

She pressed one of her clenched fists to her forehead, thudded the pale flesh with her hand. She gently pulled it away and held her by the wrist, not wanting her grief and frustration to further harm her.

Zoe looked at Anna, their glances locking, hers filled with anguish and anger. "I can't remember. I've tried. It's all a blank."

Anna pulled her phone out to add a distraction. "No service. I think the storm is to blame."

"Probably." Zoe sighed, her voice sounding tired.

"You need to rest. I'm going to the truck and get my emergency kit. We need to clean your wounds."

The cabin was getting warmer. She hurried outside to retrieve the emergency bag when a loud cracking sound echoed nearby. What the hell? She looked at the blood oozing from her coat in disbelief. She'd been shot.

THIRTY-EIGHT

Josh had spent the day running in circles. The whole department was in an uproar. First the Ferguson boy found dead out on Caribou Drive, and now a fire had partially burned down a trailer with two bodies trapped inside, one the mayor's son. And nobody so far had seen anything.

Though Anchor had its fair share of crime and criminals, this was a particularly bad run of luck. The three boys were known to pal around together, making it even more suspicious. Not to mention the mayor was nowhere to be found to inform him of his son's tragic death. Half the department was working on it, Davis pressing for answers.

He hadn't heard from Anna all day either, but to be truthful, he hadn't reached out, too busy jumping on problems and arranging things for his mother. He needed to get back on his game. Zoe needed him more than anyone did. On impulse, he dropped the file he had been studying and jumped to his feet.

"I have to go," he said aloud.

"Be careful. Something strange is going on in Anchor today," Jack said, looking up from his computer screen.

"Always. If you need me, give me a shout."

"You shouldn't be here at all. Go. See to your mom."

"Nothing new on Zoe?" he asked, shrugging on the jacket he had left hanging over the back of his office chair.

Jack shook his head, his expression apologetic. "Most of our resources are tied up at the moment."

He left quickly, more determined than ever that his sister's fate was in his hands. He didn't have the pull of a mayor or a chief of police with a whole department at his back. He only had Anna. Maybe Jack Browne. Though Anna was worth more than a few others combined, she was just one person and was suffering her own torments.

Where to go first? Instinct said if Zoe was still alive, she was hidden somewhere no one expected her to be found. If he were the bad guy, he'd take her outside city limits to a nice quiet location where he could deal with her at his leisure. The thought disgusted him, sending shooting pains to pierce his brain. But at least he had a direction to go.

The storm was quickly making the roads difficult to navigate, even with the four-wheel drive. Sleet clung to the windshield and rivers of ice crystals ran down the side windows, pooling and building up on the doorframe. He knew he should turn back, but he couldn't. Every cell in his body was fighting reason, forcing him ahead, sending him into dangerous territory.

He kept the wipers turned on high, the storm reducing visibility to only a few feet ahead. The line between the roadway and the ditch blurred, making it near impossible to see. He kept his bearings with great concentration and difficulty, feeling the presence of a hand on his shoulder. It comforted him, like his mother was still right there with him, encouraging him forward. *We need to find your sister.* The words whispered in his ear only increased his drive to get to the cabin in the woods.

To rescue Zoe.

THIRTY-NINE

Zoe remembered now. It all came back in a head rush that left her reeling. Aaron being shot. The woman being strangled. That smug face. The mayor. *The Buck*. She'd seen him preening on a news broadcast often enough. Now she just wanted to take him down. Make him pay for what he had done.

The piercing shot that resounded outside the cabin had sent her reeling back in time, providing a reminder of how it had begun. Gunfire. The man strangling the young woman with his bare hands. The terrifying look on his evil face. Then the bastard had hit her with something hard as a rock when she'd tried to run away.

She sat up straighter, looking toward the doorway, expecting Anna to come bursting through it at any second. But it remained closed. Fear struck again. Who had been shooting? Was Anna okay?

She scrambled to her feet; her legs as wobbly as a newborn foal's. She had to help her. She'd rescued her and now she could be lying outside the cabin. Hurt.

She stumbled to the door, pulling it open and peering

around. At first, she couldn't see anything, only the storm raging on and sending ice pellets into her face that stung and burned her eyes. Then she emerged, covered in a white crust, the only thing with color a large bloom of blood on her parka and the gun she clutched in her hand.

She tried helping her, but she was too weak to do much. She locked the door, and they aimed for the sofa, falling down together in a tangle of limbs.

"What happened? Who shot you?"

"I couldn't see them...the storm...they had to have been hiding somewhere nearby." Anna winced in pain, working to undo her coat. She helped her with the zipper, pulling it down and easing the fabric away from his chest.

"I remember everything now. It was the mayor, Buck Duffy, who killed Aaron and that woman." The words were hard to say, harder still to have lived.

"That woman was his new, younger wife." Anna probed her upper chest with her fingers. "I think it's a shoulder wound. We need to check if it went right through or not."

"He strangled her with his bare hands. He's a monster."

"I believe it's Buck who shot me. Or the other guy who took Tia and now Joy Evans, one of the nurses from the hospital."

"Joy's missing? What, you don't think they're the same person?" Her words confused her. Surely Anchor didn't have two such evil operators working at the same time?

"I think the mayor copycatted the original crime. But I don't know who the other guy is. He's been very elusive, but he made a point of taking Joy right after you, like he was saying the two crimes were different. It probably angered him, the mayor taking credit for his crimes. Josh's working that angle as well. The mayor doesn't fit the profile of a serial killer, not that there isn't a lot of leeway. Always a possibility of an outlier."

"Josh! He must be worried sick." Zoe bit her thumbnail at the mention of her brother. "No way to call him either."

"I want you to take my gun. Keep it pointed at the doorway. If the bastard decides to break in, I want you to shoot him before he shoots us. Can you do that if I pass out?"

"I think so. Let me look at your wound first." She leaned forward and checked her back. "It went right through you."

She grunted, obviously in pain though relieved at her words. "Thank goodness for small favors."

"I'll get some bandages. Did you think to bring in that emergency kit?"

Anna pointed at her parka pocket. "In there."

She tugged it out, opening the white case branded with the red cross with trembling hands.

"I should be bandaging you, not the other way around," Anna said, with a rueful twisted smile she appreciated. You could always count on her in any situation. Proof in point, she was there with her right now, risking her neck to help save hers. The least she could do was rise to the occasion. Shoot the bastard that was looking to harm them.

She went to work, using the basic training she'd received to keep her mom okay to clean and bandage the wound. The bleeding had slowed down somewhat, but the hole through Anna's shoulder was sizable.

"We need to get you to the hospital as soon as we can."

"Not going to happen with a storm raging outside, even if we could contact the authorities. I wonder if there's any alcohol around this place? I could use a bracer."

"I'll look." She got to her feet, trying to be brave, but the room spun alarmingly. She hung on to the sofa arm for a moment, getting her bearings, then worked her way around the room, trying to find a bottle hidden somewhere. In the cupboard beside the sink, she found what she needed. A large bottle of high proof dark rum.

"Hallelujah," she said. She slowly made her way back to the couch and plopped down.

She unscrewed the top lid, holding it out to Anna. Just the sharp odor of the liquor strengthened her resolve. When she took the bottle from her, she picked up the gun again, holding it pointed at the doorway, held between her two hands.

The next hour or two was probably going to be the most critical of all the time she'd been in captivity. It was do or die time. And she didn't intend to die.

FORTY

Josh had slowed the vehicle to a crawl, trying desperately to watch where he was going. He occasionally stuck his head out the side window, trying to find the edge of the ditch, blinking away the ice crystals stuck to his eyelids. He couldn't be too far away from his destination. The odometer reported he'd traveled twenty-nine miles from Anchor already.

What the hell! Was that gunfire? *Oh Lord, please keep Zoe be safe*, he prayed, stepping on the gas pedal. The SUV spun out, its tires trying to grip the graveled roadway. He held on to the steering wheel in a life-and-death struggle, the police cruiser seeming to have a mind of its own, wanting to head straight for the ditch. Then he hit a solid bank of snow and ice and the steering wheel twisted sideways, bringing the vehicle to a sudden stop. He brought his fists down on the dash in frustration, needing to pound something.

"Crap!" What a mess. He was stuck in the middle of nowhere.

He checked her cell phone. It had one bar—worth a

try. He texted his location back to Jack Browne at the station, letting him know he was stranded and had heard a gunshot. Hitting Send, he prayed it would reach its destination.

Now what? He had to try to get to the cabin. Nothing else for it. He pulled on a department-issue wool toque and thick, heavy gloves, then stepped out of the cruiser.

Sleet assaulted him and he pulled up the hood on his parka, tying the cords dangling on each side of the fur tightly under his chin. Plowing through the thick banks and ridges of ice and snow took a great deal of energy, and within a quarter mile he was breathing hard, his legs straining inside his heavy snowpacks with each bracing step.

The wind came on in wild gusts, the screeching sound far too much like a banshee for comfort. The call of a northern storm wearied the spirit, forced a person to take stock of their resources. Out there in the barren wilderness, he no longer felt his mom's presence. Just him, against the elements. And he had no doubt at all that one misstep would mean certain death.

He trudged along, putting one foot in front of the other, Zoe's image the only thing sustaining him.

Another gunshot, nearer now, punched through his fog. He began to run, falling down, then getting up and running again. It couldn't be far. Then he saw the dark smoke rising above the hazy white tree line. It had to be a chimney. He ran harder, sweat dripping in his eyes and freezing, half-blinding him.

A half-ton vehicle came into view. Anna's truck. He stumbled to it, found the door locked and continued onward, pounding against the solid wood of the cabin.

"Let me in, it's Josh!" he screamed, trying to be heard over the thundering voice of the blizzard.

FORTY-ONE

Anna drank a few sips of the potent rum, not wanting to become incapacitated any more than she already was. Could she have found Zoe only to lose her all over again? The bastard was out there somewhere, and here they were trapped inside. What if he decided to burn the cabin down? They'd be left to the mercy of the elements until the storm ended. And though she was hurt, she knew Zoe was in even worse shape. No food and just a few sips of water for days along with a severe head injury. She should have brought help. Other than Charlie, and maybe Josh who might figure it out from the list of locations she'd given him, no one knew where she was. Knew that his sister Zoe had been found and needed a doctor's care.

More than anything she was angry that the asshole had gotten the drop on her. Shooting her from a concealed location. The damn storm and worry over Zoe had made her less cautious than usual. Sergeant Carter would be disappointed in her, but no more disappointed than she was in herself.

"I'm sorry about all this," Zoe said, her tired, sad expression touching a chord deep inside her.

"In what universe is any of this your fault?"

"I shouldn't have left Mom alone that night. And now she's dead and it's all my fault." Tears trickled down her face and her sorrow cut her to the bone. Survivor's guilt. She lived with it every day of her life.

"You've taken really good care of your mother. *None* of this is your fault. It's that coward hiding outside that's the cause. You deserve to have a life. Everyone does. Never apologize for it, Zoe."

"What about you?" She gave her a solid look, her brows coming together in a frown.

"What do you mean?"

"Are you going to live your life again? Stop drinking and keeping to yourself like you've been doing since Tia disappeared?"

"I've lived most of the good parts of my life."

"But you just said everyone deserves a life!" She continued to look at her, a spark of anger clear in her eyes now.

"Josh said something similar. He reckons I need to find a mission. Go after more of the bad guys. No lack of them anywhere in this world." She shrugged. All she was worried about was living through the next few hours, praying the storm stopped. That she could somehow get Zoe home safe and sound. The coward lurking outside had to have come in a vehicle. Once the snow stopped falling, they could take a look around. See if they could find transportation.

The sounds of glass breaking at the back of the cabin woke her from her thoughts. *Crap, now what?*

"Give me the gun," she said, the adrenaline flowing

through her system enough to give her the strength to confront whatever was next.

Zoe handed it over, her eyes dark with worry. "Be careful, Anna, please."

"Don't worry. I don't have a death wish. At least not anymore." She realized she spoke the honest truth as she said it. She did want to go after more of the bad guys and teach them not to mess with good people. But first, she needed to live through this.

She got to her feet and crept to the back of the cabin, alert to any movement. A flash of fire racing toward her made her duck down quickly. *What was that?* A loud pop came as the missile hit the floor behind him and exploded. The coward had thrown a Molotov cocktail inside the broken back window of the porch! She looked frantically around for a fire extinguisher, her fears for Zoe getting hurt even more than she was keeping her own fear of fire at bay. Spying one attached to the back wall, she jerked it off its metal hanger and released the contents, keeping the fire from spreading.

She dropped to her knees and crawled along the floor to the open doorway and into the snowstorm, her gun braced in both hands. A sudden movement to her right and she raised the Glock, aiming and firing.

A loud grunt and she knew she'd hit the assailant. She waited, focused. There was silence all around. Was the guy dead? The icy cold penetrated her as she lay still on the ground, and then a loud shout and pounding erupted from the front of the cabin.

"Let me in. It's Josh!"

Josh. He'd found them. Thank God. He could see to Zoe.

She crept back toward the door on all fours, not wanting to be a target if the asshole was still alive. She was just about inside when a hand grabbed her ankle. She kicked, trying to shake it off.

Another grunt came as her foot connected with flesh. Good. It felt like a face got slammed by her steel-toed boot. The satisfying crunch of bone or cartilage followed her actions. She hoped the broken bone had jabbed her assailant in the brain. Not nice, but an effective way to end things. That or poking out an eyeball or two.

She looked up, half-blinded by snow, recognizing Josh standing over her. He leaped onto the still figure lying nearby, securing his hands with cuffs.

He then helped Anna to stand up. "You okay?"

She looked at the prisoner lying on the ground. Yes, The Buck, blood streaming from his nose, still alive. The guy had a gunshot in him and might die yet though. But she needed answers first.

"Yeah, I'll live. Go see to Zoe."

"Zoe's out front. I want to make sure the fire is completely out. Can you wait here? Keep an eye on that piece of shit?"

"Sure thing."

He hurried away, wading through the banks of snow.

Anna bent down, ignoring the sleet blasting them from all directions. This might be her last chance. A moment when she might be able to sleuth out the truth. "Who is the Black Rose killer?"

"Fuck you," Buck growled.

"You want to get stuck with all the crimes? Keep it up. *The Buck stops here, asshole.*" She'd never grow tired of saying it.

Buck went silent. Blood began burbling from his mouth.

She grabbed the man by the shoulders. "Tell me what I want to know. Did you take Tia? My sister?"

Anna had to lean down to hear the half-whispered words. "No, it wasn't me."

"Who was it? Tell me!"

"I'm going to hell for doing what I did. Killing my own wife. I'm sorry, Teresa...I shouldn't have left you alone so much...I didn't mean to..."

Anna shook him, her patience at an end. "Fucking tell me who it was!"

But Buck seemed lost in the memory of the night he'd murdered Teresa. "Richard helped me, you know, drove Zoe's car out there on the highway. Got me a black rose and helped with the fake note. Ask the doc, she's related to..."

The words stopped on a death rattle.

"Richard who? What doctor? Who helped you, Buck, tell me and I'll hold him accountable. Make him pay for his crimes."

But the man's limbs had gone slack, his eyes murky, staring at nothingness.

"No!" she shouted, sickened to the very depths of her soul. No closure. No knowing. *How could I live with that again?* She couldn't. Somehow or other, she had to get to the bottom of what had happened to Tia and now Joy. And anyone who got in her way would be damned sorry by the time she was through with them. But she did have one named accomplice. Richard. And a mysterious character called doc.

She'd hunt down every person in Anchor if she had to find them. Squeeze the truth out by whatever means necessary.

FORTY-TWO

"The snow has stopped," Josh said, his nose pressed to the glass of the front window of the cabin. "It shouldn't take long before help arrives."

He'd been pacing back and forth for the last hour, making Anna dizzy, poking at the fire, and constantly checking they were okay. She and Zoe rested on the sofa after Josh had aired the place of smoke, though the smell lingered inside her nostrils. The young woman resting against her undamaged shoulder had been through so much. It made her heart squeeze at the pain and danger Zoe had endured these past three days, all without complaint. The living angel was more worried about her mother and how her sister was faring.

Like Josh had willed it, flashing lights appeared through the front picture window.

Richard who? Then it came to her, one of the names on the cigar list. Richard Strobel. Cousin of the guy, Elvis Strobel, who ran the funeral home out on Caribou Drive. Richard was in the right age group, though Anna didn't know much else about the guy. They'd never run in the same crowds. But he did give off rather sleazy vibes the one or two occasions their paths had crossed, like he wasn't good at being around people, making comments off the cuff. One time came to mind when Richard said something about all women were good for was a good time. And not in those exact words. Not incriminating in itself, but if the cigar DNA matched after his name came up, then look out.

"I need to check something out something," she said, not even realizing she'd said it out loud.

"You're not going anywhere but to the hospital to have that wound tended," Josh said in his sternest tone of voice. So like his dad Alex at that moment.

"You don't understand. I have a new lead. Buck gave me a first name and he's on the list of guys who smoke those expensive cigars. Richard Strobel. Buck also mentioned a doc, but that's not much to go on. Best to focus on Strobel."

"Richard Strobel, the guy related to the man who runs the funeral home?"

"Exactly. He helped Buck that night. Left his cigar butt at the scene. Something I'm certain DNA will prove. Buck swears he had nothing to do with Tia's and Joy's abduction, and I believe him. Deathbed confessions are usually accurate—a dead man has nothing left to lose. I'm almost a hundred percent positive we can glean the rest of the truth from Strobel. Hell, he might even be our guy. At the very least, he knows something, something that can lead to the truth."

"Haven't you done enough for one night? Rescuing Zoe and getting yourself shot. Oh, and killing the bad guy."

Though he joked, his serious expression spoke of the hours of paperwork ahead for him. She'd be hung out over the coals on the mayor's killing, soon as she was bandaged up, no doubt. But Anna couldn't delay on acting on this feeling that had taken possession of her. Her gut roiled with the need for speed, an unknown force pushing at her. Tomorrow might be too late. Every instinct she had was flashing warning lights that it had to be handled now, tonight.

But when they arrived at the Anchor Hospital an hour later, escorted by police vehicles and snowplows, she was whisked into surgery before she could protest.

FORTY-THREE

Josh watched the doctors, nurses, and orderlies rush Zoe and Anna away on separate gurneys down the long hallway that led to the OR. He tried to sit down for the wait to hear how things went, but it was impossible. He kept getting up and pacing. The intel that Anna had shared with him at the cabin was eating away at him. And if he went back to the station now, he'd be hamstrung with questions and paperwork. The last thing he wanted to think about was planning his mom's funeral. Besides, he wanted Zoe's input.

"I might as well check up on Anna's idea." But when he glanced at his phone, it was the middle of the night again. His inner clock always got so screwed up with the constant changes of shift work.

Hell, why not head over to the funeral home? The guy would be taken unawares. Not a bad thing. Might spill a bit of the truth, make it worth the trip.

In the parking lot, he found his police cruiser had been left for him. Someone had been thoughtful. He slipped in behind the wheel and started the motor.

Minutes later, he pulled up in front of the Strobel Family Funeral Home. Though the large squat building looked deserted, the front foyer window was lit up with a prominent sign saying to ring for service after hours. Great. That was exactly what he wanted, help after hours to catch a killer. He pressed the button and waited impatiently, stomping his feet. His fingers and nose were chilled from the frigid air mass that had replaced the snowstorm.

Then the door opened and he was face to face with Elvis Strobel. He remembered him from high school. An unfortunate teenager who'd suffered from acne and bullying. And that dreadful presentation in middle school, about his great-grandfather being a medical doctor at one of the concentration camps during the Second World War, that had turned him into a pariah. He'd been shut down early by a shell-shocked school staff.

Poor guy had also grown up in that awful cult north of Anchor that had finally been charged with child neglect and abuse a few years back. The twins had aways been nice to him, trying to cheer him up on occasion, figuring he wasn't to blame for who his relatives were while Josh had taken a more wait-and-see approach. They'd taken a few classes together, but after high school, he'd only seen him on formal occasions. Realizing with a surge of fresh grief he had a legitimate excuse to be there as well, he led with it.

"Hi, Elvis. I guess you heard about my mom?"

The tall, ungainly man, his complexion still badly scarred from teenage acne though he did an admirable job of hiding it when he sang as an Elvis impersonator on stage, looked stunned to see him, as if he was an apparition rising in the mists.

"I'm sorry to bother you. If it's a bad time, I can come back?"

"No, please, come in. I am so honored you chose to come to us at this difficult time in your life." The statement rolled smoothly off the man's tongue, a bit too glib for Josh, but maybe it was the business the man was in. All fake platitudes most likely, easy to hide behind.

Elvis's expression changed as well to a more appropriate look, serious and humble. But underneath it all he sensed something off, that something that had always kept him at a distance in high school. He'd even warned the twins once, but they'd laughed him off, saying he was a sad case, nothing more. That maybe theirs were the only smile he'd see some days. That was his sisters, too kind for their own good. Thank God, Zoe had been found okay. He prayed there was still hope of finding Tia alive, though it had been six months.

He ignored his misgivings about the man. He was a police officer, armed, and Elvis was a business owner, his family having lived in the area for decades now. He had nothing to fear from him. It was Richard they had to be careful of.

"I hope I didn't wake you?" He did not look like a man who had just gotten out of bed. Maybe he too suffered from insomnia?

"No, I was having a drink. Long days and longer nights it seems."

"I hear you. I don't sleep much either. Overrated anyway, right?"

He followed him into his office. It was a peaceful room, tastefully decorated. Well-appointed furniture offered comfortable seating for grieving relatives. He sat down on the sofa to the side of his desk, wanting to keep the visit on the casual side.

"Does Richard live with you here?"

"My cousin? No, out back. Why? Oh, where's my manners? Can I offer you anything? A drink or coffee?" He rubbed his hands together in an odd way, like he wanted to wash them. Then he remembered in school how he was constantly showering or cleaning himself, his hands always reddened and chapped. Another reason to be bullied. A nerd afraid of germs.

He shook his head. "No, I'm fine. Thanks."

Elvis took a seat on the armchair to his right. He waited for him to speak, a fevered look in his eyes made him uncomfortable. Was he high?

"I don't know if you've been told, but my sister's been found. Zoe. We discovered her whereabouts tonight. She's in the hospital."

"No, I had no idea. Is she okay?"

"She suffered a head wound and is badly dehydrated. But the doctors are optimistic she'll be fine in a couple of days."

"Where did they find her? Did they find the other woman, Joy Evans, who went missing the other day?"

"No, unfortunately not. We're still looking for her. I was wondering if we could speak of your cousin, Richard, off the record? Has he been acting any differently lately?"

"Why? Is he a suspect?" Elvis frowned. He'd gone very still, so still it spooked him. He sat up straighter.

"His name came up tonight and I need to check it out. Have you noticed anything at all out of the norm in his behavior?"

"Richard's a lazy sod, but he wouldn't harm anyone. I can take you to him, if you like? He's a night owl, stays up till all hours playing games on his iPhone."

He debated. Maybe he should call for backup? If he was the Black Rose perp, he could be dangerous.

"That's all right. I'll come back in the morning when it's light out."

"No worries. I have brochures about what kind of funeral you might want to choose for you mom. Wait here a moment and I'll get them for you. Then you can come back later after you've decided things. It's important to take your time and not rush these things."

"I want Zoe to be in on the decisions. A pamphlet would be helpful, thanks."

"I want to thank you for being decent to me when we had classes together. No one else would talk to me, but you always had a word or two. Your sisters were extra kind, very thoughtful. You are blessed to have them in your life. Anyway, thank you and them for that. It meant a lot to me."

His words struck a chord. The poor guy must be so lonely out here with only his cousin for company. And the dead.

"It wasn't your fault about how you lived as a kid. You did all right for yourself. Got a business now and everything." He tried to put a positive spin on his life. It was obvious he was still very insecure.

"Are you sure I can't offer you something? A glass of water, perhaps? You don't want to get dehydrated like your sister."

Elvis seemed so sincere and the room was so warm he was thirsty now in his parka, he gave him a nod. "Water would be good."

"I'll right back." He vanished from the room, reappearing a couple of minutes later with a tall glass of water in a dark-green tumbler. He'd expected it to be bottled, but automatically took the offering from his outstretched hands.

"Thanks." He took a sip, noting it was fruit-flavored. "It tastes good."

"One of my favorite flavors too. Cranberry-orange vitamin water. Chock-full of vitamin C. It will make you feel invigorated in no time. I'll look for those brochures for you."

He went away again and he sat, sipping at the refreshing drink.

It was taking longer than expected, giving him time to give the room a closer inspection. But nothing appeared out of the ordinary. It looked exactly what a funeral home reception area should be. *Was it getting hotter in here?*

He stood up and unzipped his parka, suddenly feeling a rush of warmth flood through him. He was tired, that was all. Three days of running on little sleep trying to find Zoe. But now his sister was safe. Anna too. Not that they could rest until Tia was found as well. But these past three days had brought Anna back to herself, he could tell. She had been so instrumental in getting Zoe home to her family. She deserved a medal, not a damn inquisitor session in an interrogation room. He'd have a word with the officers in charge soon as he could.

The heat of the room was making him sleepy, and he worked to shake it off. What was taking so long? Brochures should be readily available for a business, not hidden away in the back somewhere. He swayed drunkenly on his feet and he knew. He'd drugged him. *Oh my god.* He staggered, fell back down on the sofa.

Soft footfalls came close to him. He stared up at Elvis's face. He looked different now. His complexion somehow smoother, his hair black, thick, and shiny. Old-fashioned sideburns down the sides of his cheeks. *What the hell?*

"You bastard! What did you give me?" His words sounded slurred. His tongue thick.

"Don't fight it, Josh. You and I, we understand each other, men of the world. I've known that since high school. We both know how special your sisters are. And tonight, you proved you don't really want me harmed. Showed up here instead of sending other cops. All by yourself too. He's still protecting me." He looked upward like he was personally talking to God. Why had he not seen it before? He was certifiable.

"You won't get away...with...it. They'll come...for... you." His mind was growing foggy. He blinked rapidly, trying to clear his dimming vision.

"Won't matter. I'll be far away by then. Good old Buck will take on all the blame. I kept his DNA in vials after he blackmailed me then placed it back where it belonged when it was time for them to depart this world permanently. You know, I always wanted to live at the end of the world. Somewhere no one knows me. Fresh start. It will be Joy that will become part of the newest chapter in my life. I'll never be alone again."

"Wh...at?" He was talking gibberish. The sensation of falling into a giant rabbit hole grew stronger and he slumped over, his head resting on the sofa cushion.

"No matter, I'll be long gone before you're found. They'll blame you on Buck too."

He couldn't hold on any longer. His eyes would not open now, his eyelids too heavy. His mind was fuzzy, nothing left.

Then the world turned to nothingness.

FORTY-FOUR

DAY FOUR

A quote from the philosopher Edmund Burke called to Anna as she came to and found herself alone in a hospital bed. *The only thing necessary for the triumph of evil is for good men to do nothing.*

Thinking about that strong belief helped to focus her and ease the pain that was more emotional than physical, though the body's pain was purer than inner turmoil and one she accepted. *I cannot live without a cause now, a reason for being.* No hesitation if and when she was called upon to do the unthinkable. Sometimes her actions would be what some people would consider a greater evil than what the bad guys had done, but she would always know that what she did was for the right reasons. And if one day, she found she was unable to get back to the other side after crossing the line, so be it. It was what a woman called upon had to do. There had to be a reason for all the difficult lessons in her life. A person called upon to cull the evil. A woman who would go the full distance to help others felt right to some force she had buried inside her, brought into existence by the events and circumstances of her life.

Her anger flared, and she felt her spirit animal rise, allowing the strong, protective wolf inside her to come to the surface, willing to kill the evil to protect the innocent. All it took was thinking of how badly Zoe had been treated. And Tia before her, along with all the others who would never go home again. She'd dedicate her life to that creed, with Tia most likely dead and gone months ago. *Tia.* She needed to speak with Josh right away. Check out the lead on Richard Strobel. Figure out the last pieces of the puzzle.

You have to get up. Josh needs you.

The figure of Tia appeared at the end of her bed, reinforcing her thoughts. She looked stronger, less hazy than ever before, riveting her with her message and worried demeanor. And she was alone this time, no baby in her arms. She sat upright, ignoring the tug on fresh stitches. Where were her clothes? She pulled the annoying tube out of her arm and shambled over to the closet. Josh needed her. *Now.* Every cell in her body screamed with panic. She dressed as fast as she could manage, her head throbbing with each jar.

"What do you think you're doing?"

Anna turned to see a nurse glaring at her, her hands on her hips. "I have to go. My friend's in danger. I was warned by…someone." She couldn't very well say her missing sister.

Her face softened with understanding. "It's just the effects of surgery, hon. People often see or hear things that aren't real when they come around. Now, let's get you back into bed, shall we."

Anna allowed her to steer her back to the bedside though her actions were delaying her, making her want to scream with frustration. She pretended to understand her concerns as she tucked her in.

"Take the damn tubes out, please. I don't need them anymore."

"But the morphine will help with the pain."

"Pain is a good thing. Means you're healing."

"Bit early for that, hon. But okay, if you need something, press the cord. We can offer oral medication. Don't be a hero. Ask for painkillers if you need them, all right?"

She nodded, longing to see the back of her.

When she had vacated the room, she once more got herself upright, dressing as quickly as her wounds allowed. She tied on the wolf talisman they hadn't allowed during her surgery, and tucked it inside her collar. She checked the hallway before slipping from the hospital room. It was clear of traffic and she found herself outside and flagging down a taxi in short order. The storm had ended, but the cold was mind-numbing. She shivered as she hurried to get into the back seat of the cab. *Maybe I am certifiable? So be it.*

"Where to, miss?" the driver asked, his wool cap pulled down low over his ears.

She pulled out her phone and texted Josh. No answer. Her concerns for his safety only grew stronger. Where had he gone? And then she knew what he would do.

"The Strobel Funeral Home."

"It's not even five o'clock in the morning, but okay, if that's what you really want?"

"Yes, sir, that's what I want."

She waited impatiently, her mind conjuring up a host of dire images of things that could happen at the funeral home. What if Richard attacked him, tried to silence him when he came around asking questions? Could his cousin, Elvis, be involved? The guy was an odd duck, only accepted by the community for the service he provided. Perhaps his weirdness suited the profession, though other funeral providers around town were more personable.

Her cell phone rang and she checked the number before answering. George Stubbs. What did he want in the middle of the night?

"Anna, I'm calling in my favor. Jason's missing. Three of his pals have met their end today. I'm worried sick about the kid. I promised my brother I'd look after him. I need your help. *Now.*"

"All his pals are gone?" The information stunned her. Who would kill all those teenage boys? It defied explanation.

"Yes, a hit and run this morning claimed Moose, then Mikey, The Buck's kid and Cutter died in a fire this afternoon, and now Jason's missing. I have every right to be worried. And you owe me."

Hating to do it, but needing to be a woman of her word, and sick at heart of hearing such tragic news, she spoke to the driver. "I need you to take me to the Yellowbird Motel first." Surely this was all just coincidence? What kind of inhuman monster would kill three teenage boys in such a short period of time? This would be taking the reality of sociopaths to a whole different level. And now his nephew was missing. The man had a right to be worried if what he said was true and George had no reason to lie about such an unthinkable thing.

"Sure," the driver nodded.

"I'm on my way, George. Be there in ten minutes."

What if the delay caused harm to Josh? She was ready to climb out of her skin with worry, each second an agony. Being pulled in two directions at once was one of the worst experience imaginable, her body vibrating with dread.

"You want me to wait?" the driver asked as he pulled up in front of the motel.

"Yes, I won't be long. Don't go anywhere and there's a big tip in it for you."

She climbed stiffly out of the taxi and make her way inside the motel office.

"You look like hell. What happened to you?" George Stubbs said by way of greeting.

"Gun shot in the shoulder, but the bullet went straight through."

"Tonight?"

"Happened when we found Zoe Pace alive. Our deceased mayor didn't like my poking my nose in."

"No kiddin'." George whistled through his teeth. "The mayor's dead and he was the black rose guy?"

"Not sure, but he did abduct Zoe. She's recovering in the hospital."

"Where you're supposed to be, right? I appreciate your coming on short notice." The assessing look in the guy's eyes suggested she'd earned some respect for that. No need to point out she'd been on the move anyway. Like old times, her inner drive taking over and running her physical body into the ground if need be. Was that a healthy attitude, absolutely not. But it got the job done.

"No problem. Have you called the cops to let them know about Jason's disappearance?"

"Yes, but I need more than they're providing. I need you on the case."

"When did you last see him?" Anna wanted just the facts now. The clock ticking in her head was growing louder by the second.

"Around midnight. He said he was going to bed. We

live out back." Stubbs jerked a thumb in the general direction. "He was feeling down about losing his pals today and wanted to go to sleep. I thought he'd be okay. I mean, it's only a hundred feet behind the motel and I see everyone coming and going for the most part. But when I checked on him an hour or two later, he was gone. Not a trace. No backpack or anything. He usually leaves a mess, makes himself a snack, but nothing, so I'm not sure he even went inside. I waited, thinking he had changed his mind, gone out somewhere. But he's not answering my texts and my gut is saying something's wrong."

"No camera feed?"

Stubbs didn't blink an eye. "No, not on my place. I like my privacy."

"Don't we all. Okay. I'm working a case and it might be related to Jason's disappearance. I'll stay in touch. Let you know if I find anything out."

"What case? You just said the mayor did it and he's dead. Never trusted that smug bastard. Did he kill his wife? Teresa was a nice girl. She didn't deserve that."

She made herself answer, though she could barely stand still, itching to get back in the taxi. "He may have had help. I need to go. I promise you I'm taking this seriously."

"Don't you want to check the house for clues or something?"

"No need. You said he's not there."

"Aw, there's something else I need to tell you."

She tried to not let her frustration break through. Not easy.

"Okay, what is it?"

"Jason was upset by something he saw at the graveyard the other night, you know, the one over on Elm Street? The guys were initiating another member—the mayor's kid of all people—and they threw him into an open grave to make the kid show his true colors."

"And?" Kids played terrible pranks on each other all the time.

"Well, something out of the norm happened. Scared the bejesus out of the kid."

"What?"

"Jason clammed up. I couldn't get any more out of him. But he was scared out of his wits. Said he needed product to pay the guy."

"What guy?"

Stubbs shook his head.

"Tell anyone else about it?"

"No, Jason made me promise not to. He was even more frightened of retaliation."

"From whom?"

"He wouldn't say. But I want to know the bastard's name. Likely had something to do with what's been going on."

She filed the information away. No time to dwell on it now. *I need to find Josh.*

She turned and was about to head out before George could delay her further, and had another thought. "Do you have a gun I can borrow for a few hours? Mine was confiscated tonight."

To his credit, George didn't question it but nodded sagely. "Sure. Handgun or shotgun?"

"Handgun and extra bullets if you got them."

George leaned down and pulled what he needed from under the counter. "Glock 19 or Smith & Wesson Model 41?"

"Glock." The guy had his uses. She slipped the gun into her pocket along with the extra bullets.

Anna was relieved to see the cab parked at the curb a

few minutes later. Now she just needed to stay on her feet long enough to see it through. She climbed back inside the vehicle, wincing at the pain in her damaged shoulder. Of all times to get shot.

"Now where?" the driver asked.

"Strobel's."

It was a short ride to the funeral home, but every second felt like an hour to her, so impatient to find Josh her heart was racing uncontrollably. *Please, please, don't fail me now.* Last thing she needed was another medical emergency.

The funeral parlor was in complete darkness when the taxi pulled up front.

"Sure about this?"

"Yes. I'll pay you now." Anna handed over the fee plus a generous tip of an equal amount.

"Thanks. I can wait if you need me to. No problem."

"No, I'll be a while. Best you leave."

The man nodded. "Whatever you say, buddy."

She vacated the vehicle and moved as fast as her wounds allowed to the front door. She rang the bell, waiting impatiently. She could hear her own heart whooshing in her ears with every beat. Not good.

She pressed the button again, but the seconds slipped by and no one answered. It was time to step it up a notch. Using the gun barrel to break the etched glass on the door, she reached inside to unlatch the lock. No one robbed funeral homes as a rule so it wasn't nearly as well secured as other businesses.

A loud scraping noise occurred as she stepped over the threshold. *Threat assessment: high.* She crept slowly down the hallway, the borrowed gun braced between her two hands. The stance made her shoulder wound ache like mad, but she welcomed the pain. It meant she was still alive and capable of doing what had to be done. What must be done.

She checked the reception area first, scanning the room for occupants. No one. He moved into the hallway and made her way toward the back of the building, checking each room as he went. The last one on the left had a light on, the reflection visible under the doorway on the hardwood floor.

Pulling open the door quickly, she surprised Elvis Strobel loading a coffin onto a metal cart. She glanced around, checking for anything amiss. The room had a large garage-style electric door. It would be easy work to load a hearse. The man held his ground, though his eyes glanced briefly at the gun Anna held pointed toward him.

"What do you think you're doing?" Elvis asked, his eyes dark pools in the low light. The guy appeared impatient. Like he'd been interrupted doing something important. Why would the guy be dealing with coffins at this ungodly hour? Business that good?

"Need help? I heard an odd sound."

"I'm fine. What are you doing in here?"

"I want to talk to you and you didn't answer the bell though it says rather prominently to ring it no matter what time it is."

"Strange way you have going about it, bringing a weapon along. Come back when I open at eight and I'll answer your questions then. I don't take well to being threatened."

"Why are you loading coffins at this time of the morning?"

"What business is that of yours?"

"I'm making it my business and you didn't answer the question."

"How did you get in here?" Elvis asked, his eyes

narrowing. He reminded Anna of a rattlesnake, about to strike. His muscles looked tight and a sheen had broken out on his pale forehead. The guy was made up to look like Elvis, the long-dead singer, and it only added a sense of discombobulation to the situation. *I mean, who does such a creepy thing in the middle of the night? Or maybe the guy had a gig earlier and hadn't bothered to change yet?*

"I'm looking for two missing people. And I need answers now. They may be in mortal danger. If you won't talk, maybe the police can help you see reason?"

"No need for that. I'll answer your questions. And I assume you will take full cost and responsibility for breaking into my place of business?"

She ignored the dig. "Bill me. You've been named as the last person to see either of the missing people alive." A lie, but it might prove useful.

"Who are they? I can't help you if I don't know their names."

"Where were you today? Can you account for your whereabouts this morning out on Caribou Drive when Michael Ferguson was struck by a motorist, or at noon when his friends were set on fire as they ate lunch?" She hit him hard with the cruelest of facts, looking for a reaction.

The guy peered at her with cold unblinking eyes, remaining silent. She observed the total lack of empathy and it chilled her to the marrow. Why had she not noticed the predator eyes of a shark before? Or maybe it was the hazard of working in the death industry, trying to hide behind a wall of protection? Strobel had also had a terrible childhood, growing up in a cult. If memory served her correctly, he had been a loner at school, an easy victim for bullies. That didn't make him a killer though and she was here to see Richard, the only name

Buck had shared before he died. She was also desperate to know the identity of the mysterious doc. Unfortunately, it was too generic to help.

"And now Jason Stubbs has gone missing. And Officer Josh Pace. Know anything about that?"

Strobel pursed his lips, clicking his thumbnail against his front teeth. "You should talk to my cousin, Richard. He's been acting strangely these past few days, like he's keeping a secret. My bet, he knows something. He lives out back. Why not question him? I've got work to do, work that Richard leaves to me, which is why I'm still here at this god damned time of the morning."

It was a plausible excuse, but the guy's demeanor still bothered her.

"Okay, let's both go talk to him." She waved the gun. She was not going unarmed. "Now."

"I need to get my coat. It's freezing outside."

"Where is it?"

"I keep a jacket on a hook around the corner." Strobel pointed in the general direction.

Anna moved to follow him, keeping a close eye out. But the guy didn't look bothered, just slipped his arms into the coat sleeves, and zipped up the front.

Strobel pushed an electronic button and the large overhead door began to rise, letting in the arctic air in a mist of swirling fog. Crystal ice skidded across the cement floor, collecting in the cracks.

She kept her distance as she walked slightly behind the man, gun kept at the ready. Her every instinct told her this was not a man to be trusted. Elvis Strobel had no empathy for others. Most people would have been upset at learning what had happened to teenage boys, that a law officer was missing as well. Were the two cousins in on it together? She tilted sideways like she was boarding a listing ship, making her all too aware of her recent wounding. How long was her strength going to hold out? She hated the sensation of physical weakness with every fiber of her being. *I'll need all the strength I can muster before this day ends. Risk assessment: extreme.*

FORTY-FIVE

Josh woke up with a sickening lurch. He rubbed his aching head. *What happened?* His memory felt fuzzy, something that had never occurred before. Zoe. Oh, thank God, she was safe. Right. Then he'd followed up on a tip Anna had given him about Richard Strobel, the man The Buck had named as he lay dying in the snow. The last thing he remembered was Elvis Strobel getting him a glass of flavored water. Damn it! He'd drugged him. But why was it so inky black?

He reached out with one hand and hit an obstruction a scant six or seven inches away from his face. He attempted to sit up but knocked the top of his head on the bottom of something hard, making his mind spin even worse than it already was. *What the hell!*

Panicking, he struck out with his fists, encountering a quick end to all avenues of escape, sweat dripping into his eyes. Horror slammed into his chest. He was inside some kind of freakin' box. No, this couldn't be happening, not again. He had claustrophobia so bad he couldn't even go down the steps into a fully lit basement without having a drink or two first. He'd managed to keep his condition hidden from most people with only his family knowing of his irrational fear.

It was residual PTSD, caused by being accidentally locked in an old frig when he was a kid. It was only a stroke of luck he'd been found before the air ran out. The dubious gift of HSAM also contained its own built-in curse. He'd never forgot any second of the experience, any day or hour of his entire existence. He had to get out of there or go stark raving mad.

He began pounding at the box, screaming at the top of his lungs, tearing at the silky fabric it was covered in, ripping chunks of it away. Then it dawned on him. Elvis owned a funeral home. Was he in a coffin? The terror of it made him want to redouble his efforts, to get out or die trying. But then his air would run out that much sooner.

Stop. I need to calm down. Find a way to keep my mind occupied. Getting hold of an irrational fear was the only way to save on oxygen. Not that it felt irrational to fear being held inside a box and unable to get out, but it wasn't going to help him, only end his life that much quicker. Wait, wasn't there a prisoner who had spent a lot of his time building a house in his mind, brick by brick? Yes, he dimly remembered it, but he had something equally as useful. An entire life behind him that read just like turning the pages of a novel.

What was my first memory? His first memory was of his third birthday. March 7, 1990. The day it had all begun. From then on, each day had been cataloged securely in his mind. What had turned one of the rarest human abilities on? He had no idea. No one else in his family had it. Josh had been called a freak often enough at school to learn to hide it from others. Not until he was an adult had it come in useful on occasion.

But it had been a later birthday party when he turned seven that was the most pronounced in his memory bank. The wonderful afternoon party shared with friends and family, the events that had started out with his favorite special pancakes their mom had made upon waking. It had ended with the weird girl from next door barging in with blood streaming down her face. It had been his first introduction to his neighbor, the sweet gangly girl who slowly but surely earned her way into all their hearts.

Her mom and dad had tried to shield him and the twins and had quickly taken charge of the situation. Her mother had ushered Anna out of the room and cleaned her up somewhere. Next time he saw her, she was wearing a too-large T-shirt of his dad's and eating a plate of food left over from the party like she was starving to death.

He flash-forwarded the timeline, to his first day of middle school and what had happened with his twin sisters. A boy who had failed grade six had been held back and was now in their class. Marvin Lockwood had taken an immediate dislike to them being twins, calling them out for hanging around each other so much and showing off in class when they always had the answer to any question. One day, October nineteenth, to be exact, things came to a head when the teacher asked him to solve a problem on the board and he did it wrong.

Laughter ensued when Zoe had marched up to the whiteboard and erased his answer and filled in the correct one, at the behest of her favorite teacher.

On their way home that day as the twins told it, he'd come out of nowhere, waiting until they were in a quiet stretch of street shadowed by thick bushes. He'd slammed into Tia and knocked her to the ground, then raised his fists to Zoe. He outweighed her by a good thirty or forty pounds, but she'd stood her ground. She shouted and rushed him, pounding him with her fists.

He'd laughed, holding her off easily while tearing her backpack off her shoulders. She was shoved off balance and fell down, skinning both knees.

He pulled her beloved iPad out of her backpack and grinned at her. "This is mine now, stupid Miss Know-It-All."

Then suddenly Anna was there, grabbing Marvin and twisting his arm behind his back. "We don't hurt girls."

Marvin turned beet red. "Get off me you piece of— *ow.*"

Anna had locked onto his arm all the harder. "We don't swear in their presence either. Say you're sorry and you'll never do it again."

He had a renewed respect for Anna from that day forward. There was nothing he wouldn't do for her. Maybe that was even part of why he'd gone overseas. He'd carried a torch for her all his life and probably would until the last second of his life. And if that was this day, he'd been a fool not to tell her sooner what she'd meant to him.

FORTY-SIX

Anna kept her eyes on Strobel as she knocked on his cousin's front door. She couldn't afford any slipups now. Maybe she should call for backup? She was seeing double at times, never a good thing if things went south.

Every instinct said Josh was on the property somewhere. She just had to stay alert long enough to find him.

"Richard," Strobel called out, knocking louder. "It's me. Elvis."

No answer.

"I can open it with my key?"

"Go ahead." She gestured, impatient to get inside.

The funeral director walked in first, banging his snow-covered boots on the rough floor mat before proceeding across the area rug toward the back of the house.

"Richard, are you here?"

Anna could hear him asking the question. She followed, watching Strobel's every movement. But the guy didn't try to pull a fast one, just went into each room of the residence to check on his cousin.

"It appears he never came home last night," Strobel said.

"When was the last time you saw him?"

"Hmm, he came in and did a few hours of work in the early afternoon. Guy's not an early riser. Then he headed out, saying he was going to meet up with a friend."

"What friend?"

"I don't know." He shrugged. "Richard and I don't always see eye to eye and we don't run in the same crowds."

"Does this place have a basement?"

"Yes, a cellar with a cistern. You want to have a look?"

"Let's go."

"It's not very well lit and the steps are kind of iffy. I don't want to get sued if you fall or anything. But sure, we can check. The entrance is off the kitchen." Strobel moved off to lead the way.

In the kitchen, Strobel hesitated. "You sure you want to go down there? Like I said, the steps are old. I can't vouch for your safety."

"I won't sue. You have my word. Grab a flashlight. You go first."

Strobel rummaged around in a cupboard, pulling out a heavy-duty silver-colored flashlight he turned on to check the batteries. "It's working."

He opened the narrow door to the cellar and began to descend the steps. Anna could hear them creaking under his weight.

"I need to have these replaced," Strobel said, his voice muffled. "Okay, I'm down. Oh my god! Richard! What have you done!"

Then complete silence. Anna's heart began to race. What had Strobel found? Was it Josh? Time to call for backup. But her need to know outweighed the logic for caution. What if Tia was down there as well? Needed her? She couldn't think past that. She clambered down the rickety steps, a ringing echoing in her ears.

But when she reached the bottom of the stairs and observed the low-ceiling space, all she saw was Elvis Strobel's back as he stood inside the doorway to the cement cistern that took up the length of one wall. A rickety old ladder sat leaning against another wall. Otherwise, the basement appeared empty.

"What is it? What can you see?" She rushed to Strobel's side so quickly her head ached from the sudden assault to her brain. She was existing on adrenaline now, nothing else. There would be hell to pay for her actions later when she crashed. But what would it matter if she didn't find out the truth, find Josh.

To his credit, the funeral director looked stricken when he turned back to briefly lock eyes with her, before stepping out of the way to allow Anna to look inside. The man has switched on an overhead bare light bulb, making it easier to see.

On the uneven floor lay the prone body of a woman. She was dressed all in white, like she was wearing some kind of a wedding gown, her face turned away from the doorway. Who was it? It was only in that moment she realized that she still had a faint hope she would be found alive, though her spirit visited her on occasion. She bent down and carefully turned the woman's face toward her, her thoughts in turmoil.

She didn't know what to feel at the moment of recognition. It wasn't Tia, her sister, but Joy Evans who lay dead on the cold cement floor. Her face was reposed in death, still beautiful, her cheeks blooming with color. She checked her pulse to be certain, so lifelike she appeared to be sleeping. If she believed in vampires, Joy would be the closest to such a supernatural creature she could envision. Even her lips appeared a natural cherry red.

"We have to report this," she said, getting to her feet and slipping the gun inside her parka pocket before fishing out her phone.

"I don't understand any of this," Strobel said. He shook his head as if he couldn't believe what he was seeing. "My own cousin—a kid I grew up with. How could this happen?"

"We don't always know those closest to us as well as we think," she said, throwing the man a bone. "All serial killers have a family, friends, parents at least. Lots of people are fooled."

She hit 9-1-1 on her phone, waiting for the operator to pick up.

"Yes, I want to report finding a body, in the basement of the house behind the Strobel Family Funeral Home."

"What's your name, ma'am?" the operator asked.

"Anna Hale." She kept an eye on the funeral director, but he seemed harmless now, thinking about his cousin Richard, no doubt.

"Do you know the name of the deceased?"

"Yes, one of the missing women, Joy Evans."

"Have you checked to be certain she's dead?"

"I have. I'll wait right here for the police to arrive."

"We'll alert a unit and it should be there soon. It's been a busy night and we've had a lot of calls. But hang tight, help will arrive shortly."

"It's a narrow, dangerous staircase to descend into the basement where I am. Let them know that. Tell them to be careful," she added.

With Joy gone, the chances of Tia being found alive had pretty much died with her. She felt the deepening chill of the unheated basement seep into her weary body.

She stamped her feet in effort to keep them warm, then startled at the pain it caused her unhealed shoulder.

"I had nothing to do with this," Strobel said. It seemed all his earlier confidence had evaporated. She even experienced a slight twinge of sympathy for the guy.

"You'll be interviewed as a matter of course." She shrugged. "Me too. They have always suspected I had something to do with Tia's disappearance. Better prepare yourself; the cops can be pretty invasive in their questioning. They'll tear apart everything in your life, looking for answers. And they have the right to. It's a serious crime taking another person's life. I intend to scorch the earth to get to any person that's hurt Tia if that's what it takes. Until I find her, I will never let *any* of this go."

She heard the conviction in his voice and knew it to be true. All her old drive was back. There was nothing to stop her digging into this further. *As God is my witness, I will discover the truth. The entire truth, no matter how much it hurts or how long it takes.*

Elvis Strobel's expression shifted; his eyes wary. "I need to check in with my lawyer. Sounds like I might need one." Strobel moved away and began to text on his phone, his fingers flying over the screen.

She wanted to sit down, her light-headedness worse, but there was no place to sit, and climbing the stairs seemed beyond her capability at the moment. Hell, at this rate, she might need an ambulance to take her back to the hospital.

"Can I get you anything? You don't look so good."

Strobel had rejoined her, his hands in his pockets. He looked smug now, like he had things well in hand. The guy must have a good lawyer on retainer.

"I'll be okay. Just a bit tired. Got shot last night of all stupid things." She gave a rueful snort. Maybe sharing would loosen the guy up. Strobel probably had guilty knowledge he wasn't aware of about his cousin.

"Really? Who shot you?"

"Doesn't matter." She dismissed his concerns. "I need to find Josh Pace. He might have come here earlier looking to speak to you or your cousin. I'm worried Richard may have him. He could be in immediate danger."

"Soon as the police get here, we'll tell them about him."

She took out her phone again.

"Who you calling now?" Strobel asked in an impatient tone of voice. He appeared a bit antsy, like he expected things to be over soon and didn't want anything to change.

Grow a pair, buddy. Things would be in flux until all the facts were in. No getting away from it. He was going to be thrust into the limelight whether he liked it or not. A far cry from being a quiet funeral director who hovered mostly in the background. But on second thought, he did do events as the king of rock and roll, so maybe he could manage to keep his head above water. But he should ditch the Elvis gear if he wanted to give a decent impression to the cops. Maybe she should say something?

"I need to check in with Charlie, alert her to recent events. Tia was a friend and she has a right to know about Joy as well, they were cousins. It may help prepare her if Tia's..." Her voice trailed off. It was harder to say it aloud than to think of her dead sister.

"I can't let you do that."

Suddenly her phone was not in her hand, but flying across the room and striking the cement wall opposite them. It flew into a dozen pieces, damaged beyond repair.

"What the hell! Why'd you do that?" The guy had reflexes like a cat.

"I was going to be a nice guy and let you live. I know about your childhood, your connection to that guy they executed down in Texas, almost as bad a one as my own. I was going to give you a pass. But then I realized you'll never cease trying to find your sister or your friend Josh. And I want to get away from here clean as a whistle. So, change of plans. I'm not leaving any loose ends. Yes, Richard and The Buck will be blamed for the missing and dead women, I've made sure of it. But you, Anna Hale, are a wild card, too dangerous for me to allow to roam free. You'd just become a thorn in my side, following me to the ends of the earth where I was actually headed until you broke into my place of business."

"You're a damned psychopath." Stunned by the revelation, she spat the words at the beast hiding in human form. She was prepared to throttle the answers from him. Her hands clenched into fists. "What did you do? Did you hurt Tia and Josh? Where are they?"

"Did your sister feel any pain would be a more important question. The answer to that is no, she did not. Tia was my faithful companion to the end. I wouldn't come any closer if you want answers."

"What did you do to her? Where's Josh?" Anna had no doubts now that *this* was the Strobel who had masterminded the whole thing. Then she remembered the Strobel family connection to the Nazis and the past and why the bastard had become a pariah in his teenage years. He'd adored his great-grandfather, a former Nazi who had hidden in the commune up north like the coward he was.

She dimly remembered it had something to do with the secret Paperclip Program, that had allowed former

Nazis into North America if they had a useful skill to the government, and that had been the ticket for the man's escape. Then the eventual move up to Alaska. The bastard she was now confronted by was as sick and twisted as his great-grandfather had ever been. Genes, unfortunately, won out in this case. *At least I wasn't related to the monster that raised me.* Soon she would have to confront that reality and consider going in search of her own roots. Just not now. She pushed all such thoughts aside, focused on the sociopath in front of her.

"Somewhere that you can never find them. I've seen to it." The smug expression was back. All Anna wanted to do was to strike the man down, squeeze the facts from him with her cold bare hands. It was all she could do to hold on to her rage. The wild animal within pushed hard at her, but she kept them contained. She could never kill a man in cold blood. It had to be justified.

It was obvious by his stance Strobel had regained his confidence. Even with the fact Anna still had a gun in her pocket, he appeared fearless. The distant sounds of a siren alerted her to help arriving. The need for speed. If she wanted the truth, it was now or never.

She quickly pulled out the gun and pointed it at Strobel's black heart. "I don't know if you've noticed, asshole, but I'm the one holding the gun."

"No need for obscenities. What, you going to shoot an unarmed man with the police on the way? Not to mention the cop coming is, well, let's say, is not on the side of justice. You know, money talks, and some policemen can be bought. Expensive, but worth the price. I wish I could deduct it on my taxes, but whatever. You've heard of bent coppers. I mean, who hasn't? We have one right here in town and he's the guy coming to arrest you as a favor to me. You did break in, right? Oh well, if you don't admit it, it will be on video. The front door is under 24-hour surveillance. For breaking and entry alone, you'll do time. By the time they sort it all out, I will be long gone."

"Who's coming?" She narrowed her eyes at Strobel, her adrenaline kicking in further. The man was a serial murderer. The kind of killer than kept everyone up at night, worrying about the safety of those they cared about. He would never stop. Until the day the man was dead in his grave, he'd be a menace to the human race.

"Does it matter? Wouldn't you rather use your one question to ask me something more important to you personally?"

She knew what and who Strobel was referring to, but she couldn't quite make all the pieces fit. She desperately needed to know, and this might be her last chance. In her experience, intelligent criminals loved to talk about their crimes, bragging about how clever they were. In this case, there was truth to it. "How are you going to pin all the crimes on Buck and Richard? And how does the doc feature into it?"

"I don't know nothing about any doc. But DNA. That's the great get-out-of-jail-free card. Our mayor was greedy. Once he knew what I was up to, he wanted access while they were still alive. Disgusting man. Hence the trail of breadcrumbs will lead straight back to him. No way any of this can be pinned on me. I've made dead certain of it." He smiled at his little play on words.

"How many times have you done this? Were there others before Tia and Joy?"

"What do you think? I let Him choose." Strobel punctuated his remarks with a sanctimonious upward tilt of his head.

Disgust churned the bile in her stomach, making her

forefinger itch to pull the trigger. "What's to stop me shooting you right here and now?" Anna wasn't certain if the question was for Strobel or herself. The wolf within screamed this would be a justifiable killing.

"*Phttt*, you're the good guy. The person with the white hat who comes charging in to save the day. You want justice done. I can see right through you—"

Sirens sounded closer now. Time was running out. She only had a scant minute or two to get answers before the tide could turn in Strobel's favor if what he'd said about a bent copper proved true.

Now's the time. Anna aimed at Strobel's arm, the recoil of the gun sending shards of pain through her damaged shoulder. An instant sense of wetness probably meant she'd just torn her stitches all to hell.

Strobel shouted out in shock or pain. Probably both. He staggered, blood dripping from the wound in his arm visible through the large hole in his jacket. Anna had to hand it to George Stubbs—he really knew his ammunition.

"Next one is to your head if you don't tell me where Tia and Josh are."

Strobel looked confused. "You shot me."

"I winged you. You'll be fine. And you hurt women and children. No bigger crime than that." She shrugged with indifference. "I want to know where they are. You have ten seconds to tell me, or you're a dead man." She locked eyes with the man to prove her intentions.

"Ten, nine, eight, seven, six, five..."

"*To me belongeth vengeance, and recompence; their foot shall slide in due time: for the day of their calamity is at hand, and the things that shall come upon them make haste.* Deuteronomy 32:35."

"You're spouting Bible verses about vengeance? *At*

me?" Offended wasn't a big enough word for what she felt.

Loud bootsteps echoed on the floor above them.

"Four, three, two, one—"

"Okay, okay. He's fine. Alive. In a coffin. You have my word."

"What coffin?" Horror filled her. Josh didn't know it, but she knew of his condition, his fear of tight places. She swallowed against the bile that now rose to the back of her throat. *I have to get her out of there right now.*

The heavy footsteps thudded at the top of the rickety stairs. The creaking did not bode well for the cop on them, who took a couple of steps downward. It sounded like the structure could collapse at any second. Part of her wished the stairs would disappear beneath the police officer, if indeed it was a bad cop on the take coming to join them.

"Now, that's the rub, isn't it? Which coffin?" Strobel's look of glee was too much.

"Police. Put down the gun, Anna." Cecil Karloff's voice rang out from above them. Only his black boots were visible from the stairs when she looked over. There was no way Karloff had seen her yet. He had to be the bad cop. Why was she not surprised?

"Stay where you are, Karloff. The stairs are unsafe. They won't take the weight of your body," she half-shouted back, her eyes never leaving Strobel who had taken the opportunity to creep closer. It turned out she didn't actually want to see the man falling to his death now that the possibility was real.

"What are you playing at?" Karloff asked, sounding annoyed.

"I got the guy who killed Tia and Joy and who knows who else right here. You sure you want to play it his way?

Keep a serial killer alive for money when you swore to uphold the law? *For what shall it profit a man, if he shall gain the whole world, and lose his own soul?* Mark 8:36. That goes for you too, Strobel." She knew her way around a Bible verse or two, her mom having insisted on church on Sundays when she'd been alive. However, her stance on forgiveness...that was not something they shared anymore.

"Drop the gun. Then we'll talk."

"I can't do that. He was about to tell me which coffin Josh's hidden in. I take my gun away and he's going to clam up. Did you kill those boys as well, Strobel?" Anna asked, wanting Karloff to hear the answer, to be made fully aware of all the horrid facts. Surely, he would come back round to the right side of things if he knew?

"What does it matter? They were a group of delinquents. No loss there." Strobel dismissed her words.

The man was one of the worst narcissistic sociopaths on the planet. Shooting him dead would be a favor to humanity, not to mention save the taxpayers the cost of his long incarceration and many lengthy appeals.

"I'll triple your payout, Cecil, if you end this thing with Anna right now for shooting me and for breaking in and threatening me," Strobel shouted out to the policeman still hesitating on the stairs.

The stairs creaked louder as Karloff began to descend again, one careful step at a time.

"Tell me where Josh is and I'll let you live. I'll even plead your case in court." As much as it pained Anna to say it, Josh was all that mattered now. She knew in her heart Tia was long gone, but Josh could still be alive.

"Right. Like that's enticement. You'll never find him. He'll die soon if I don't get him out. Your best bet is to go along with all this. Maybe I'll let him live for your sacrifice. We'll let Him decide."

A loud cracking imploded her eardrums, taking all her attention away from Strobel. The room exploded. Debris and dust flew around the space, boards clunking against the stone walls. A body hit the cement floor with a horrible sickening wet thump of breaking bones and exploding tissue.

She was stunned by the new development, though she should have expected it. The stairs had given way under the excessive weight of the detective.

She looked over at Strobel. The man was covered in gray dust, only his dark eyes visible. Strobel yanked off the black wig, exposing colorless hair plastered to his scalp. He looked shocked, trying desperately to shake the film of dust off like it was a rain of bugs covering him. Neither of them had been hit hard enough to be knocked out, but one glance over at Karloff and Anna knew the game was up for the man. His neck was cranked at a horrible angle. No way anyone could survive that.

"Looks like you're on your lonesome now, asshole. This is your last chance. *Where. Is. Josh.* Wrong answer and you're a dead man."

"Not like it's going to do you any good. How are you going to save him now?"

Enough.

She shot Strobel again, this time in the other arm, winging him twice. She'd worry about explaining it later if she lived through this.

"Last chance, asshole."

Strobel moaned in pain, his eyes black and angry though he managed to stay on his feet. He was stronger than he looked, but he had only himself to blame.

"Okay, okay. Outside, on the Cessna I overhauled. I loaded him earlier. Now take that gun off me."

"Good answer. But I don't trust you or your intel so the gun stays." Anna moved slowly over to Karloff, confirming he had no pulse, then looked to see if the detective's phone had survived the fall. She needed to call for backup. She prayed Josh was really on the plane, that it wasn't a ruse to keep from being shot again.

It was sad to see the man in blue dead, but Anna didn't feel as much sympathy as she would have thought. The man had brought it on himself. However, she did feel badly for the man's family. She knew all too well what it felt like to be a pariah and she'd never wish that grief on anyone. Maybe it would be possible to keep his being a bad cop off his record? Allow the family closure and a pension. She remembered the guy had a nice wife and a couple of kids. Why did he do it? No amount of money was worth it.

She found a cell phone in the detective's breast pocket. The screen was cracked, but it lit up when she tried the power button. She picked up the detective's revolver as well and thrust it in her parka pocket.

She was about to hit 9-1-1 again when she hesitated. How to explain this mess? It would take hours and hours and she needed to be out searching for Josh, confirm he was on the Cessna or not. Strobel and the police would try to stall her at every turn. It wasn't like they would take her word for it upfront. Hell, she could be in handcuffs for breaking into the joint. And look what had happened with Tia when all the focus was on trying to prove she did it. Maybe by then it would be too late. She had to make the hard call now. Every second counted. Any delay could cause his death. She knew this right to the very depths of her being. But how to bring this situation with Strobel to a head that she could live with?

"Where is my sister Tia?"

"You'd like to know that, wouldn't you? But you got nothing left to bargain with. I've given you Josh's whereabouts. Tia, you will have to find yourself. Not like you're going to kill me—"

She kicked Karloff's gun over to Strobel. "Pick it up."

"That's not fair. You're an expert and I'm wounded," he protested.

"So am I. Your accomplice saw to it. I won't shoot until you have it in your hands."

Strobel bent over and rapidly retrieved the gun, keeping his eyes on Anna the entire time. He pointed it toward her, the monster's eyes filled with the hot fire of certainty as to what he planned to do.

The moment.

All her life, it had been building up to this. In a few seconds there would be no turning the clock back.

God. Is this something I can live with? Crossing the line forever?

Every instinct screamed the answer: *Yes.*

Without thinking about it any further, Anna fired a shot straight between the perp's eyes, functioning totally on automatic pilot, like she'd done when necessary overseas in the warzone. She may have been stateside now, but it was still a war. And just because this was a war without end, didn't mean she couldn't step up and do what needed doing.

Now she'd bought the time necessary to save Josh. She'd probably spend years in jail, but it would be worth it to save him. In her heart, she knew it was a justified killing. She could live with that as it was the principle that mattered the most, even if some of the world would never agree with her. With her decision. If you haven't walked the talk, you don't really have a say in it. Always. *Death before dishonor.*

She ignored the dead men, put her gun in her pocket for safekeeping, and went to retrieve the old ladder. She pulled apart the legs of the wooden ladder, praying it would support her for the short distance to the main floor.

Fortunately, she got the one break she needed when the ladder held her weight. She stumbled along the hallway to the front door and hurried in the direction of the outbuildings nearest the tarmac. Surely one of them held the Cessna and the coffin ready for a quick departure. *Please, dear God, please let him be telling the truth about this one thing.*

FORTY-SEVEN

Josh knew he was going to die. Very, very soon. He sucked in gasps of air as his lungs fought valiantly to work. He was beyond exhausted, his arms gone limp at his sides, unable to move a muscle. His whole body ached from the initial fight of trying to get away before he'd grabbed hold of himself. But even the mind trick of living through so many memories had abandoned him. His fingers were still bleeding; he could feel the stickiness. Would his body ever be found? Was he already in a hole in the ground? The horror surrounded him, left him roiling with despair. The only saving grace was Zoe was alive. Anna too.

He kept himself focused by thinking of Anna these last few moments of remaining air. She was a good woman. She'd saved Zoe. She didn't deserve the life she'd had to lead. First her mother, then her sisters, now him. Why did such monsters exist? It made no sense to him. If he could, he'd wipe them off the face of the earth. He'd read somewhere about the differences between a normal person's brain and a psychopathic brain. Was there any truth to it?

Was it possible to pinpoint those who would go on to carry out their evil intentions? If he survived, he would do his research, find out if such a thing existed. What the world needed was a test to find out who was capable of such things, and keep a close watch on them. Or maybe there were just too many? He thought of how often now in the news mass shootings were reported and other forms of evil perpetrated on the innocent.

He felt himself refocusing his priorities as he lay there in the blackness. Maybe not for the better but embracing the reality that the world at large was changing and not in ways that improved it. He vowed, then, if he lived, to dedicate his life to tracking such evil and eradicating it.

He was so tired now. So weary. It was such a struggle. His chest hurt with each gasping intake of stale air, his mind spinning from lack of oxygen. He was dying.

A gleam of light pinpointed and began to grow in the distance. *Was this what everyone talked about?* A light that moved closer slowly and brightened with every heartbeat? But it felt good, like a warm hug in the worst of times. Was that his mom, the lady dressed all in white moving closer to him? And she was with someone. Another beautiful woman. Tia, his sister. Josh was overcome by the sensation of complete love and acceptance. Moving on would be okay if it felt this good...

What was that?

A sudden series of odd, ringing squawks filled his ears. It hurt, slamming him back from the warm, loving light. *What?* Was someone pounding nails above his head? The squeaking sounds made him cringe, the noise grating to his ears. The world screamed at him again. Oh, but then the realization hit full force. He was back. The light and the two women had vanished. He wasn't dead after all.

The lid was lifted away and he was staring up at Anna. She was covered in dust, but a better sight Josh could not imagine. He gasped in a full breath, filling his lungs with cold, vital, life-giving air.

"Josh, I'm here. You're safe," she said. The words were the sweetest he'd ever heard in his entire life, or probably would ever hear again. The reluctance at moving away from the light dissipated in a head rush of intense over-whelming emotion. He watched her toss aside the pry bar she was using to lift the nails before assisting him out of the coffin. They were in the back of a small airplane, with cramped space around them for maneuvering. Anna pulled him in for a tight hug as his senses reeled drunk-enly. He clamped onto her with both arms, never wanting to ever let her go.

"Your poor hands. Are you okay?" Anna asked, taking note of his bruised and bleeding fingers when he reluc-tantly pulled away. He could barely feel his torn hands in his joy at being alive. Of being here for friends and family. To see all their dear faces again sent a starburst of pure joy to his core. It had been so close. A few more minutes and he'd never have come back.

He was still dressed in his parka, unzipped, though his scarf and gloves were long gone. "I'm fine. How did you find me? And what are you doing here? I thought you were in the hospital?"

"I was. But I had this terrible feeling that something bad was happening to you." Then she looked a bit rueful before confessing, "It was Tia's spirit that sounded the alarm. She insisted I get up out of that hospital bed and go looking for you."

"I believe in ghosts, by the way. Did you see him? Elvis Strobel? He drugged me and put me in the..." He had a hard time admitting it out loud. He'd wait to tell Anna later about seeing his mom and Tia, once he'd found time to process it.

"He's dead. I shot him. So is Cecil Karloff. The stairs leading to the cellar in Richard Strobel's house collapsed, killing him. He was on the take, in Strobel's pocket. But that's enough talking. Let's get you to the ER for treatment. And I think I may need my stitches redone."

They began to move slowly to the front of the plane. "Lying there in the pitch black, all I could think about was going after the bad guys."

"You're in the right job to do that."

"Yeah, maybe. I'd also like to help you any way I can going forward."

"You already have. But there's another problem I hesitate to mention, but I'm probably going to be arrested for killing Strobel. He was bragging about how he was pinning it all on The Buck and his cousin Richard. I shot him after making him pick up Karloff's gun. I didn't give him a choice. Though the pair were also in on it, Strobel was the mastermind, even if the evidence is going to point otherwise. I didn't want a delay finding you after he told me where you were. I couldn't be certain he was telling the truth or if I would find you in time. It's not an excuse, but a fact. I'll take my lumps for it now that you're safe."

"I'd be a dead man if there had been a delay. I can't thank you enough for shooting him. He didn't deserve to live. We can fix this. Let me help."

"I can't let you do it. You're a good, clean cop, sworn to uphold the law. Helping me will change all that. You can't *ever* uncross that kind of line. It's too late for me."

"I don't care and you're still on the right side of things. It was a justified killing, in my opinion, and I know you, what you stand for. No, this has to be done. The universe owes you one. Let me help. We can figure it out together. Let's go take a look at the crime scene."

They placed their arms around each other and crossed the open space together, propping each other up as they walked toward the funeral home. The air had never smelled sweeter to Josh. For once he didn't mind the cold, instead embracing it with every fiber of his being. *I'm alive.* Alive like he'd never been before. He was drunk with the sensation, fueled by hope. He would use all his skills to make an even bigger difference now. Protect the innocent at all costs and bring closure to grieving families.

"I fundamentally changed in that box. Or it brought out who I really am. I can't go back to the old status quo. It's too late. If you hadn't done what you did, hadn't broken a few rules, I wouldn't be here now. You'll just have to take my word for it that the time has passed."

"Okay, but let's just take this one step at a time."

FORTY-EIGHT

Anna opened the door to Richard Strobel's house, preceding Josh to the kitchen where the entrance to the cellar was located.

"You used a ladder to get out?" Josh peered over the rough edge of the floor where the stairs had broken away.

"I was darn lucky it was there. Otherwise—"

"I'd be dead," he said, finishing for her. "I owe you a debt that can never be repaid. I was slipping into unconsciousness from lack of oxygen. Hell, that's a story in itself. But later. Let's get this done. I have no idea how long before they send someone else out to follow up on Karloff."

"He must have turned the cops away that were going to come out initially, made up some kind of story so he could be here. I have no idea what." She shrugged. She would have to accept that some parts would remain forever a mystery, much as it bugged her.

"Probably something simple like he was in the area and could get there first, check things out. And if we're lucky, no one else is coming. It won't be until Karloff is missed that people will start asking questions. When did Strobel have the opportunity to call him?"

"When I thought it was his cousin that had done it all, he texted Karloff under the guise of calling his lawyer."

"Okay, let's head down there. See how we can spin this."

"I'll go first." Anna moved to the top of the ladder, careful to check it was still braced, and then descended into the shadowy world below. She'd always felt hell was certain places on earth, just like heaven. The pit below was one of those manmade hellholes.

Josh followed her down while she held on to the ladder at the bottom, securing it to make sure it stayed put. He made a wide berth around the detective and stood back, checking out the scene.

"Okay. Explain how it all happened."

She laid out the facts.

"Too bad you didn't think to use Karloff's gun on Strobel. That would have made this easier."

"I love hindsight. Always twenty-twenty."

"Well, Karloff could have used your gun to shoot Strobel. Pulled it off you at some point during a struggle. Then the ladder collapsed when he was trying to get back up. We need to put it in his hand and shoot one bullet to leave a residue. Are there any bullets left in the Glock?"

"Yes." Anna pulled it from her pocket. "How do we explain the residue on my hands?"

"You mean the GSR and the SEM/EDX method of testing? Cross contamination happens all the time. And it will mostly be gone now anyway after you put on your gloves. Washing with water or alcohol wouldn't hurt. It's going to turn up all over this cellar, is my best guess. Especially with all the debris that contaminated this scene when the stairs fell down. Forensics will have their work cut out for them. I don't envy them trying to sort out this mess, but it means we can spin this our way. No one left to suggest otherwise, right? Here, use this when we're done." He pulled a wet nap packet from his pocket and handed it over, wincing at the pain from his bruised and battered fingers. Blood still oozed from several of the cuts.

"I have another idea. A simpler solution. What if Strobel fired at me before I shot him? He held the gun for a second or two before I finished him. I was just quicker."

"Yeah, that is a lot simpler. But it puts it on your record. It looks like you shot him three times, like you were interrogating him. Will that affect your PI license going forward?"

"Don't know." She shrugged. "Not the biggest problem right now."

Anna could see herself taking a few steps and bending down to place the borrowed Glock in the detective's right hand, pointing it at the wall behind them in the direction of where Strobel had been standing, pulling the trigger, then throwing the weapon down beside the body. But her whole being rejected it. No. The facts were the truth of it. Something that mattered more than her life. She'd never let Josh pay for her sins. She could never live with it. *Death before dishonor.*

"No, it lays as it is. I stand behind what I did, playing the death card as it was presented to me. It's over, Josh, and I'm not going to let you jeopardize your future."

"I wish you would have let me help you more than just a character endorsement." He let out a deep sigh of resignation. "But I understand. We shouldn't wait too long to call this in."

"You are one impressive man, Josh. Glad we're on the same team." she said, shaking her head with admiration.

"Ah, one last thing and I hate to ask you this…"

"Go ahead, I think I know already what it is."

"Tia. Did he say where she was being held?"

She shook his head to the negative, unable to speak for a moment.

"We'll find her, Anna, I promise. Just like you did Zoe."

FORTY-NINE

Anna stood at the graveside of her second mother, flanked by Zoe and Josh and Charlie. It was a rare day of bright sunshine with a slight rise in temperature. The past two days, recovering in the hospital and then at home, had left her exhausted from all the questioning. But she hadn't been arrested so far, and there was even grudging respect from the department for solving both cases, though mostly for saving one of their own.

Anna was still reeling from getting a letter from the Pace's lawyer about her inheriting a third of what turned out to be a fortune earned in gold mining. A lot of good to be done with that kind of money. She looked around the cemetery, at all the gravestones. She was overcome with the need to have one for Tia. *Where are you?*

She blinked, staring at a ghostly white figure forming over a gravestone nearby. She startled, drawing the attention of the Josh, as she recognized her sister Tia.

"You all right, Anna?" Josh asked, turning to look at her, concern overriding some of the grief in his blue eyes.

Stubbs's intel came back to her in the moment. The

young boys who had been initiating a new member in the graveyard. The fear at what they had found. How scared Jason had been. And rightly so, for there was no word yet of the teenager's whereabouts. His uncle was pressing Anna for answers, and she'd promised right after the funeral to give the case her undivided attention. It was like the kid had vanished into thin air, according to the APD. She knew they were doing all they could to locate Jason, but it was hard convincing Jason's uncle of it.

"Yeah, just processing something." Doubt turned instantly into a near certainty. Over there, where Tia hovered above the ground, that was where she was buried. Her body lay under a coffin not fifty feet away. She was pointing it out by materializing over it. She had been for some time. She swallowed hard. Tears stung the backs of her eyes. *Oh my god, Tia, I'm so sorry.*

She kept her feet planted, working to keep herself focused. Now was not the time. Later, after they had seen Cindy properly buried, she'd come back and do what had to be done.

"What is it?" Josh asked, glancing from her over to where she was staring off into space.

"Later."

"It's Tia, right? I see her too. Floating above that newly dug grave," he whispered in her ear.

Shocked Josh could see her too, she nodded without thinking. The police had found Strobel's journal hidden in an antique desk and were busy compiling a list of his victims after Anna had broken the strange code for them. The using of Elvis Aron Presley, king, wife, and CD in replacement for the twenty-six letters of the alphabet plus a few nonsensical words didn't confuse her just by Strobel's leaving out the doubling of letters.

It did however resemble the Cesar Shift that Strobel

ported was the inspiration behind it, because each time he wrote about a new victim, he shifted the code over two spaces, adding a layer of complication that had taken some sleuthing on her part to figure out. The worse thing, though the diary was filled with biblical quotes and information on his monstrous experiments, it didn't mention where he had buried the bodies. The bastard was one of the sickest of the sick. But now she knew.

"I'll help you," Josh whispered.

———

Hours later, aided by a bright full moon, they approached the recently dug grave that contained the earthly remains of Giles John Larson. Josh carried a ladder and Anna a pair of shovels.

"Why do you think we could both see her?" Josh asked. "Do you think it's because we've both been to the other side? You know, seeing the light and all. I've always believed in ghosts, just never had it proven to me before."

"I didn't see a light—it wasn't like that for me." Anna stopped to think about his words. She was still fired up from the argument she'd had with him earlier. She'd lost that one, his insisting there was no way in hell she was doing it alone.

"What did you see before the paramedics brought you back?"

"It was like I'd gone through a wall. Then suddenly I was riding in some kind of open-aired conveyance. I could see the stars and planets flashing by, bigger than life. Then I jumped off into the darkness and came back into my body. I actually watched my pixels reform from the waist up, like a shower of bright light. I learned an odd thing on the other side. My own expiration date." She pulled up her sleeve to reveal her mom's name, Sarah Jane Hale 1973-2003 on her inner arm. Then her own tattooed beneath hers: Anna Jane Hale 1989-2064. She would now have Tia's added. "Apparently, I had to come back because my time wasn't over." Even though she had tried to circumvent fate and considered leaving a second time, a fact that now made her shake his head. She had too much to do now to ever imagine again wanting to leave this life prematurely.

"You were brave even in near death. So much like you," he said with a shake of his head, running a fingertip over the black-inked dates. "No, I didn't get my own expiration date. Though I have my own motto I live by tattooed on my arm: *carpe diem*, seize the day. But I have to admit, it felt good on the other side. All warm and fuzzy. It's going to help going forward knowing that. There's one more thing that I need to say about it."

"Okay."

"I saw Mom and Tia, both dressed all in white, coming toward me. They looked beautiful, full of love. It helped me—knowing that. I hope it helps you?"

She looked into his eyes. He wasn't lying. It was his truth. Maybe hers now.

But no matter how she looked at it, they both had been taken too soon, died too young. "You ready to do this?"

"Let's pray the ground isn't frozen solid again," he said.

"I'm going to get the backhoe. We're also going to have to bring up the coffin anyway and lay it to the side before we check below." She couldn't say what they were checking for out loud. *Just do what needs to be done.*

"Right. And pray like mad no one comes out to ask why the backhoe is being used so late at night," Josh said.

"I've seen work being done here at night before. Not often, but with any luck, we'll be able to do this thing and get our answers." She didn't care if they were interrupted after the fact, or if she was charged with a crime. Though she did worry about Josh. "If anyone comes by you say you were trying to stop me. Are we clear? I don't want you implicated in this thing. And I'm not waiting for any damn court order to bring our sister home."

"Yes, Anna."

The answer was too glib. "I'm not kidding around here, Josh."

"Fine. I promise. Now, go get the backhoe already and let's get this over with. It's not going to get any warmer or easier."

She loped off across the field, careful to stay on the path between the headstones. The grave was next to an empty one, which was a boon. They needed some place to lay the dirt and coffin. In short order she was back, driving the heavy equipment. One of her summer jobs growing up had been helping around a construction site, giving her vital lessons on operating machinery. She had never been a girly girl and too late now to start.

In twenty-five minutes, she had the grave excavated of dirt and the coffin safely laid to the side. Ignoring her elevated heart rate, she climbed down off the machine and joined Josh at the graveside.

"Okay, are you ready? There's no going back. Maybe you should let me do this?"

"No, I need to be there. Have you got blankets ready for her?"

"No, let me get those." Josh rushed off and she slipped

the ladder into the hole, climbing down the steep steps to stand on the bottom. Swallowing hard, she began to carefully move the soil away from the center of the grave toward the sides.

FIFTY

Josh heard the moans of an animal in acute pain. He quickened his pace though weighted down with a thick stack of quilts and blankets. He found Anna with Tia in her arms, rocking back and forth at the bottom of the hole. His chest squeezed so tight at the gut-wrenching sight he was certain he was going to have a heart attack. *Now is not the time to be weak.* He clambered down the ladder and kneeled at her side.

"Let me help you."

He gently laid a quilt on the body that was dressed in some kind of white garment and carefully took up her feet, waiting for Anna to start back up the ladder with their sister. It was awkward and hard, but eventually they had her topside and covered in a swaddling of blankets.

"I'll finish up here."

"No, you don't know how to work the backhoe. We'll lay her on the back seat, then I'll come back and finish this up. You go home, Josh. You could lose your job over this. You've been more than a friend tonight. I've got this."

They carried their sister together across the landscape

back to the SUV and laid her gently inside. He didn't like the look of Anna. Like maybe she'd given up hope again. No way was he leaving her alone tonight. He knew how much she blamed herself for Tia's disappearance, having been living with her at the time. She needed human companionship more than anything now. The memory of another night, the day Zoe had disappeared and he'd gone asking for her help, then discovering later on what Anna had been preparing to do, that was something he'd never forget. He'd never forgive himself if he wasn't here for her now.

Anna came back a few minutes later and shook her head when she saw him still frozen to the same spot of ground. She climbed onto the machine and retraced her steps, refilling the grave and packing the earth smooth. The only saving grace was no one had come by and gotten in the way.

They walked side-by-side to the waiting vehicle, and without saying a word, got inside. She drove them home.

"How are we going to explain this?" he asked, thinking ahead. He hated to ask at such a terrible time, but the tough question was necessary.

"We don't have to tell anyone other than Zoe. Everyone else is gone now. Our parents, just the three of us left, and Charlie, of course. We could bury Tia right here on my property. No law against burying someone on personal property in Anchor. This was her home. She loved this place. It's prettier than the cemetery. Not to mention far better memories and a fitting place to pay her visits for you and Zoe. I intend to live here all my life. Keeps me rootbound, something I desperately need, I think. I've learned that much as least in this lifetime."

"I can help with that. I'll need to talk to Zoe, of course,

she what she thinks is the right thing to do. But I think this is a good idea."

She nodded. "Thank you."

"I hate to bring this up, but what are we going to do about the fact that there could be other bodies buried under more graves? Other families without closure?"

Anna turned, eyes shadowed deeply by grief and concern toward him. "I've broken laws doing what I did tonight."

"Me too."

"I'll swear to it that you weren't there," she said, her tone of voice growing stronger. Anna was the strongest woman he knew, bar none. He admired her more than anyone, especially at moments like this. Maybe one day he would tell her how he felt. The idea helped him, gave him hope.

"But I will have to go in and tell them about all this— what I did. Soon."

"Okay. I'll help you carry her inside."

———

In the garage, Anna and Josh tenderly lay their sister on the table she'd prepared earlier. She'd needed to wash her first before transferring her to the coffin she'd purchased after Cindy's funeral, knowing she would most likely need it. Were her mom, adopted mom, and sister together in the afterlife? The thought was comforting. She'd once checked on social media, researching near-death experiences, and found more than eighty-nine thousand people in one of the groups that believed. Lots of testimonials.

Josh stayed back, hovering, like he didn't want to interfere, but offered comfort. They ended up doing the job together when she gave him a curt nod. Taking Tia's body inside the house, stripping off the offensive borrowed wedding gown, and washing her gently in the bathtub.

From their shared bedroom closet, she pulled her favorite dress, the one she'd worn the past two Christmases. A lovely red velvet number with a white lace shawl collar that brought to mind an angel.

Redressed, with her hair brushed, she looked lifelike. And it broke her heart all over again to place her in the white padded coffin she'd set on sawhorses in the double garage. But taking care of their own felt right, like it had been done for hundreds of years before funeral homes came along and turned it into a business.

"I think we both need a drink," Josh said. He looked so white and tired. She felt the hand of guilt. He'd been there for her so much lately it was wearing him down. He must be so torn, between his duty as a police officer, and his loyalty to family.

"Yes, we do."

They sat in silence at the kitchen table, Friday subdued at their feet like he understood the solemnness of the occasion, and drank down the raw whiskey Anna sat out for them.

"Sorry there's not much to offer in the house right now. I haven't been to the store for a while, except for dog food."

"This is fine. I ate earlier."

"Tomorrow, after we bury her where they can never find her and do unspeakable things to her beyond what has already been done, I'll turn myself in."

He nodded. "I think they'll go easier on you now. Maybe just a fine or probation for disturbing the grave. The family might sue you. But the Larsons are good people. I think they'll understand the need for you to do what you did, not taking the time to wait around for permission from the courts."

"It goes as it goes," she said, feeling philosophical after the evening's hard work.

Josh swallowed down the last of the whiskey. "I'll come back tomorrow and we'll see her properly buried together. If Zoe agrees. I'll text you later."

"Yes. I'll ask Charlie as well. She needs to be here. There's an abandoned mine shaft on the land that will keep her safe until spring when I can build a proper home for her. We can all say a few words."

"That will work." He got up and came over and kissed her on the forehead.

"What's that for?"

"For being a good woman who does what's necessary. I'm glad we're all sharing in that unexpectedly substantial fortune my dad left. I had no idea how lucrative gold mining can still be, or that they had so many millions stashed away. Did it blow you away too?"

She shrugged and recapped the bottle of whiskey. "I'm grateful once more to your family, though I think the money should be split equally between you and Zoe."

He shook his head. "Never going to happen. You deserve it as much as anyone. They both loved you. We all love you."

"It will make it far easier for me to run the kind of operation that allows what needs to be done without worry of finances. Not much else for it, is there." It wasn't a question. "Thank you, Josh, for today and everything. Not many people would have stepped up and did what you did."

"It was only right. You saved my life. I wouldn't even be here if it wasn't for you."

"I hope I can count on your help in the future? I'm

prepared to chase the bastards to the end of the earth, if necessary. I want to dedicate my life to finding justice for others, to be that independent outsider that isn't part of the establishment. Like the old western stories wrote about. It's the only way I can ease this survivor guilt, knowing I can help others. It must be why I'm still hanging around this planet."

"You have that, whatever you need, just ask. But why are any of us here? There's no easy answers. Only to keep moving forward, do what one can. My mother's condition made me realize how short life is. I may inherit it, and if so, *now* is what matters, this short time we have on earth to make some kind of difference. And yes, I want to do that—bring closure to others. Hopefully together we can do some good."

"Tia was big on that word. Closure. I finally get it. But I wouldn't need it if I had been here for her and not in Texas."

Josh's expression changed, his eyes drilling into her like he wanted her to believe his next words. "You don't know that. She could still have been taken. I don't think it would have changed the outcome at all because nobody knew what we were dealing with. Not one, but two homegrown monsters—it defies logic." He shook his head. "But I'm grateful to have known her, to have been her big brother. Tia was one of a kind."

"She was one of the most beautiful souls ever to live on this earth. An angel."

A pensive look came over his face as he stood for a couple of seconds before speaking.

"Yesterday, after the funeral, one of the men I served with over in Afghanistan came up to talk. Corporal Tom Jackson. His sister's remains were found recently, about two hundred miles due north of Anchor. The body had been given a tree burial—off the ground and in the fork of a tree and had been shot with an arrow right through the back of the skull. She was only found because a hunter was out tracking game. He needs help—he wants to hire someone to look into it. I gave him your card. Laura, his sister, was only twenty years old. And from the photos he shared, one of the most beautiful girls I've ever seen."

Anna's stomach roiled with distaste to think of such a tragic end to a young woman just beginning her life. Friday whimpered at her feet as if he too picked up on the horror of it. She repeated his words in disbelief. "Shot with a bow and arrow in the back of the head and left to rot in the top of a tree. What kind of inhuman monster does that?"

"Okay, enough said. I'll be back in the morning."

She watched Josh leave without really seeing him go. She slid her laptop across the table and opened it. Research. That would keep her mind busy until she was too tired to keep her eyes open any longer. After all, they needed her, a woman willing to cross the line for them. And maybe in time, it would ease her grief, doing for others. The women who deserved to come home and the people who waited for them. Thoughts of the elusive doc came back to her. She hated loose ends. *But I promise I'll find you too, doc, and if you had anything to do with this, you'll pay dearly as well.*

A wolf howled nearby and her blood answered. Like an ancient warrior from another time, she had gone through her own trial and had earned her vision.

No turning back now.

ACKNOWLEDGMENTS

I want to thank everyone at Rough Edges Press for their wonderful support, especially Mike Bray, Jake Bray, Rachel Del Grosso, Amy Briggs, Jason Bates, Patience Bramlett, John Buck, Brent Towns, Thonie Hevron, Darrel Sparkman, and all the other authors who blessed me with not only a warm welcome, but a wealth of wonderful stories to read and enjoy!

And to you, dear reader, thanks for taking the time to read and perhaps review with thoughts of sharing my work with others. Absolutely nothing beats word of mouth! And if my story gave you some entertainment or respite while captivating you to another world or touched your heart, that's the best an author can hope for.

A LOOK AT BOOK TWO:
DEATH TRAP

A gripping tale of mystery, intrigue, and survival against the backdrop of Alaska's unforgiving wilderness.

Corporal Tom Jackson, hardened by the brutal terrains of Afghanistan, steps into Anna Hale's office, desperate to find out who is responsible for killing his sister and burying her beneath a tree on sacred land.

The investigation leads Anna from the deceptive calm of snow-blanketed landscapes to the dimly lit alleys of human depravity where contempt for women festers, striking at the very core of Hollywood and Washington's hallowed power structures. Governed by men shrouded in secrecy, their willingness to preserve their status knows no bounds. Murder is merely a tool in their arsenal.

But then Anna uncovers the darkest secret of them all: The Order of Blood and Bone, a sinister cabal of thirteen families with ties that trace back to the Illuminati and Freemasons, families that wield unfathomable power and wealth, believe themselves to be untouchable and above the very fabric of the law.

When another young actress vanishes, her disappearance a ticking clock against the midnight sun. With The Order setting a cunning trap, framing her as the perpetrator, Anna is forced to tread a path fraught with danger. Going undercover, she stands as the lone barrier against the encroaching evil.

Can Anna stop the evil invading her town and save the young girl's life? Or does this death trap spell doom for the intrepid Anna Hale?

AVAILABLE AUGUST 2024

ABOUT THE AUTHOR

January Bain is an award-winning author who firmly believes that stories unite us, that good stories help us to discover the commonality of the human experience by supporting values, empathy and understanding. She has had the pleasure of select novels being turned into games, and her work is also available in different languages.

She and her husband live in rural Canada on peaceful acreage where a variety of wildlife comes to visit regularly and expect to be fed and paid attention to.

Printed in the USA
CPSIA information can be obtained
at www.ICGtesting.com
CBHW011736020724
11025CB00010B/155

9 781685 496135